EX LIBRIS

VINTAGE **CLASSICS**

THE GENERAL OF THE DEAD ARMY

Ismail Kadare, born in 1936 in the mountain town of Gjirokastër, near the Greek border, is Albania's best-known poet and novelist. Since the appearance of *The General of the Dead Army* in 1965, Kadare has published scores of stories and novels that make up a panorama of Albanian history linked by a constant meditation on the nature of the human consequences of dictatorship. Kadare's works brought him into frequent conflict with the authorities from 1945 to 1985. In 1990 he sought political asylum in France, and now divides his time between Paris and Tirana. He is the winner of the inaugural Man Booker International Prize.

ISMAIL KADARE

The General of the Dead Army

TRANSLATED FROM THE FRENCH VERSION
OF THE ALBANIAN
by Derek Coltman

VINTAGE BOOKS
London

Published by Vintage 2008
24

French version © Albin Michel 1970 and Librarie Arthème Fayard 1998
English translation copyright © W.H. Allen 1971
and The Harvill Press 2000

Ismail Kadare has asserted his right under the Copyright, Designs and
Patents Act, 1988 to be identified as the author of this work

First published in Albanian in 1963 and in France in 1970 by Albin Michel
with the title Le Géneral de l'armée morte. An edition revised by the
author published in France in 1998 by Librarie Arthème Fayard

First published in Great Britain in 1971 by W.H. Allen and in paperback
in 1986 by Quartet Books.

This edition, based on the revised 1998 text, first published in Great
Britain in 2000 by The Harvill Press

Vintage
Random House, 20 Vauxhall Bridge Road,
London SW1V 2SA

www.vintage-classics.info

Addresses for companies within The Random House Group Limited can
be found at: www.randomhouse.co.uk/offices.htm

The Random House Group Limited Reg. No. 954009

A CIP catalogue record for this book
is available from the British Library

ISBN 9780099518266

Penguin Random House is committed to a sustainable future for
our business, our readers and our planet. This book is made from
Forest Stewardship Council® certified paper.

Printed and bound in Great Britain by Clays Ltd, Elcograf S.p.A.

Look, I have brought them back.
The going was rough, and the weather
was on our backs all the way.

THE GENERAL
OF THE DEAD ARMY

PART ONE

I

RAIN AND FLAKES OF SNOW were falling simultaneously on the foreign soil. The concrete runway, the airport buildings, the soldiers guarding them were all soaking wet. The plain and the surrounding hills were covered in melting snow and the water had made the black asphalt of the road shine. At any other time of year this monotonous rain might have been thought a dismal coincidence. But the general was not really surprised by it. He had come to Albania to search for the remains of his country's soldiers killed in various parts of Albania during the last world war and to supervise their repatriation. Negotiations between the two governments had begun the spring before, but the final contracts had not been signed until the end of August, just when the first grey days normally put in an appearance. Now it was autumn. And autumn, the general was aware, was the rainy season. Before leaving, he had looked up the country's climate. This time of year, he had discovered, was usually damp and rainy. But, even if his handbook had told him that the autumns in Albania were ordinarily dry and sunny, he would still not have found this rain untoward. Quite the reverse. He had always felt in fact that his mission somehow required bad weather as a precondition of its success.

He had spent much of the journey gazing out of the plane window at the menacing mountains. He felt that one of their sharp peaks was bound to rip open the plane's belly at any moment. Jagged rock on every side. Sinister escarpments sliding swiftly back into the mist. At the bottoms of those abysses and on those abrupt slopes, beneath the rain, lay the army he had come to unearth. Now that he was seeing it for the first time, this foreign land, he was suddenly much more clearly aware of the vague fear that had always begun coalescing inside him whenever he tried to confront the feeling of unreality that seemed bound up with his mission. The army was there, below him, outside time, frozen, petrified, covered with earth. It was his mission to draw it up from the mud, and the mission made him afraid. It was a mission that exceeded the bounds of nature, a mission in which there must be something blind, something deaf, something deeply absurd. A mission that bore unforeseeable consequences in its womb.

The land that had at last come into view, below him, far from inspiring him with a certain feeling of security – simply because of its reality – had on the contrary served to increase his apprehension. It had merely added its own indifference to the indifference of the dead. But it was not only indifference, it was something more than that. Those racing peaks just visible through the mist, those contours seemingly torn into jaggedness by grief, expressed nothing but hostility.

For a few moments he felt that the accomplishment of his mission was an impossibility. Then he tried to pull himself together. He tried to neutralize the effect of that seemingly hostile earth, and above all of the mountains, by consciously evoking the feeling of pride that this mission inspired in him. Passages from speeches and articles, fragments of conversations, hymns, sequences from films, ceremonies, pages of memoirs, bells, a whole treasure trove of elements buried beneath the level of awareness and now slowly rising to the surface. Thousands of mothers were waiting for their sons' last remains. And it was his task to bring those remains back to them. He would do everything in his power to acquit himself worthily of such a sacred task. Not one of his fellow countrymen should be forgotten, not one should be left behind in this foreign land. Oh, it was indeed a noble mission. During the journey he had repeated to himself the words a very great lady had spoken to him before his departure: "Like a proud and solitary bird, you will fly over those silent and tragic mountains in order to wrest our poor young men from their jagged, rocky grip."

But now the journey was almost over, and, since they had left the mountains behind them and begun flying over valleys and plains, the general had felt a slight sense of relief.

The plane touched down on the streaming runway. The red and mauve lights slipped by on either side. Bare trees. A soldier in his heavy cape. Another, more stock still than the first, all seemed to be fleeing in a panic. Only the dignitaries who had come to meet them were walking in a tight cluster towards the plane.

The general emerged first. The priest accompanying him on his mission followed. A damp wind struck them violently in the face and they turned up their coat collars.

Fifteen minutes later the whole party was being driven swiftly towards Tirana in two cars.

The general turned his head towards the priest who was seated beside him with a face devoid of all expression as he gazed in silence through the car window. The general felt he had nothing to say to him and lit a cigarette. Then he turned his eyes back to the world outside. His eyes perceived the outlines of this foreign land refracted, distorted by the rivulets of water snaking down the glass.

A train whistled in the distance. The railway track itself was hidden by an embankment and the general wondered in which direction the train would pass them. Then he saw it emerge from the cutting and gradually overhaul the car as it picked up speed. He continued to watch it until the guard's van was no longer visible through the mist. Then he turned back towards his companion; but the priest's features still seemed to him as immobile as before. Again he felt he had nothing to say to him. And, what was more, he realized, he had nothing left to think about. He had exhausted every possible subject of meditation during the journey. In any case, what was the point of reflecting further just now? He was tired. Enough was enough. Wiser just to check in the mirror that his uniform was in order.

Dusk was falling as they drove into Tirana. There seemed to be a thick fog suspended just above the buildings, above the street lamps, above the naked trees in the parks. The general began to feel more himself again. Through the window he could make out quantities of pedestrians scurrying through the rain. "They have a lot of umbrellas in this country!" he observed aloud. He felt he would have liked to exchange a few impressions now; the silence in the car was beginning to weigh on him. But he didn't know how to set about breaking through his companion's taciturnity. Beyond the pavement, on his side, he noticed a church, then a mosque. On the priest's side there were buildings still in the course of construction, corseted with scaffolding. The cranes, their lights blazing, looked like red-eyed monsters moving in the mist. The general called the priest's attention to the proximity of the church and the mosque. But he showed not the slightest interest. The general concluded that for the moment there was absolutely nothing he could do to arouse his companion from his apathy. As for himself, he was now feeling in a somewhat better humour; but who was there for him to talk to? The Albanian official sent to escort them was sitting in the front seat, over on the priest's side. The politician and the ministry representative, who had met them at the airport, were following in another car.

Once they had disembarked at the Hotel Dajti, the general began to feel more at ease. He went up to the room that had been booked for him, shaved, and changed his uniform. Then he asked the hotel switchboard to put through a call to his family.

After that he rejoined the priest and the three Albanians, who had settled themselves around a table in the lounge. Various subjects of no particular interest were discussed. Everyone avoided broaching political or social topics. The general succeeded in being both affable and grave. The priest spoke little. The general made it clear that he was the more important of the two emissaries; although the priest's reticence nevertheless allowed a certain doubt to subsist in this respect. The general alluded to the pride that humanity has always taken in the ceremonial interment of its warriors. He instanced the Greeks and Trojans, who concluded truces solely for the purpose of ensuring that their dead received the funeral rites that were their due. The general made it clear that he was filled with a great zeal for his mission. It was a pious task, an arduous task, and one that he intended to carry out successfully. Thousands of mothers were waiting for their sons. They had been waiting for twenty years now. It was true that their expectation had altered somewhat in its nature. They were no longer expecting living sons to come home to them. But is it not equally possible to anticipate the return of the dead? It had fallen to him, the task of bringing back to all those grieving mothers the remains of the children those idiot generals had lacked the wit to lead properly into battle. He was proud of the fact, and he intended to do everything in his power not to disappoint them.

"General, your call . . ."

He rose briskly to his feet.

"Excuse me, gentlemen," he said, and strode off towards the hotel offices with loping yet majestic steps.

He returned with the same lofty bearing. He was radiant. His companions had ordered coffee and cognac. The conversation had livened up. The general let it be known once again that he was in charge of the mission, while the priest, though holding the military rank of colonel, was in fact merely a spiritual adviser. He was the leader, and as such it was his privilege to direct the conversation onto the subjects he cared to discuss, such as brands of cognac, the differences between various capital cities or certain makes of cigarette. He suddenly felt filled with confidence there in that lounge, warmly protected by those thick curtains, listening to the foreign, the very alien music. In fact he was rather astonished himself at this abrupt attachment he perceived in himself for physical comforts, for all the things he could see around him in that place, from the padded armchairs to the pleasant gurglings of the café-filtre in front of him. Except that it was perhaps less of an attachment and more a sort of foretaste of regret for something he would shortly be saying goodbye to for a long while.

Yes, the general was radiant. Even he himself was unable to understand the reason for this unexpected wave of wellbeing. It was the joy of the traveller luxuriating safely in some haven after a perilous journey through rough weather. The little amber glass of cognac was gradually erasing the memory of those menacing mountains that even now, as he sat there at the table, were coming back – occasionally, disturbingly – into his mind. "Like a proud and solitary bird! . . ." He was suddenly suffused with a sense of his own power. The bodies of tens of thousands of soldiers buried beneath the earth had been waiting so many long years for his arrival, and now he was here at last, like a new Messiah, copiously provided with maps, with lists, with the infallible directions that would enable him to draw them up out of the mud and restore them to their families. Other generals had led those interminable columns of soldiers into defeat and destruction. But he, he had come to wrest back from oblivion and death the few that remained. He was going to speed on from graveyard to graveyard, searching every field of battle in this country to recover those who had vanished. And in his campaign against the mud he would suffer no reverses; because at his back he had the magic power conferred by statistical exactitude.

He was the representative of a great and civilized country and his work must be greatly worthy of it. In the task he was now undertaking there was something of the majesty of the Greeks and the Trojans, of the solemnity of Homeric funeral rites.

The general drank another glass of brandy. And from this night onwards, every day, every night, far though he was from his country, all those awaiting his return would be saying as they thought of him: "At this moment he is searching. We are here, out strolling for our pleasure, going to the cinema, to restaurants, while he is over there, leaving no path untrodden in that foreign land in order to recover our unhappy sons. Oh, truly that man's task is a heavy one! But he will make a success of it. He will not have been sent in vain. And may God be with him!"

II

THE EXHUMATION OF THE army began on 29 October at 1400 hours.

The pick sank into the ground with a dull thud. The priest made the sign of the cross. The general gave a military salute. The old roadmender, lent to them by the local government association, raised his pick and brought it thudding down a second time.

There, the task has begun, the general thought to himself with emotion as he watched the first clods of damp earth roll to a halt at their feet. It was the first grave to be opened, and all those involved were standing around it in silence, like figures of stone. The Albanian expert, a blond and elegant young man with a very thin face, scribbled in his notebook. Two of the other workmen were smoking cigarettes, a third had a pipe in his mouth, and the last, the youngest, wearing a roll-neck pullover, was leaning on the handle of his pick and simply observing the scene with a pensive air. All four were closely following the opening of this first grave so as to learn the correct procedure to be observed in their work – the exhumation procedure described in detail in the contract: appendix 4, paragraphs 7 and 8.

The general's eyes remained fixed on the steadily growing pile of clods at his feet. They were black and friable, and as they crumbled they gave off faint wisps of vapour.

So there it is, that foreign soil, he said to himself. The same black mud as everywhere else, the same stones, the same roots, the same vapour. Earth like earth anywhere. And yet – foreign.

Behind them, on the road, the cars flashing past occasionally sounded their horns at one another. The cemetery, like most military cemeteries, flanked the road with one of its sides. Beyond the road there were cows grazing, and occasionally one would send a peaceful moo floating across the valley.

The general was uneasy. The pile of earth was perpetually growing, and now, after half an hour, the old workman was buried up to his knees in the trench. He climbed out to rest for a moment, just long enough to allow one of his comrades to shovel out the earth he had just loosened with his pick, then he climbed back into the hole.

High in the sky a flight of wild geese passed over their heads. A lone villager, leading his horse by the bridle, walked solitarily past along the road. Apparently unaware of the nature of their labours, he shouted down: "Keep at it!"

No one replied, and the peasant continued on his way.

The general gazed in turn at the dug earth and the calm, grave faces of the workmen.

"What can they be thinking of all this?" he wondered. "Five of them, just five, and they are about to dig up a whole army."

But there was nothing to be learned from their expressionless features. Two of them lit further cigarettes, the third pulled yet again on his pipe, and the fourth, the youngest, still leaning on the handle of his pick, was looking on with the same absent gaze.

The old roadmender, now only visible from the waist upwards, was listening to the expert explaining something. After a few moments' discussion he resumed his task.

"What did he say?" the general asked.

"I didn't quite catch it," the priest answered.

The entire group resumed its deathly silence.

"We shall be lucky if it doesn't rain!" the priest remarked suddenly.

The general raised his eyes. The mist concealed the horizon on every side, and it would have been impossible to say whether the darker shapes distinguishable in the distance, far in the distance, were thicker banks of mist or enormous mountains.

As he continued to dig, the workman sank deeper and deeper into the earth. The general kept his eyes fixed on the snowy head as it moved back and forth in time to the blows of the pick.

You can see he knows his job, he thought to himself. Naturally. If he didn't they presumably wouldn't have given him to us as a foreman. But the general would have liked to see the old roadmender dig even more quickly, to see all the graves opened up as quickly as possible, and all those dead men found. He was impatient to see the other workmen begin digging too. Then he would be able to take out his lists and start covering them withlittle crosses – one little cross for every soldier found.

Now the pick was striking the earth with a muffled sound that seemed to spring from the very bowels of the earth. The general suddenly felt alarm run through every fibre of his being. What if they didn't find anything down there? What if the maps were wrong and they were obliged to dig in two, three, ten different spots? Just to find a single soldier!

"What if we don't find anything?" he said to the priest.

"We tell them to dig somewhere else. We can pay them double if necessary."

"It's not a matter of money. The only thing that counts is to find all the bodies on our lists."

"We'll find them. We can't afford not to."

After a moment the general spoke again, perplexedly:

"It's as though there had never been a battle here, as though this ground had never been trodden by anything but those brown cows grazing so quietly over there."

"One always has that impression afterwards," the priest said. "Remember, more than twenty years have gone by."

"Yes, it was a long time ago, it's true. And that's what worries me."

"Why? Why should it?" the priest asked. "The earth here is firm enough. Anything buried in it wouldn't move for a great many years."

"Yes, that's true too. But I don't know, I just can't get used to the idea of them being down there at all, so close to us, only six feet away."

"That's because you were never in Albania during the war," the priest said.

"Was it really so terrible?"

The priest nodded.

The old workman had by now almost completely vanished into the earth. The little circle had tightened more closely around him. The Albanian expert, doubled over at the waist, continued to pour instructions down into the trench.

The shovel produced a harsh, dull sound as it scraped against the pebbles. The general felt as though he were hearing fragments of the stories he had been told by the ex-soldiers who had come to see him before he left, hoping to be of help to him in his search for the graves of their comrades, dead and buried here in Albania.

The noise of my dagger grating against the pebbles made me shudder. But no matter how hard I tried I could make no impression on the ground with my makeshift tool. After a tremendous effort all I'd managed to get out was a wretched fistful of dirt, and I thought to myself sadly: "Ah, if only I'd been sent to the Engineers I'd have a shovel, and then I could dig faster, really quickly!", because only a few yards away my best mate was lying on his belly with his legs sticking out over a ditch half full of water. I pulled out the dagger from his belt too and began digging again with both hands. I wanted the hole to be really deep, because that's what he'd asked for. He'd said to me: "If I'm killed when I'm with you, then bury me in the ground as deep as you can. I'm afraid those dogs and jackals will find me. Like that time outside that little town. Tepelene wasn't it called? You remember those dogs there?" "Yes, I remember them all right," I answered, taking a drag at my cigarette. And now he was dead, and I kept saying to him as I went on digging: "Don't worry, don't worry, your grave's going to be deep, really deep!" And when I'd finished everything I flattened the earth down as best as I could, making sure not to leave any clues behind, for fear someone might just notice something and dig his body up again. And then, turning my back on the machine-gun fire, I made off into the darkness and, after I'd walked a little way, I turned just once to look back into the blackness where I'd just left him, and I said to him in my mind: "Don't be afraid, they won't find you."

"Still nothing, apparently," the general said, failing to disguise his nervousness.

"It's still too early to say," the priest answered, "but there's no reason to give up hope yet."

"All the same, it's unusual in wartime to bury the dead so deeply."

"Perhaps this was his second burial. They were sometimes exhumed and reburied a second, or even a third time."

"Possibly. But if all the graves are as deep as this we shall never finish."

"We'll have to take on extra workmen sometimes, that's all," the priest said. "Even if it is only for short periods."

"But what are they doing, for goodness' sake?" the general broke out after a pause. "Haven't they found anything yet?"

"They have reached the maximum depth," the priest said. "If there is anything to be found, it is now or never."

"I'm afraid we're off to a bad start."

"Perhaps there has been a subsidence of the subsoil," the priest said, "though the map doesn't show any seismic zone."

The expert leaned even further down into the trench. The others moved closer.

"Here we are! I've found him!" the old workman cried in a voice that came up to them sounding cavernous and muffled, for he had shouted the words with his head lowered, into the bottom of the grave.

"He has found him," the priest echoed.

The general uttered a deep sigh. The other workmen emerged from their torpor. The youngest, the one who had been standing so pensively leaning on the handle of his pick, asked one of his companions for a cigarette and lit it.

The old workman began depositing the bones, shovelful by shovelful, on the edges of the grave. There was nothing very impressive in these remains. Mixed with the crumbling soil they looked like pieces of dead wood. All around there hung the aroma of the freshly turned earth.

"The disinfectant," the expert cried. "Bring the disinfectant!"

Two workmen hurried over to the lorry parked behind the car on the side of the road.

The expert, who had found a small object of some kind among the bones, held it out to the general, gripped in a pair of pincers.

"It's an identity medallion," he said. "Please don't touch it."

The general brought his face closer to the object and with difficulty made out the figure of the Virgin Mary.

"Our army's medallion!" he said in a low voice.

"Do you know why we wear this medallion?" he said to me one day. "So that they'll be able to identify our remains if we're killed." And there was irony in his smile. "Do you really imagine they'll bother to look for our remains? O.K., so let's suppose they do search one day. Do you think I get any consolation out of that thought? There's nothing more hypocritical, if you ask me, than going around looking for bones when the war's over. It's a favour I can certainly do without. Let them just leave me be where I fall, I say. I shall chuck this rotten medallion of theirs away." And that's what he did in the end. One fine day he just threw it away and never wore one again.

The disinfecting done, the expert took the measurements of each bone in turn, spent a short while making calculations in his notebook, his pen held aslant in his long, thin fingers, then lifted his head and said:

"Height five foot eight."

"Correct," the general said, after checking to see that the figure tallied with that on his list.

"Pack the bones!" the expert told the workmen.

The general followed the roadmender with his eyes as the old man walked over to the road and, obviously tired, sat down on a stone, pulled his tobacco pouch from his pocket and began rolling a cigarette.

Why is that man looking at me like that? the general thought.

A few minutes later the workmen began digging in five different places at once.

Chapter without a Number

"NOW THERE'S NO knowing where we are," said the general smiting his brow. "This looks to me like a complete dead-end."

"Why don't we take another look at the maps?"

"Because they're meaningless. Because none of our references seem to refer to them!"

"And it looks as though the sketch-map of the cemetery was made in a terrible hurry. While they were actually retreating."

"Quite possible."

"Why don't we try over there, to the right? Where does that track lead to?"

"Those are all fields belonging to a co-operative. In cultivation."

"Well, let's try that way."

"It's a waste of time."

"And this damnable mud on top of it all!"

"We shall have to try over to the right there eventually, you know."

"Very well, but it won't get us anywhere."

"This isn't a search, it's a wild-goose chase!"

"What's that you said?"

"Oh, this blasted mud!"

"We're stuck."

The fretful voices and the footsteps moved off together across the plain.

III

AT THE END OF twenty days they returned to Tirana. Dusk had fallen. Their green limousine drew up outside the Hotel Dajti, at the foot of the curtain of great pine trees that tower in front of the building. The general emerged first. He looked tired, depressed, drawn-featured. His fixed gaze halted for a moment on the car. If only they'd at least wiped off that mud, he thought irritably. But they had only just arrived back, so he could hardly blame the driver because the car was dirty. The general realized that, but he brushed such rational considerations aside.

He walked swiftly up the entrance steps, collected his mail at the desk, asked for a call to be put through to his family, and continued slowly on up to his room.

The priest had gone up to his without even pausing at the desk.

An hour later, having bathed and changed, they were both seated at a table in the ground-floor lounge.

The general ordered brandy. The priest asked for a hot chocolate. It was Saturday. The sounds of a dance band could be heard from the taverna in the basement. Young couples going down into the taverna or coming up from it were visible from time to time at the other end of the lounge. There were people, who were coming in and going out, in the lobby too. The lounge, with its dark curtains and its deep armchairs, had an austere air about it.

"Well, our first tour is over at last," the general said.

They rehearsed the same discussions they had had time and again on their dreary trip: mulling over whether they'd get it all done inside a year, unexpected snags, sudden spells of bad weather.

"Up in the mountains it's going to be tough."

"Yes, I'm very much afraid it is."

"Tomorrow I must get my maps out again and plan the best itinerary for our second tour."

"I only hope the weather is not too unkind to us."

"Well, there's nothing we can do about it. It's the time of year."

The priest sat tranquilly sipping his chocolate, the cup held between thumb and forefinger of one long, slender hand.

A good-looking man, the general thought to himself as he sat looking at the priest's severe profile and impassive, masklike features. Then suddenly he wondered: What was his relationship with the colonel's widow? There must be something between them. She is pretty, quite ravishing in fact, especially in a bathing suit. He remembered that when he had alluded to the priest on one occasion she had been unable to stop herself blushing and had lowered her eyes. What can their relationship be? the generalasked himself again, still watching his companion's face.

"Despite all our efforts we have been unable to find the remains of Colonel Z.," he remarked in a detached tone.

"All the possibilities haven't been exhausted yet," the priest answered, bowing his head. "I have high hopes."

"It will be difficult though, since we know nothing about the circumstances of his death."

"No, it won't be easy," the priest agreed curtly, "but we are still only at the beginning of our mission, we have plenty of time ahead of us."

How far did he manage to go in his relations with the colonel's widow, the general wondered yet again. He was itching to know just how far this reverend father was able to try conclusions with a pretty woman.

"We must find the colonel's remains at all costs," he went on. "The remains of all the other high-ranking officers were repatriated a long time ago. He is the only one who has not been brought home yet. And his family, as you know, is waiting most anxiously to hear the results of our researches. His wife especially."

"Yes," the priest said, "she is very interested in our efforts."

"Have you seen the colonel's tomb? The sumptuous marble tomb they have erected for him?"

"Yes, I went to see it before we left."

"A truly imposing monument," the general continued, "with its statue and those beds planted with red and white roses all around it. But it is empty."

The priest made no answer.

Both men remained silent for some time. The general sipped at his cognac and let his eyes wander about him, realizing as he did so how foreign the whole atmosphere of this place was to him. He suddenly felt quite alone. Alone among the graves of his dead countrymen. Dammit! he wanted to rid his mind of the sight of those graves – those places where his "brothers" lay buried – and not think about them again at any price. He had spent three weeks wandering amongst them. Three weeks on end, day and night, every hour, every minute spent giving himself up solely to those graves. And now he wanted to free himself from them. He had looked forward avidly to this day of rest. It was Saturday and he desperately wanted to relax. After all, he was still alive. It was a right conferred by nature itself. From the basement he could hear the sound of music. They were drinking down there, drinking and dancing.

"We ought to rest," he said softly. But as he said "rest", so he thought "enjoy ourselves".

The priest raised his eyes. No, they said.

It was true. He was a foreign general, and here on government business. Moreover that business was of a particularly lugubrious nature. And lastly he was in the midst of a people who had killed and been killed by his own soldiers in the war.

The general lowered his gaze to the ashtray filled with cigarette ends. He knew inside himself that in the weeks and months ahead, throughout the long pilgrimage that had only just begun, he would never say those words again. His brief rebellion had been nipped in the bud. From now on he would be with his dead alone. All the time.

Yes, he was really very tired. All those worn-out roads, those muddy graves, piled one on top of another in some places, scattered yards apart in others, that eternal and depressing mud, those half-ruined blockhouses – reduced to skeletons, like the soldiers, and then the confusion when the graves of other nations' soldiers overlapped with theirs, the reports to be made out, the receipts to be written and checked with the rural district councils, the complications created at the bank over his foreign currency, so many difficulties one on top of another! The trickiest part was sorting out their own dead from those of the various other armies. Often discrepancies appeared between the statements. The old men confused the events and battles of the last war with those of preceding ones. Nothing that offered even asemblance of certainty. The mud alone held the truth.

The general drank another glass of brandy.

"That shed, out there, in the plain," he said in a low voice, as though talking to himself. "With that sinister storekeeper."

They were forbidden to bring the bones into the towns, so before coming back into Tirana they had delivered all the remains they had collected to a shed erected for the purpose, according to the terms of the contract, on a stretch of waste land on the outskirts.

"A shed, a storekeeper . . . and a dog in front of the door."

The priest did not speak.

In the course of the preliminary discussions they had had with the Albanian officials, there had been notable problems in agreeing on taking the loads of bones through the towns. The authorities had reckoned that this was unacceptable. The mission had never been able to establish precisely why they took this line, but in the end they had to live with it. So each time they reached a town they had to leave the main road to find some sinister shed out on a piece of waste ground, and even now the mere thought of it made the general heave a sigh of exasperation.

He glanced around him. The lounge was quiet as usual. The only exception, only a little way away from him, to one side of the big room, was a group of young men apparently telling stories and laughing from time to time. He could see only their backs. At the far end of the room a young man and a girl, engaged by the look of it, were sitting side by side. They were looking into one another's eyes, only rarely exchanging a few words. The boy had a regularly shaped head, a high, sloping forehead, rather broad lower jaw. An Alpine type, the general said to himself.

The barman's serene round face, as he stood behind his bar, looked like a cut-out moon between two dishes piled high with oranges and apples.

A slim man came in carrying a briefcase. He sat down at a table over by the radio.

"The usual," he said to the barman.

While his coffee was being prepared, the man drew a large exercise book from his briefcase and began to write in it. His jaw was narrow and his cheeks flat. When he drew on his cigarette his cheeks were sucked into hollows.

"So here they are, these Albanians," the general said, as though he were continuing some interrupted discussion. "Men just like anyone else. You would never believe that in battle they would turn into wild beasts."

"True, the transformation in them, once they begin fighting, is quite astounding."

"And to think there are so few of them."

"Not so few as all that," the priest said.

Another man with a sloping forehead walked into the lounge.

"What a damned business this is we've got on our hands!" the general said. "I can't even pass anyone in the street or see anyone in a café now without automatically checking to see what type his skull is."

"I hope you will forgive me for venturing the observation, but I think you're drinking a little too much," the priest said amiably, fixing him with his grey eyes.

At that moment the general saw the colour of those eyes as somehow the same as the television screen at the other end of the lounge. The colour of a television that never lights up! the general said to himself. Or rather of a television screen perpetually showing the same utterly incomprehensible programme.

He looked down for an instant into his now colourless glass as he twisted it round and round in his fingers.

"And what else should I be doing, in your opinion?" he asked with a certain amount of irritation. "What advice have you to offer me? Should I be taking photos to show to my wife when I get back, or keeping a diary and making notes of all the places of interest? Eh? What do you think?"

"I didn't say that. I simply pointed out that you are perhaps drinking a little too much."

"Whereas I find it astonishing that you don't drink. Very astonishing in fact."

23

"I have never drunk alcohol," the priest said.

"That's no reason not to drink it now. Do as I do: drink every evening in order to forget what you see all day long."

"And why should I forget what I see during the day?"

"Because we come from the same country as all these poor wretches," the general said, tapping with his finger on his brief case. "Don't you feel sorry for them?"

"Please don't attack me," the priest said. "I am just as attached to my country as you are."

The general smiled.

"Do you know something?" he said. "I've noticed that our conversations during the past three days or so have the oddest way of sounding like dialogues from some of the modern plays I've seen. Extremely boring ones, I might add."

The priest smiled in his turn.

"That is in the nature of things. Any conversation is bound to bear a resemblance to the dialogue in some play or comedy."

"Do you enjoy the modern theatre?"

"Yes, to a certain extent."

The general looked into the priest's eyes for a long moment before averting his gaze.

"My poor soldiers," he said suddenly, as though waking from a dream. "It tears at my heart when I think of them. I feel like a foster father trying to make it up to children that others have abandoned. You can sometimes feel even fonder of other people's children who have been left by them than of your own. But what can I do for them? How can I avenge them?"

"It tears my heart too," the priest said.

"We are so powerless. We have nothing but lists and reports in our hands. All we can do is hunt out their graves. And one by one at that. It is sad to have been reduced to such impotence."

"That is fate."

The general nodded.

Again just like a play! he thought to himself. He acts as though he's made of metal, that priest. But I'd be curious to know, all the same, whether he was as metallic as this when he was alone with Colonel Z.'s beautiful widow. And he tried to picture to himself how he would have to pull up his cassock in order to kneel down in front of her. Did she just find him attractive, or was there an ulterior motive that made her encourage him? Did anything really happen between them . . . ? But, after all, of what interest is it to me?

A voice emerging from the television in the lounge drew his attention. He turned his head to listen. Albanian struck him as a harsh language. He had heard it spoken quite a lot by this time by the country people who came to help with their excavations in the local cemeteries. And those dead soldiers, he thought, they must certainly have heard it too – a fatal tongue for them. This must be the news now by the sound of it, he thought. And then he did in fact begin to catch familiar syllables: Tel-Aviv, Bonn, Laos . . .

So many cities scattered all over the face of the earth, he thought to himself, and his mind harked back once more to all those soldiers who had come to Albania from so many different countries, to the inscriptions on the rusty metal labels, to the crosses, to the marks on the earth, to the clumsily printed names. But most of the graves had no distinguishing marks over them at all. Worse still, the majority of the dead men they were seeking hadn't been given proper burial. They had simply been piled up in common graves, thrown into hurriedly dug trenches, just dropped into the mud. And there were some who had even been deprived of that muddy ground as a resting place – those that existed solely in his lists.

They had found the remains of one of their soldiers in a

museum case in a tiny little town towards the south. The museum had been founded by a little group of citizens passionately proud of their native town's history. In a deep dungeon below the ancient citadel, among other vestiges of the past, they had unearthed some human remains. For weeks on end, sitting in a local café, these amateur archaeologists had argued over their conflicting theories as to the origins of these remains. Two of them were even in the process of writing an article for a magazine, expressing their learned and audacious theses, when the little group of bone-hunters arrived. Having wandered into the museum quite by chance, the expert had of course recognized the skeleton immediately for what it was by the regulation medallion. (In their article, the local archaeologists were advancing two possible hypotheses on the origin of this object: it was, they said, either a coin or a personal adornment dating from Roman times.) But the expert's visit to the museum put an end to all such conjectures. Only a single point remained to be elucidated: how had the soldier managed to find his way into the impenetrable labyrinth beneath the citadel, and why?

He asked the priest, but he had no clear recollection of the episode.

"You're right," said the general. "One remembers so many stories, and many of them are strangely similar, just as the names are. Really the lists are too long, and sometimes I feel I don't remember a thing."

"He was just a soldier, no different from any of the others," the priest said.

"What is the good of all these names, all these cards covered in details and descriptions?" the general said. "When all is said and done, can a pile of bones still have a name?"

The priest shook his head as though to signify: There is nothing we can do. That is the way it is!

"They should all have the same name, just as they all wear the same medallion round their necks," the general went on.

The priest did not reply.

The sounds of the band were still reaching them from the basement. The general continued to chain-smoke.

"It's horrible, the number of our men they managed to kill," he said as though in a dream.

"It is indeed."

"But we killed a lot of theirs too."

The priest remained silent.

"Yes, we certainly killed a lot of theirs," the general said again. "You see their graves everywhere too. It would have been depressing and humiliating to see nothing but lonely cemeteries filled with our own soldiers everywhere."

The priest made a movement of the head, but without making it clear whether he was agreeing with the general or not.

"A meagre consolation," the general added.

Once again the priest made that movement of the head that seemed to say: There's nothing we can do about it.

"What do you mean?" the general said. "Do you think their graves are a consolation or not?"

The priest spread out his hands.

"I am a man of religion. I cannot approve of homicide."

"Ah!" the general said.

The engaged couple had got to their feet and were leaving the lounge.

"We fought one another like wild beasts," the general went on. "Those devils really were savage fighters."

"There's a reason for that," the priest said. "It's not a matter of conscious courage with them. It's ingrained in their psychology."

"I don't understand you," the general said.

"There's nothing difficult about it," the priest continued. "In

27

war, some are guided by their reason, however reliable or unstable it happens to be, others follow their instincts."

"Yes!"

"The Albanians are a rough and backward people. Almost as soon as they are born someone puts a gun into their cradle, so that it shall become an integral part of their existence."

"Yes, you can see that," the general said. "They even hold their umbrellas as though they were guns."

"And by becoming from earliest childhood an ingredient of their very being," the priest went on, "a fundamental constituent of their lives, the gun has exercised a direct influence on the Albanians' psychological development."

"How interesting."

"But if you cultivate what amounts to a sort of religion around any object, then naturally you feel a desire to use it. And what is the best use to which you can put a gun?"

"Killing, of course," the general said.

"Exactly. And the Albanians have always had a taste for killing or getting themselves killed. Whenever they haven't been able to find an enemy to fight they've turned to killing one another. Have you heard about their vendettas?"

"Yes."

"It's an atavistic instinct that drives them into war. Their nature requires war, cries out for war. In peace, the Albanian becomes sluggish and only half alive, like a snake in winter. It is only when he is fighting that his vitality is at full stretch."

The general nodded approvingly.

"War is the normal condition of this country," the priest went on. "That's why its inhabitants are so wild, so formidable, and why when they have once begun to fight there is no limit to how far they are prepared to go."

"In other words," the general said, "if what you say about this

28

thirst for destruction – or rather for self-destruction – is true, then as a people they are doomed to disappear from the face of the earth."

"Of course."

The general took another drink. He was beginning to have slight difficulty in articulating his words.

"Do you hate the Albanians?" he asked suddenly.

The grimace the priest gave was intended as a smile.

"No. Why do you ask?"

The general leant forward to whisper into his ear. The priest gave a tiny start of revulsion as he smelt the alcohol-impregnated breath.

"What do you mean, 'Why?'?" the general said very quietly. "I know perfectly well that you do hate them. Just as I do. But you're right, it's not in our interests to go round saying so just now."

IV

WHEN THEY HAD WISHED one another good night and the general had closed the door of his room behind him he sat down at a little table lit by the light falling from a shaded lamp. Despite the late hour he did not feel sleepy. His briefcase lay on the table, and he stretched out a mechanical hand to pick it up. He pulled out the lists of dead soldiers and began leafing through them. They made a big bundle, stapled together in batches of four, five – up to ten sheets. He glanced through them, re-reading for the hundredth time the headings typed in capitals at the beginning of each list: "Old Glory Regiment", "Second Division", "Iron Division", "3rd Alpine Battalion", "4th Regiment of Guards", "Victory Division", "7th Infantry Division", "Blue Battalion" (a punitive unit) . . . He paused for a moment over this last one. The first name on the list was that of Colonel Z., followed by the names, listed in alphabetical order, of all the other dead, officers, N.C.O.s, privates, all classified according to their troops and companies. "Blue Battalion" – a pretty name, the general thought to himself.

The typing of the lists had been started in the spring. Young girls, their hair and clothes strictly in accord with the latest fashions, had sat in the long offices at the Ministry, by the tall windows, tapping at the keys of their machines with slender fingers. It was almost as though, beneath the indifferent stares of those mascaraed eyes, the soldiers were being machine-gunned down yet again.

He laid aside the master lists of names and drew out another bundle, this time copiously annotated and bearing occasional little red crosses in the margins. These were the lists containing all the available facts that might be of help in the search for the remains. On these lists the dead soldiers were no longer grouped according to regiment, division, etc., but according to the places where they had fallen; and beside each name there was a set of co-ordinates referring to one of the maps, together with the man's height and a description of his dentition. The names of those already recovered were marked with small red crosses; but these were still very few in number.

I ought to transcribe these results onto the master lists and work out the figures of our first tour, the general thought to himself, but it is very late.

Unable to think of anything else to do, almost without think-ing he continued his perusal of the lists. On those giving the location details, all the place names were followed by transla-tions in brackets, and the names of all those valleys, passes, plateaux, rivers and towns seemed to him somehow extraordi-nary and macabre: the Deaf-mute's Ditch, the Bride's Brook, the Five Wells, the Church of Psalms, Sheho's Mother's Tomb, the Screech Owl's Crevice. He had the feeling that these places had shared out the lists of dead men among themselves, each taking a different quantity, and that he was now here to wrest the bodies away from them again.

Once more his eyes came to rest on one of the lists. It was the "Missing" list, and again Colonel Z.'s name stood at the head of it. Six foot one, right number one incisor gold inlay, the general read, and continued right on to the end: five foot eight, two premolars missing; five foot five, upper molars missing; six foot two and a half, incisors on metal bridge; five foot eleven, dentition complete; six foot ten . . . ! He must certainly be the tallest on the list, the general thought. I wonder how tall the tallest soldier in our army was. I know quite well how small the smallest will have been: five feet, because that's the regulation minimum. The tallest are usually from the 4th Guards Regiment, the shortest from the Alpine Regiment. But really, why am I sitting here letting all this absurd nonsense run through my head like this?

He switched off the light and lay down. Sleep wouldn't come. Oughtn't to have drunk that damned coffee so late in the evening, he thought ruefully.

He lay staring up at the white ceiling of his room, watching the headlights of the passing cars sweep across it. Penetrating the still partly open blinds, the light was projected onto the white surface in a fan of wheeling stripes, and he felt he was gazing up at an X-ray screen upon which an endless succession of strangers was appearing and demanding to be examined.

He thought of the lists lying scattered on the table and shuddered. I ought to have brought my wife with me, he thought. We should be lying here side by side now in the darkness, we should be talking in low voices, and I could tell her all my worries. But she would be afraid, the way she was those last days before I left to come here.

Those last few days had been very different from his usual way of life, filled with an element of the unexpected and the unknown. The fine weather had broken and he had scarcely got home from their holiday at the sea before the first visitor had presented himself at his home. He was reading in his study when the maid came to tell him that someone was waiting to see him in the drawing-room.

The man was standing by the window. Outside, the day was waning and the shadows, moving shapes, wandered haggardly about. Hearing the door open, the visitor turned towards the general and greeted him.

"I apologize for disturbing you," he said in a deep, hoarse voice, "but I have been told that you are about to leave for Albania in order to bring home the remains of our countrymen still buried there."

"That is quite true," the general answered. "I expect to leave in a fortnight."

"I have a request I'd like to make to you," the man went on, and he pulled a crumpled map of Albania out of his pocket. "I fought in Albania during the war, as a private. I was there for two years."

"Which unit?" the general asked.

"Iron Division, 5th Battalion, machine-gun section."

"Go ahead," the general said.

The stranger leaned over the crumpled map he had unfolded and after studying it for a moment laid his forefinger on a particular spot.

"This is the place where my battalion was wiped out during a big attack by the Albanian partisans. It was the middle of the winter. Those of us who escaped being killed dispersed in all directions as soon as darkness came. I had a wounded soldier with me, a friend. He died shortly before dawn, just as I was dragging him towards a deserted village. I buried him as best I could on my own, just behind the little village church, and then I left. That's all. No one has any idea the grave is there. That's why I've come to see you. I want to beg you, when you go that way, to search for his remains."

"His name must certainly figure on the 'Missing' list," the general said. "The lists are extremely accurate. But nevertheless you did well to come and see me, since the chances of finding missing bodies are always slight. Success in such cases is often simply a matter of luck."

"I have also made a little sketch, as well as I could," the man said, pulling out of his pocket a scrap of paper on which he had scratched out something with a fountain pen that vaguely resembled a church, and then, just behind it, two arrows with the word grave written in red ink below them. "There's a fountain not far away," the man went on, "and further still, on the right, two cypresses about here," and he made a fresh mark on the map, near the church.

"Good," the general said. "Thank you for your help."

"Oh, it is for me to thank you," the other said. "He was my best friend."

There was something else he wanted to say, perhaps some further detail about the position of the grave, but the general's stern and serious air prevented him from doing so. He took his leave without the general having even asked him his identity or his profession.

And that had been just the start. Every afternoon he would hear the doorbell ring again and again as more and more visitors came pouring into the drawing-room. They were people of all sorts, from every walk of life – wives, aged parents, ex-soldiers – and they all had the same timid air, the same reserved expression on their faces. Then others began to filter in from the more distant towns and provinces. These newcomers waited in the drawing-room with an even more embarrassed air than the others and had great difficulty getting out what they wanted to say, especially since the information they were able to provide about their relations or their friends killed in Albania was usually bothvery limited and unreliable.

The general made notes of everything that was said to him and then told them all the same thing:

"Don't worry. The lists drawn up by the War Ministry are extremely accurate, and with the detailed information they provide we cannot fail to find all those we are looking for. But I have in any case made a note of the information you have brought me. It may prove useful."

They thanked him, they left, and next day the whole thing began all over again. Another batch would appear, in dripping raincoats. It didn't matter how carefully they picked their way across the thick carpet, they still left footprints on it. Some were afraid that their relations weren't included on the lists, others brought telegrams received from commanding officers during the war bearing the date of death and the name of the place where the soldier had "fallen for his country", still others – the old parents especially – unable to believe that their sons could be recovered solely with the help of the information provided by the lists, left in despair, having once more begged the general to spare no effort in his search.

All had their little story to tell, and the general listened to them patiently, each in turn, from the wives who had now remarried and wanted to do their best for their first husbands without their new husbands knowing, to the young twenty-year-olds in sweaters and duffle coats who had never known the fathers who had died in the war.

The last week before his departure, the number of visitors had increased even further. When he came back from his headquarters at mid-day the general would find his drawing-room crammed with people. The room had the air of a hospital corridor filled with patients waiting to be examined; but the silence here was even more complete. The visitors remained utterly silent for hours on end, sitting with their eyes fixed on the patterns in the carpet. Some, country people who had come a long way, appeared with bundles in their arms, which they then set down at their feet. And the general always knew they were waiting for him, even before he got out of his car, because of the bicycles leaning against the railings, and sometimes a strange car parked outside. He would go directly into the drawing-room, where the bitter odour of damp wool from the peasants' thick clothes, mingling with some elegant woman's scent, would make him catch his breath. At his entry they all respectfully rose to their feet, but without saying a word, knowing that this was not yet the moment to speak to him.

Then, when lunch was over, he would go through into the drawing-room and one by one the visitors would put their cases before him. How little the stories differed! The things they said to him had soon become so familiar that each day seemed like no more than a reliving of the previous day in his mind. Often there were women whose grief over their lost sons or husbands was such that they could not restrain their sobs, and that made the general even more on edge than ever.

"Now that's enough of that!" he cried one day to one of these weeping women. "This is not the place to bring your tears! Your son fell on the field of battle, fighting for his country."

Another day there was a tall man who had scarcely entered the room before shouting:

"This mission of yours is nothing but a hoax!"

The general turned white with anger.

"That is traitor's talk! Get out of here!"

Towards the middle of this last week, among the visitors waiting for him he noticed a very old woman accompanied by a little girl. The old woman looked as though she was in a state of exhaustion, so he went over to her first.

"My son is still over there," she said in a faint voice, "my only son."

And taking a little bag out of her pocket she pulled it open with trembling hands. It contained a telegram, yellowed with age, which she held out to him. His eyes flicked through the usual phrases employed by commanding officers to convey the news of a soldier's death to his relatives, but stopped abruptly at the words: " . . . fell on the field of battle at Stalingrad."

He tried to explain to her: "I'm very sorry, my dear, but it's not Russia I'm going to, it's Albania."

The old woman rested her dulled eyes on him for a moment, but apparently without having grasped the meaning of what he said.

"There is something I want to ask you to do," she went on. "Could you manage to find out where he died, and how? And who was with him, who brought him water, and what his last wishes were?"

The general attempted once more to make her understand that he wasn't going to Russia, but the old woman, still unable to understand, simply went on repeating her request while all the other occupants of the room eyed one another in silence.

"Set your mind at rest, my dear lady," someone gently interrupted at last, "the general will do everything he can to help, you may be sure." And at that the old woman thanked him and left, bent almost double, supporting herself with one hand clutching her stick and the other on the shoulder of the little girl beside her.

Another afternoon, two days later, a man with a particularly sombre look about him waited till everyone else had gone.

"I was a general once too," he said in a tone that betrayed suppressed anger, "and I took part in the Albanian campaign." The two men looked at one another for an instant with mutual contempt, the one because he was looking at a defeated general, the other because he was dealing with a mere peacetime soldier.

"What is it you want?" the general asked his visitor.

"Nothing at all, really. Because I'm not expecting you to get very far anyway. To tell you the truth I have no confidence in you, and also I find this whole scheme basically ridiculous. But given that you've taken it on, this mission, well it might as well be done properly, damn it!"

"Could you explain yourself more clearly?"

"I have nothing more to say. I simply wanted to warn you. Be always on your guard. Keep your head high, and never let them see you bow it. They will try to provoke you, they may try to make a fool of you, and you must know how to answer them. You must be on the alert all the time. They will try to insult our soldiers' remains. I know them too well. They often jeered at us. They didn't give a damn even then! Imagine what they will be capable of now!"

"I shall not tolerate such behaviour under any circumstances," the general said.

The ex-general looked at him with an air of commiseration, as though he was just on the point of saying: "Poor fellow!", then he suddenly turned and walked out without even taking his leave.

For the next three days, the last before he was due to leave, the general's drawing-room was packed with people the whole time, and the general himself, worn out by these preliminaries, longed only to leave as soon as possible. Meanwhile, his wife had become extremely nervous and agitated. One evening, as they lay side by side talking, she told him what was really on her mind:

"Why can't you just refuse to go on this mission? I feel . . . I feel as though death has come into the house."

He soothed her as best he could. But that night he scarcely slept a wink himself. He had the feeling that he was going into battle next day.

He received the last visitor of all on the very morning of his departure. He was up just after daybreak, because he had to be at the airport very early. As he went out through the garden to open the garage doors he noticed figures outside. They were squatting down asleep against the railings, wrapped in a thick blanket – an old man and his young grandson. They had come from one of the most distant frontier districts. The journey had taken them several days and they had only arrived on the last train the night before.

Since they hadn't dared to ring the bell at such an hour they had simply huddled down on the pavement outside and dozed off while waiting for the dawn.

The general repeated for the last time the words he had uttered so often: "The lists have been drawn up with the utmost care, don't worry, we shall find them." The old countryman thanked him with a nod of the head, then bent to pick up the blanket that he and his grandson had let fall at their feet when startled into wakefulness by the squeaking garage door.

That is how it had been, and that was how the general's two weeks at home, before he left for Albania, had been spent.

V

THEY WERE ON THE road again. There was a fine rain falling. For weeks now they had been journeying through rugged country with only scattered villages. The car drove in front. The lorry carrying the workmen and their tools brought up the rear. The road was a very busy one. Villagers, dressed in their tightly fitting suits of thick black wool, were passing continually in both directions, on foot, on horseback, or perched on the backs of lorries. The general observed the lie and contours of the hills they passed with great interest. He tried to envisage the tactics that would have been adopted by successive armies during all the country's various wars.

Not far from the centre of one small town there was a newspaper kiosk. There were quite a number of people crowding around it, others were standing nearby reading, and some were glancing through their newspapers as they walked away.

"The Albanians read a great many newspapers," the general commented suddenly.

The priest emerged from his torpor in the other corner.

"That's because they are so politically conscious. Now they've quarrelled with the Soviet Union they are completely isolated in Europe."

"As they always have been."

"But now they're under blockade. And with things as they are it's going to be hard for them to hold out."

"All the same, having to blockade so small a country . . ."

"It's odd!"

"Exactly. They'll be hard put to hold out, in the circumstances."

"It just shows what stubborn devils they must be," the general said. "It looks as though it's impossible to subdue them by force. Perhaps they would succumb to beauty?"

The priest laughed.

"What are you laughing at?"

The priest continued to chuckle without answering.

The general looked out at the dark landscape swathed in mist, at the denuded flanks of the mountains and the multitude of stones of all sizes scattered everywhere over the ground. He felt a profound sadness well up in him. It was a week now since they had seen any other sight but rock-covered slopes just like these, and he began to feel that beneath their stark wildness they were concealing some awful secret.

"It is a tragic country," he said. "Even their clothes have something tragic about them. Look at those black cloaks, and the women's skirts."

"What would you say if you heard their songs, I wonder? They are even more lugubrious. It is all tied up with the country's whole past. Down the centuries, there can be no people that has experienced a sadder destiny. That is what accounts for the roughness, the harshness we see today."

The car was making its way down a mountain road. It was cold. Every now and then they heard the sound of lorries furiously revving their engines. At the top of a slope there rose the outline of a big factory still in the course of construction. Because of the bareness of the landscape the half-finished building stood out gaunt and gigantic against its backdrop of mist.

"It's a copper-processing plant," the priest said.

Every now and then, when they came to crossroads, they would pass square, or circular, or hexagonal blockhouses with gun-slits pointing down at the road. At each bend the car emerged into their line of fire, and the general sat staring back into those narrow, deserted slits with the rain dripping endlessly across them.

We're past! he would say to himself every time the car passed out of the line of fire. But then at the next turn yet another block-house would seem to rise up out of the earth, and the car seemed once more threatened by its potential fire. The general let his eyes relax and focus on the rain streaming down the car window; but every now and then, as he began to sink into a doze, he imagined the car windows shattered into a thousand shards by bullets, and he would wake up again with a sudden start. But the blockhouses were all silent and deserted. If you studied them carefully from a distance they looked like Egyptian sculptures, with expressions that were sometimes cold and contemptuous, sometimes enig-matic, depending upon the design of the gunslits. When the slits were vertical then the little forts had a cruel, menacing expression that conjured up some evil spirit; but when the slits were horizon-tal, then their strange petrified mimicry expressed only indiffer-ence and scorn.

At about noon they came down at last into the plain and eventually arrived at a village composed of two lines of houses strung out on either side of the road. The rain had stopped. The usual crowd of children began gathering about the car. They could be heard calling to one another in the distance as they ran towards the main street along parallel paths. The lorry drew up a few yards behind the car, and the workmen, leaping out over the tailgate one after another, began jumping up and down and waving their arms in order to get the circulation going again in their numbed limbs.

Passing villagers stopped to stare at these strangers. But they did not seem to be unaware of the reason for the visit. You could tell that from their faces. From the women's especially. The general could recognize it easily now, that indecipherable expression in the villagers' eyes. We remind them of the invasion, he thought. Wherever we go, you can always tell what the war was like there just from their expressions. The fiercer the fighting was the more enigmatic their faces.

At the edge of the village, in a piece of fallow land, a considerable number of graves had been arranged in rows. The cemetery was surrounded by a low wall, breached in places. The men lying there are all ours, the general said to himself. And he drew his long waterproof cape closer about him to keep out the chill of the thought. A little ahead of him, standing quite motionless, the priest had the appearance of a black cross in a Mexican engraving. It's easy to see how they came to get themselves surrounded, the general thought. Then they must have tried to escape by that bridge over the river there, and that's where they will have got themselves wiped out. What idiot of an officer could have led them into a hornets' nest like that? There's nothing on the graves to tell us.

The Albanian expert began the customary formalities. Further on more graves appeared. They were all very much closer to the village and had red stars at their heads. The general recognized it immediately as a "martyrs' graveyard", as the natives of the country called the plots where the partisans were buried. In this one, seven of his countrymen had been buried beside the Albanians. Despite the spelling mistakes it was still possible to make out the names of the seven on the little metal labels with their red stars, together with their nationality and the date of their deaths – identical for all seven. On a stone plaque nearby was the inscription: "These foreign soldiers died heroes' deaths, fighting beside Albanian partisans against the forces of the Blue Battalion, 17 March 1943."

"That Blue Battalion again," the general said as he walked between the rows of graves. "This is the second time we've come across Colonel Z.'s tracks. And according to our lists there should be two men of his battalion buried in this very village."

"We must ask the villagers whether they know anything about the colonel," the priest said.

While the visitors were busy entering their expenses, a number of men from the village had unobtrusively gathered along the graveyard boundary. Then a few women had appeared too. The children had even ventured further forward and were now standing there whispering in one another's ears and shaking their little blond heads. All eyes were on the little group walking up and down between the rows of graves.

An old woman carrying a keg on her back joined the villagers.

"Are they taking them away?" she asked in a low voice.

"Yes, yes, they're taking them away," several voices murmured in reply.

Her burden still on her back, the old woman surveyed the scene in the cemetery for a while with the other villagers. Then she walked forward several steps and spoke to the workmen:

"Make sure you tell them not to mix those seven up with the others. We mourned those with our own, according to the custom."

The general and the priest turned round to look at the old woman, but she had already turned and was walking away. They watched her little keg swaying from side to side for a moment, then she was hidden by a bend in the road.

The villagers strung out along the edge of the cemetery were so still that it would have been easy not to notice their presence there at all. They all stood watching with the utmost concentration, determined not to miss a single movement made by these men walking up and down inside the cemetery, their coat collars turned up against the cold, apparently searching for something, though without success.

"Work in both cemeteries will begin tomorrow," the general said. "Today we shall try to find the two Blue Battalion soldiers and the crashed pilot."

Everyone in the village knew about the pilot. The wreckage of his aircraft had been strewn all through the little wood on the far side of the village. The pilot had been buried by the peasants themselves, near his plane. There was hardly any sign of the grave left now, except for a big stone that presumably marked its head. As for the plane, there was nothing left of that but a pile of rusty metal. One of the villagers told them how they had gradually stripped it of all the items that could be of any use to them, from the tyres and other rubber components – burnt during the war in place of candles – to the heavier metal parts, which had been put to innumerable different uses.

Two of the workmen started digging straight away. The others began making their way back to the village.

The rain had stopped long before, but the ruts left in the track by carts and tractors were still full of water. Here and there half-used haystacks loomed, still dripping wet. Between the cypress trees, the steeple of the old church stood out in the distance against the sky, and from a field even further away there came the muffled roar of a tractor.

They ate lunch in the vehicles, then went to have coffee in the co-operative club. The room was very smoky and there were almost no tables to be had. A little radio was shrieking its head off, the volume turned full up. The villagers were all chattering at the tops of their voices. It was easy to see, from their sun-bleached hair and their creased skins, that they were plain-dwellers. Also, the timbre of their voices was different from that of the mountain people – gentler, more melodious.

45

As he sipped his coffee, the general let his eyes wander round the walls, trying to read the slogans blazoned there in bright red print. All he could make out were the words "imperialism", "revisionism", "plenum", and the name Enver Hoxha at the bottom of a brief quotation.

After a short while, the expert rejoined them in the club. He was accompanied by a young man wearing a very wide-ribbed corduroy jacket. Both men came over to the table where the general was sitting and the expert did the introductions.

The young man fixed his grey, slightly astonished eyes on the foreigner for a moment, then turned back to the expert.

"It's very simple," the latter began. "This week we expect to be doing exhumations in the two military cemeteries outside your village. We have our own workmen of course, but to get the job done quicker we should appreciate some help from you as well, if it's possible."

The young man paused for a moment in what appeared to be embarrassment before replying:

"The fact is our men are rather busy just at the moment. It's right in the middle of ploughing for one thing, and also our tobacco and cotton aren't doing too well this year. And apart from that . . ."

"But it would only be for a few days," the expert broke in. "And of course all the co-operative workmen we use will be properly paid. These people" (and the expert indicated the general and the priest with his eyes) "are prepared to pay thirty new leks for every grave opened and fifty for each opened grave that proves to contain one of their men."

"We pay well." The general emphasized the point.

"It's not a question of that," the head of the co-operative said. "I'm wondering whether this kind of work is authorized by the government . . . . I mean, if . . ."

"Oh, you can set your mind at rest on that score," the expert interrupted him again. "I have a permit from the Presidency offices. Take a look."

The young man read the document held out to him, then thought for a moment.

"As far as I'm concerned, I can let you have ten men for three or four days."

The general thanked the young man and the visitors rose to go.

No one in the village had even heard of the existence of the two Blue Battalion soldiers who had been killed and buried in the area.

The general spent over an hour with the Albanian expert trying to work out, with the help of the information on the map, the precise location of the graves. Finally they succeeded. The spot turned out to be inside the co-operative's calf shed. Accompanied by a group from the co-operative, they made their way there, and having cleared the animals away from the presumed burial areas they began digging. The calves gazed at the intruders with their beautiful, tranquil eyes, and the pleasant smell of hay hung in the shed.

Before nightfall the remains of the pilot and the two soldiers had been recovered. Those of the pilot had been found without difficulty, but before unearthing those of the two soldiers they had been obliged to open up trench after trench, and when the general finally departed the floor of the calf shed looked as though it had been under heavy shellfire.

The workmen filled in the trenches without hurrying; they were going to sleep in the village. The general, the priest, and the expert, however, had decided to spend the night in a small town about thirty kilometres away.

It was already dark when they set out. Their car started off slowly, avoiding the ruts, its headlights sometimes lighting up the poplars lining the road, sometimes a cart coming in from the field or a farmyard with its fence of tall reeds.

"Stop!" the priest cried suddenly, just as they were driving back past the part of the cemetery where their own soldiers were buried.

The driver braked.

"What's up?" asked the expert.

The priest pointed out to the general an inscription on the little wall bounding the cemetery.

As soon as the car was stationary he got out. The general followed, slamming the car door violently behind him. The expert also climbed out.

"What is the meaning of that?" the general cried, pointing at the low wall.

Scrawled in charcoal, in big, badly formed capitals, were the words: *Such is the fate of our enemies!*

The expert shrugged.

"It was done this afternoon," he said. "There was nothing there this morning."

"We are aware of that," the general said. "What we should like to know is what the purpose of your government is in inciting its people to shameful provocations of this kind."

"I can't see anything shameful in it," the expert said calmly.

The priest had pulled out his notebook, apparently in order to copy down the words written on the wall.

"Nothing shameful?" the general exploded. "Words like that scrawled on the wall around our dead! I shall report the matter. It is a serious provocation, a contemptible insult."

The expert turned back angrily to face him.

"Twenty years ago you scrawled your Fascist slogans on our comrades' chests before you hanged them, and now you pretend

48

to be appalled by a few simple words like that, probably put there by a schoolchild."

"We are not talking about what happened twenty years ago," the general interrupted him.

"It still applies, nevertheless."

"It's got nothing to do with what happened twenty years ago!"

"You are always talking about the Greeks and the Trojans. Why shouldn't we talk about what happened twenty years ago?"

"Talk like this will get us nowhere," the general concluded. "This is not the place for it."

All three walked quickly back to the car. The doors slammed furiously behind them, one after another, like guns firing, and the driver set off again. But in less than five minutes they were forced to stop again.

Outside the village, just over a wooden bridge, the road was blocked by a cart that had just shed a wheel. Two peasants were at work on it.

Without breaking off his struggle to get the wheel back on, the villager asked the expert:

"Where are you from?"

The expert told him.

"This morning we were told why you're here," the man said. "All the women in the village are talking about nothing else. They started the moment they saw your car and lorry driving in."

"Push, can't you, damn it!" the other peasant grunted as he strained on his side to get the wheel back on.

"They said you're going to get all the foreign soldiers up out of their graves and take them back to their own country," the first peasant went on unperturbed. "And that you're going to dig up all the *ballistes*[1] along with them, and take them away

1 Albanian nationalists, sometimes accused of collaborating with the occupying Italian and German forces.

too, into a foreign country beyond the sunset. Is that true?"

The expert began to laugh.

"That's the story they're telling," the peasant persisted. "So that even now they're dead they'll still be with the enemy, just the same as when they were alive. Collaborators yesterday, collaborators today. That's what they're saying in the village."

The expert laughed again.

"Well, it's not true," he told the man. "No one is going to bother with the dead *ballistes*."

"Hey, push, will you, I say!" the other peasant shouted again.

The wheel wouldn't stay on. There were dogs barking in the distance. Someone was approaching from the fields carrying a lantern. The light from it quivered, as though it was afraid.

"One of your wheels playing up then?" the new arrival asked, then lifted his lantern to gaze with astonishment at the strangers and their car.

After standing there for a further moment observing them, the man in the cowsheds wished them a good night and moved on. The light from his lantern threw pale patches onto the haystacks standing in a silent row along the edge of the road.

The dogs were still barking.

"Do you always do this kind of work?" the peasant asked the expert.

The expert nodded.

"Yes, I've been doing it for quite a while now," he said a moment later.

The peasant gave a deep sigh.

"Not a very happy job to be doing."

The driver began whistling a recent popular song.

"Come on! One and two and push!"

The wheel was back on at last.

"Good night!" The cry had come from a group of villagers

returning across the darkening plain, hoes over their shoulders.

"Good night!"

At last the cart was pulled clear of the road and the car continued on its way towards the main road ahead.

The October night had now descended over the plain. The moon, having given up its vain attempts to break through, was pouring its brightness down into the spongy layers of cloud and mist, which now seemed to have become saturated with its pale light and were slowly, gently, evenly letting it drift down onto the horizon and the vast open plain. The sky above them had acquired a fecund glow, and the horizon, the plain, the road, all seemed to be covered with pools of milky light.

There were those autumn nights when the sky was possessed by an aspect of strange brightness, wholly steeped in the indifferent, haunting light of the moon. And lying on the ground, on our backs, every one of us must surely have said to himself: "My God! What a sky!"

VI

THE CAR DREW UP outside the Albtourist Hotel. In the rain-soaked streets, in front of the neon-lit shop windows, the occasional passer-by was still to be seen. But the cold night wind was sharp as a knife flaying your face, and the travellers hurried into the shelter of the hotel lobby. There were plenty of rooms available because the tourist season was over.

The general went over to the window and pulled back the curtains. Across the plain the same troubling brightness was seeping down from the moon. He closed the curtains again and lit a cigarette.

The priest knocked at the door.

"The lieutenant-general we met two weeks ago up in the mountains is downstairs, in the restaurant," he said.

The expert, who was waiting for them in the bar, had the same news: "I can only assume that they have some exhumations to do in the town."

Two weeks before, they had been driving along a road running beneath the flank of a vast plateau when the general, sitting silent in his corner and fitfully dozing, suddenly noticed something very odd.

Up on the mountainside a group of what looked, from their blue overalls, like municipal roadworkers were busy digging holes in four or five separate spots. Further on, in the road stood a car with a canvas-covered lorry parked behind it. The two vehicles were identical with their own. A man in uniform, tightly belted into his raincoat, was standing beside the green car. Another man, dressed in black, was standing with his back to the road.

What is this mirage? the general asked himself, his mind still half asleep. Am I dreaming? He felt it must be himself, the priest, and their own workmen he was looking out at. He screwed up his eyes and lifted his arm to wipe away the mist obscuring the glass. It wasn't a mirage.

"Just take a look over there," he said quietly to the priest. And the latter, turning in the direction indicated, made a gesture of surprise.

"Would you stop here, please," the general said to the driver.

The man brought the car to a halt. The general wound down the window on his side and pointed over to the right.

"Take a look at those men up there," he said to the expert.

The man turned his head and screwed up his eyes.

"Who are they? What are they up to?" asked the general.

"Evidently just what we're doing: digging."

"How is that possible? They have no right to excavate without informing us."

"It is their own soldiers they are looking for," the expert said.

"Heavens! Anyone would think I'm having hallucinations."

"It is over a year since our government signed the contract with theirs, but their preparations took them longer than they expected and they did not begin work until this past summer."

"Ah! Now I understand. Is he a general too?"

"Yes, a lieutenant-general. The other man is the mayor of one of their cities."

The general smiled and said:

"All we need now is a general with a *hodja* in tow."

"There would be nothing very surprising in that. The Turks may well come to fetch their dead back one day."

While this exchange was taking place between the general

and the expert, the two strangers standing on the side of the road had turned around and were looking towards the newcomers with curiosity.

"Let's get out," the general said, opening his door. "They are colleagues of ours. It might be as well to get to know them."

"What for?" the priest said.

"We can pool our experience, since we're all in the same profession," the general said with a laugh.

As he walked closer he noticed that the other general had had his right arm amputated. In his remaining hand – the left one – he was holding a fat black pipe. The civilian was a corpulent, bald man.

The introductions over, they conversed for a while in bad English while the two lorry drivers lent each other a hand on some small matter.

Ten minutes later, having taken leave of their new acquaintances, the general and the priest set off again.

And this was the first time they had run into them again since that day.

"There they are," the general said as he and the priest entered the restaurant.

They acknowledged one another with nods of the head.

The newcomers sat down and ate in their turn, mostly in silence. The expert and the priest did exchange a few words now and then, but the general, a hint of a scowl on his face, seemed put out about something. As soon as they had finished eating the expert went up to his room.

The general and the priest left the restaurant and went out into the lounge where the other general and the mayor were sitting smoking.

"We sit here like this every evening," the mayor said. "We've been in this town a good week now, and this is how we've spent all our evenings. Where is one to go? They tell us that the place is very pleasant in summer, that there are various places of entertainment open; but at this time of year there are no foreign tourists, and also there's this icy wind blowing off the river day and night."

"We could have come here before," the one-armed general said, "but the football championship was still going on, and they wouldn't give us permission to excavate inside the stadium boundary until all the championship matches were over."

"Can you imagine a more bizarre obstacle to have put in your way?" the mayor asked.

"Oh, it was reasonable enough really," the other put in. "I know we could perhaps have begun by digging around the edges, not touching the actual field; but it wouldn't have been very pleasant. Imagine listening to all those spectators cheering their heads off at every goal while we were hunting for bones."

"And what about the spectators?" the general said. "I don't suppose they would have enjoyed the sight of graves gaping everywhere during the match."

"Perhaps not," said the one-armed general, "but I wouldn't risk my hand in the fire on it."

The general's eyes dropped to the hand, the remaining hand, with which the other was holding his pipe. Then to the empty coat sleeve tucked into the right pocket.

Odd expression, he thought. And then: The arm must have been amputated at the elbow by the look of it.

"I don't understand how they were allowed to build a football stadium on top of a military cemetery," the priest said. "It is contrary to all the international agreements. You ought to have put in a protest."

"We have," the lieutenant-general told him, "but apparently our men's bodies weren't buried by the locals but by our own forces. And what's more the job was done during the night. So no one knew anything about it."

"I must say, however, that I don't really believe that explanation," the mayor put in.

"It doesn't exactly convince me either," the lieutenant-general said, "but again, I wouldn't risk my hand in the fire over it."

The general stared at the empty sleeve again.

"We have been fortunate. We have never encountered anything of that kind," he said.

"Where are you excavating at the moment?" the mayor asked.

The general told him the name of the village.

"You have extremely accurate lists at your disposal, I believe. Whereas ours are based solely on verbal testimony."

"You might say that we are hunting in the dark," the mayor put in.

"Difficult for you."

"Extremely," the lieutenant-general said. "We shall probably find no more than a few hundred or so sets of remains. And even then we shan't be able to identify most of them."

"Identification must indeed be a problem without accurate lists."

"You, I assume, have full details as to the height and dentition of each of your bodies?"

"Yes," the priest said.

"And moreover all your soldiers wore a medallion, isn't that so?"

"Yes indeed."

"Whereas our lists do not even give the heights of the dead we are looking for, and that scarcely facilitates our task."

"Fortunately there are the metal buckles on the belts. They help enormously," the mayor said.

Two young men came into the lounge and took seats over by

the tall french windows which led out onto the hotel gardens, and, presumably, down to the river.

"What brand of disinfectant do you use on your remains?" the mayor asked.

"'Universal 62'."

"That's efficient. Though the most efficient of all is the earth itself."

"True, true. But there are cases when the earth itself has proved unable to fulfil that function."

"You have found bodies still intact?"

"We certainly have!"

"Yes, so have we."

"It's extremely dangerous."

"Yes, though the danger of infection is constant of course. The bacteria can sometimes resist destruction for many years and then suddenly recover all their virulence the moment the grave is opened."

"Have you ever had any, er, unfortunate accidents?"

"Not so far."

"Will you take coffee with us?" the lieutenant-general asked.

"Thank you, but no. I am going up to bed now," the priest said.

"I must go up now too," the mayor said. "I still have a letter to write."

They wished the two generals good night and disappeared up stairs which were carpeted in a velvety crimson. The lounge was quiet. The only sound was that of the two young men talking in the far corner, fragments of whose conversation could occasion-ally be heard.

The general glanced over at the french windows and the darkness beyond.

"We are already worn out, and yet who knows what difficulties still lie ahead?"

"It's rough country."

"Very rough. I make use of the time we spend travelling by studying the terrain and applying it to some tactical problem of modern mountain warfare. But I always run into some obstacle or another that I can't see any solution to. Yes, it's rough country all right!"

His companion seemed to have no interest at all in the subject of mountain warfare however – rather to the general's amazement.

"It's strange," the lieutenant-general began, "almost every day in that stadium, the football stadium where we're excavating at the moment, I see a girl who comes to watch her young man training. When it rains she wears a blue raincoat, and she just stands there, not making a sound, tucked away between two pillars by the players' entrance, gazing out at the footballers running to and fro on the grass. The empty stadium has a sad, you might even say a lugubrious, look about it, with all the curving tiers of those concrete stands glistening in the rain and the edges of the pitch all hacked about with our trenches. There's nothing pretty there to look at except her, in her blue raincoat. All the time she's there I spend my whole time just staring at her, while the workmen go on digging a few yards off – and that is the one and only distraction I have found in this town."

"Wasn't she horrified, seeing the remains being dug up?"

"Not in the slightest," the other said. "She simply turned her head away towards the pitch and fixed her eyes on her young man running after the ball."

The two men sat for a long moment, sunk in their armchairs, smoking their cigarettes, without exchanging a word.

Finally the general broke the silence with what was almost a laugh:

"We are the world's most skilled grave-diggers. And we shall find them, those dead soldiers, no matter where they're buried. They can't escape us."

His companion looked at him and said:

"Do you know, for several nights now I've had the same nightmare."

"Ah yes, I have bad dreams too . . ."

"I see myself in that stadium where we're digging now," the lieutenant-general went on, "only it seems much bigger, and the stands are packed while we are digging up the field. Among the crowd I can see that girl in her blue raincoat. Every time a new grave is opened up the whole crowd of spectators cheers so loud I expect the place to come tumbling down, and the whole stadium gets to its feet and starts chanting the soldier's name. I listen and listen in the hope of being able to identify the dead man, but their cries sound muffled, and the noise is so loud I'm quite unable to catch any name. Just imagine – this happens pretty well every night."

"It's understandable enough. You're just obsessed at the moment with identifying your dead."

"Yes, yes, it must be that. It is a very worrisome business."

The general was recalling a similar recurrent dream of his own. He was old and had been made curator of a military cemetery back in his own country, the very cemetery in which all the remains he had brought back from Albania were now buried. It was a large cemetery, immense in fact, and there were thousands of people walking to and fro along the paths between the graves, all carrying telegrams in their hands and looking for the graves of their kinsfolk. But none of them seemed to be able to find the grave they were looking for, because they all began shaking their heads in the most menacing way and he was filled with an icy terror. But just at that moment the priest rang his bell and all the people went away. Then he would wake up.

He was about to tell this dream, then suddenly changed his mind because it occurred to him that the other would think he had simply made it up.

"The task ahead of us is certainly no easy one," he said instead.

"Agreed," the other replied. "What we're being asked to do is a sort of carbon copy of the war!"

"And perhaps it is even worse than the original."

They were silent for a moment.

"Have you been the object of provocations at any point?" the general asked.

"No. Or rather yes, but only once. Some children threw stones at us."

"They attacked you with stones?" the general exclaimed, then, leaning over towards the other's ear, he continued teasingly: "Had you put your foot in it?"

"It was a complicated business," the lieutenant-general said. "We had mistakenly opened several Albanian graves under the impression that they were some of ours."

"Oh, I see."

"Yes, an unfortunate business all round. I'd really rather not think about it. Let's have another coffee."

"We shan't sleep a wink if we do."

"As if that mattered! It just means we shan't have to dream those dreams of ours. And like anything that is repeated often enough, they do become really very boring."

"True, very true."

They ordered two more coffees.

Chapter without a Number

WHAT ELSE IS there for me to write? What remains but a monotonous chronicle of recurring details. Rain, mud, lists, reports, a variety of figures and calculations, a whole dismal technology of exhumation. And besides, just lately something strange is happening to me. As soon as I see someone – anyone at all – I automatically begin stripping off his hair, then his cheeks, then his eyes, as though they were something unnecessary, something that is merely preventing me from penetrating to his essence; and I envisage his head as nothing but a skull and teeth – the only details that endure. Do you understand? I feel that I have crossed over into a kingdom of bones, of pure calcium.

VII

"IT ALL HAPPENED TOWARDS the beginning of the war," the café-owner began in broken English, with a slight stammer. He had worked for many years in a New York bar and his odd speech was reminiscent of the sounds and silences of a night-time bar. The general himself had insisted on being told the prostitute's story by an actual inhabitant of the old, stone-built town, and no one, he was assured, knew all the details better than the café-owner.

Never mind if he butchers the language, the general decided; the whole story evolves under the sign of slaughter.

They had read the prostitute's name only that morning, in the military cemetery on the outskirts of the town. Of all the remains they had located up to now she was the first woman they had come across and, when he was told something of how she came to be there, the general was curious to hear her whole story.

The general had in fact noticed the white headstone from quite a distance. It inevitably caught the gaze among all those twisted, blackened, rotting wooden crosses that in contrast seemed only the more crookedly set, and all those rusty helmets.

"A marble headstone!" the general had exclaimed. "An officer? Perhaps even Colonel Z.?"

They went straight over to the grave to read what was carved on the slab: "For Leader and for Country". It gave a woman's surname and Christian name, then her place of birth. She was from the same province as the general, though he did not tell anyone so.

"Yes, it happened right at the beginning," the café-owner said in the tones of someone addressing a large audience. (For since he had told this story many times he had developed a particular narrative style for the purpose, introducing frequent parentheses enabling him to insert his own comments on the events. And with it a slightly rhetorical tone that nevertheless stopped short of actual grandiloquence.) "I was one of the first to hear the news. Not that I have any particular interest in such matters, you understand but, because I was always here in the café working, I naturally tended to be one of the first to learn of any event affecting our town. And that was how it was on that particular day. The café was full when the rumour first started, and we never did find out who started it. Some said it came from a soldier who'd spent the night in our hotel here and got blind drunk before leaving for the front in Greece. Others claimed that it originated from a certain Lame Spiri, who was always positively obsessed with such things. Not that it really mattered one way or the other. We were so amazed and shaken up that we didn't really care whether it was the soldier or that blackguard Lame Spiri that the news actually came from.

"I ought to add here that it wasn't easy to surprise us at that time. It was wartime for one thing, and we were hearing incredible, fantastic stories every day. And we all thought there was nothing left in the world that could surprise us after that day when we saw the anti-tank guns and the anti-aircraft guns with their long barrels rolling through our streets for the first time, making such a terrible din that we all thought the entire town was about to come tumbling round our ears. And we were even more convinced when the aeroplanes started fighting right over our heads, not to mention a lot of other things that happened after that.

"And then for a time the whole town talked about nothing but

63

the English pilot who was shot down just outside the town. I saw his hand with my own eyes, it was all there was left of him. I saw it when they showed it to the townspeople, out on the main square, with a scrap of his burnt shirt. It looked just like a piece of yellowed wood, and you could even see the ring on his ring finger, they hadn't got round to taking it off.

"So we were used to hearing about things of that kind, and even the most unexpected events no longer had much effect on us. And yet, somehow the news that they were going to open a licensed brothel here shattered everyone no end. We were prepared for anything – but not for that. In fact the news was so surprising that a lot of people refused to believe it at first.

"Our town is a very ancient one. It has survived through many different times and many different customs but how could it ever have foreseen anything like this? How could it suffer such a terrible shame in its old age, our town that had always been a byword for honour all through the years? What was to be done? It was a terrible problem, and one that threw us all into distress and confusion. Something strange and new and terrible was creeping into our life, as if the occupation, the barracks crammed with foreign soldiers, the bombings and the hunger weren't a heavy enough burden upon us already. We didn't understand then that this was just another side of life in wartime, no different really, no better and no worse, than the bombings, the barracks, and the hunger.

"The day after the news first went round a delegation of elders walked in a group to the town hall; and that night another group met in my café to prepare a petition to the Fascist emperor's lieutenant-general in Tirana. For hours they sat there, round this very table, writing page after page, while a crowd of others stood around nearby, drinking coffee, smoking, wandering off on some business of their own, then coming back to ask how the letter was getting on. A lot of the women began to get worried and sent

64

their children to make sure their husbands weren't a drop too many. For there were not many of us who realized that writing a letter, even one addressed not to the king in person but to his lieutenant-general, could be such a difficult thing to do.

"I had never closed the place as late as I did that night. At last the letter was finished and someone read it out. I don't remember too well exactly what they'd put in it. I only know that it said how for a great many reasons, all listed at length one after the other, the honest citizens of our town begged the Duce's lieutenant-general to reverse his decision to open a licensed brothel here, in the name of the honour and the prosperity of our ancient town with its noble traditions and its origins lost in the mists of antiquity.

"Next day the letter was despatched.

"Of course there were some people who didn't want anything to do with a petition like that, and who disapproved of any kind of letter or request at all being addressed to the occupying powers. But we ignored them. We clung firmly to the hope that something would be done for us. You must remember that this was still the beginning of the war, and there were still many things we hadn't quite cottoned on to as yet.

"But of course no heed was paid to our request. A few days later a telegram arrived: "Brothel to be opened for reasons of strategic order stop". The old postmaster who was the first to read it didn't grasp the meaning of the message immediately. Indeed, some people said that it was written in one of those coded languages they were always using then, and that always did seem to be incomprehensible. In the telegram were the words "ethnic Albanian" which was deemed to mean the mayor's fat wife, and so forth. Someone even said they were all wrong to be making a fuss about the opening of a brothel, that it was all to do with the opening of a second front. But such comforting thoughts did not last for long and everything became clear: it wasn't a second front that was about to be opened but, beyond a shadow of a doubt, a brothel.

"A few days later further details filtered through. The brothel was to be opened and run by the occupying forces themselves, and foreign women were to be specially brought in.

"It was the sole subject of conversation in our town. The few men who had been abroad for any length of time pandered to the curiosity of the others, clustering wide-eyed around my tables, by telling them all manner of things on the subject. It wasn't hard to tell that they often supplemented genuine incidents in their lives with others that were less so. To listen to them talk about Japanese brothels and Portuguese brothels, you would have thought they must know those countries like the backs of their hands, and that they were on first-name terms with every prostitute in the world.

"Their listeners, especially the ones with grown-up sons, became increasingly worried and kept shaking their heads with more and more anxious looks. And the women, at home, were even more tortured by anxiety, and it was hard to say whether it was for their husbands or for their sons that they were most concerned. The older inhabitants regarded the promised event as the most fateful of omens and were now waiting, their hearts gripped by the darkest forebodings, for an even more terrible punishment to descend upon us from on high. It has to be admitted, of course, that there were some who were delighted, because as you know it takes all sorts to make a world; but no one had the face to actually display his pleasure openly. There were a number of husbands who didn't get on with their wives, for instance, and also a number who had always been given to skirt-chasing by nature. But above all there were the young men, the ones who weren't married yet, reading love stories all day long and hanging about all evening with nothing to do. Some people tried to console themselves and reassure everyone else by arguing that from now on the foreign soldiers wouldn't bother our girls any more because they'd have their own. But people weren't that easily pacified.

"At last *they* arrived. They were brought in by a camouflaged army lorry. I can recall the scene as though it was only yesterday. Dusk had just fallen and my café was full. At first I couldn't understand why so many customers were getting up from their tables and going over to the windows, peering out towards the main square. Then several of them rushed out into the street, and the customers still sitting down began to ask what it was all about. A lot of the tables were suddenly empty. It was the first time so many people had left without paying. So then I went outside myself, unable to restrain my curiosity. People were coming out of the café opposite too, and out of the hunters' club, and quite a crowd had already formed to watch the scene. The lorry had drawn up just by the town war memorial, opposite the town hall, and *they* had just clambered out of it. Now they were just standing looking around them with astonished eyes. There were six of them, and they seemed tired, numbed from the long journey. The circle of bystanders was gazing at them with popping eyes, as though they were some sort of rare animal, but *they*, as they stood there exchanging comments with one another, merely returned our stares with calm and indifferent smiles. Perhaps they were a little taken aback at finding themselves so unexpectedly in this strange place, all carved out of stone, for it is true that our town does take on a slightly phantasmagorical look in the dusk, with the buttresses of the citadel and the dreaming minarets with their metal-covered spires gleaming in the setting sun.

"By now the square was filling up with people, in particular with a horde of children, who began hurling a few of the choice foreign words they had picked up from the occupying soldiers at *them*. The grown-ups stood observing them in silence. It was difficult for us at that moment to know exactly what it was we felt in our hearts. The only thing we did realize clearly that evening was that all the things we'd been told about the brothels in Tokyo or Honolulu bore very little relation to what was now meeting our gaze, and that the reality was something very different from all the stories we had been told, something much deeper, sadder, more pitiful.

"Escorted by a few foreigners, a town hall official, and a gaggle of children, the little flock made its way meekly over to the hotel. It was there that our town's strange hostesses were to spend the night.

"Next day *they* were installed in a two-storey house, surrounded by a small garden, right in the heart of the town. A notice giving the hours allotted to civilian and military clients respectively was put up on the door, though none of us actually saw it until later, since for the first few days the street remained as deserted as though it had been struck by the plague. It was particularly awkward for the people who lived along the street. Those who could moved out; those with a back garden would go out the back way onto the adjacent street. Willy nilly the rest had to put up with the misfortune. Only the elderly, especially the entrenched old women, stayed resolutely at home, and sent messages to their friends to say, I can't come to see you and don't you come calling on me. They had taken an oath never to leave the house again except in their coffins to be carried to the graveyard. And that's how it would have been were it not that another coffin came to disrupt matters. But there you are.

"So the street seemed to be profaned in our eyes. Such was our disgust that later on, when the business was at an end, each time we needed to take this street, it seemed quite alien to us, just as a fallen woman is haunted by the traces of her shame even long after she first fell.

"Those were dark and worrying days for all of us. Our town had never known any women of ill repute before, and even family scandals caused by jealousy or infidelity had always been rare. And now, so unexpectedly, there was this black spot in the very heart of the town itself. The shock that people had felt when they first heard the news was as nothing to their utter disarray now that the brothel was actually open. The men all began going home very early, and the café was always empty quite early in the evening. If husbands or sons did stay out late then their mothers or wives became frantic with anxiety. *They* were like a kind of tumour right in the centre of the town. It was noticeable that everyone's nerves were very much on edge, and a lot of the men and the youngsters were not always able to conceal a certain guilty look in their eyes.

"At first, I need hardly say, no one ever actually went into the brothel. And probably *they* found that rather surprising. They may have thought to themselves that these people they'd landed up amongst must be an odd lot if their men were so uninterested in women. But perhaps, on the other hand, they understood that they were foreigners here, and that they were looked upon with the same eyes as the troops occupying us, whom we considered as being wholly our enemies.

"As was to be expected, the first to visit the brothel was that good-for-nothing Lame Spiri. And that afternoon of his first visit the news got round so fast that by the time he came out again all the windows of the nearby houses were crammed full of people staring at him, their eyes popping out of their heads as though Christ had just risen again. And Lame Spiri just walked on arrogantly down the street without seeming in the least bit embarrassed. He even waved goodbye to one of *them* as she leaned out of her window and watched him walking away. It was just then that an old woman threw a bucketful of water down at him from her window; but she didn't manage to hit him. The other old women all made sour faces and cursed them with that gesture so characteristic of the women in our country: the arm stretched out, the hand raised, the spread fingers sighted on the person they are cursing. But the occupants of the brothel apparently didn't understand what was meant and just burst out laughing.

"That's how it was in the beginning. But then people began to get used to the situation. There were even some men, on suitably moonless nights, who began to pay secret visits to the house and its occupants that had caused us all so much distress. You might say that they were beginning to become part of our lives.

"Quite often, in the evenings, they used to appear out on their verandah. They would sit smoking their cigarettes and gazing up with absent eyes at the mountains all around them, doubtless thinking of their own country so far away. And they would stay there for a while, quite quiet in the half-darkness, until the muezzin had finished his singsong call to prayer from the minaret and the town's inhabitants had gone home.

"So that after a while our animosity against them faded. There were even those who felt sorry for them.

"Little by little we seemed to have got used to their being there. People were no longer mortified when they encountered them by chance in a shop, or in church on Sundays – except for the old women, that is, who were still praying night and day for a bomb "from the English", as they put it, to fall and destroy that accursed house.

"And I think there were days when *they* longed for that to happen too.

"The Italian-Greek front wasn't far away, and at night we could hear the rumble of the guns. Our town was used as an overnight rest-point both for the units being brought up to relieve the battle-worn troops at the front and for the latter coming back from it.

"Quite often a notice would appear on the door of their house reading: *No civilian clients accepted tomorrow*, and then everyone knew there was a troop movement due next day. Though in fact the notice was quite pointless, since no civilian ever went near the place during the day, and would be even less likely to do so if there were soldiers there. With the exception, of course, of Lame Spiri, who came and went as he pleased at all hours of the day and night.

"On those days we sometimes used to walk along the brothel street simply to have a look at the soldiers just back from the fighting, filthy and unshaven, standing in line outside. They never broke ranks, even when it began to rain, and it would undoubt-edly have been much easier to dislodge them from their trenches than from their places in that dismal queue winding its inter-minable length along that street. To make the waiting in the rain bearable they made silly jokes, scratched at their lice, hurled foul language at one another, and squabbled about the number of minutes they were going to spend inside. It can't have been very gay for *them* inside – though of course they had no choice but to grin and bear it, because when it came down to it, they were under army orders too.

"As the afternoon drew on, so the queue would grow shorter. The last soldier would finally vanish, and the street would relapse into its usual calm. And most mornings after those overworked days *they* would appear looking sallow-skinned and even more haggard than usual. It was as though their soldier-clients back from the front were unloading onto those poor girls all the weariness, the rain, the mud and the setbacks that they themselves had suffered in the trenches; so that they could then get up and go on their way refreshed and satisfied, relieved of a great burden, while *they* must perforce stay on here perpetually, in our town, a few miles back

71

from that front, waiting for yet another batch of weary soldiers to arrive, interminably soaking up the bitterness of their retreat.

"And perhaps everything might have gone on for a long while in exactly the same way, perhaps nothing extraordinary would have occurred – for as we all know life must go on. Perhaps they would have spent the whole of the war here in our town, watching their dreary days fade into dusk with the singsong call of the *hodjas*, and receiving those long lines of soldiers before fate scattered them – who knows where? Yes, things might perfectly well have turned out that way, if Ramiz Kurti's son had not suddenly broken off his engagement one fine day.

"Our town, as you see, is not a large one, and incidents of that kind cause a great stir. For it is a fact that there are very few towns or villages anywhere in the country where fewer divorces occur than here. So that the break between Ramiz's son and his betrothed was a very shocking matter. Several nights running all Ramiz Kurti's relations met in solemn conclave at his house in order to discuss the affair and bring pressure on the son, with all kinds of threats, to renew the engagement. But the son obstinately refused. Nothing in the world would make him give in to his family's demands. But worse still, he also refused to reveal the reason for his change of feelings, and all his relations' attempts to extort it from him were in vain. He spent every day in a state of prostration, not speaking, just lying thinking, and growing visibly paler and thinner as though under some evil spell.

"And meanwhile the girl's family were demanding explanations. All her relatives – and she had just as many as the boy – were also meeting in order to deliberate on the affair. And twice they sent messengers to Ramiz Kurti to ask him the reason for the rupture. But the motive had not yet been discovered, and both emissaries in turn left again very much put out, letting it be understood that they would not tolerate their family's honour being spurned in such a way. Which meant that they intended to exchange words for weapons before very long. And indeed shots were fired, but in circumstances very different from those now generally expected and feared.

"But it was at that point, just as the representatives of the two families were holding their final discussions, just as the feeling was growing on both sides that the ancient friendship between the two families, sealed by the betrothal of the two young people in their cradles, was turning to hatred, that the true reason for the rupture was discovered. It was simple but shameful: Ramiz Kurti's son had entered into a liaison with one of the prostitutes in the brothel.

"Later we often racked our brains trying to guess the true nature of the boy's relationship with that foreign girl. Did he genuinely love her? Or was it she who had fallen in love with him? God alone knows what there was between them, for we never learned the truth.

"But on the evening of the very day we all heard the rumour, as dusk fell so Ramiz Kurti came down from the upper town, whitefaced, bareheaded, stick in hand, and made his way towards the brothel. His gaze was frozen like ice as he walked, and he must certainly have been partly out of his mind. And you can imagine the surprise they felt at seeing this whitefaced old man pushing the gate of their little garden open with his stick and walking in like that. They were sitting out on their verandah, and as the old man climbed the steps up to it one of them let out a burst of laughter. But the amused comments of the others were suddenly frozen on their lips, and a deathly quiet fell over the whole company. The old man pointed with his stick at the one his son came to see (apparently he recognized her by her hair) and the girl obediently trailed off upstairs to her room, assuming him to be just one more customer. The old man followed her. Then, as she was beginning to undress, the girl looked up and saw the old man's face, abnormally still, a staring mask, and she shrieked in terror. Perhaps the old man wouldn't have used his revolver if she hadn't cried out. Her shriek seems to have somehow jolted him out of his half-stupefied state. He fired three times, threw the gun down, then walked out like a man drunk, completely ignoring the screams of the brothel's inmates.

"Three days later Ramiz Kurti was hanged. His son just vanished.

"It was October, and there was a cold wind blowing day and night down from the passes all around. Despite the circumstances of her death, despite the weather, a funeral with flowers, wreaths, music, and rifle salvoes was laid on for the victim. The Fascists managed to round up a fair crowd of people from the streets and cafés and forced them to swell the cortège. We walked in silence with the wind flaying our faces. She had been placed on the back of a small army lorry in a fine red coffin. The military band played her funeral march, and her companions wept as they walked.

"The people of our town had never followed a foreigner's coffin before, to say nothing of the coffin of a woman from her walk of life. We felt somehow stunned, with a sensation of emptiness in our hearts. I looked up at the clouds, high in the sky that day, and as I walked I thought about her life and her fate. Who could say what destiny had driven that poor woman to follow so far in the wake of those helmeted soldiers, and then, after wandering from place to place in the hinterland of war, to arrive at last in our town – where she had been fated to end her days and drag down others with her, into ruin and even death?

"She was buried in the military cemetery, the 'cemetery of brothers' as they called it, and over the grave they put up that marble slab you saw this morning. Then they carved the standard inscription on the slab: *For Leader and for Country*. The same words you see on all the soldiers' graves.

"A few days later an order arrived from the capital and the brothel was closed. I remember it as though it was only yesterday, that cold morning when *they* came out into the main square again, their cases in their hands, to wait for the lorry that was coming to take them away. All the people passing stopped to watch them. They stood huddled together, their coat collars turned up against the cold, rootless, more adrift in life than ever.

"They clambered up into the truck, and as it began to move off so some of the people watching raised their hands and timidly waved. The girls in the lorry acknowledged those farewells; but in a way that bore little relation to what we might have expected from women of their calling. Their gestures were something very different, movements of the hand and arm that conveyed their bitterness and their lassitude. We stood there watching them go, yet without any sense of liberation. We had always assumed that we could mark their departure with some kind of celebration; but it was all turning out very differently. And what were we going to gain by their going? True, they were leaving , but nothing else had changed.

"God knows where those unfortunate creatures were sent. Undoubtedly to some other small town near the front, some place where the troops moving up to the fighting and those returning from it would be halting for the night. And once again, no doubt, their existence would be filled with those long lines of tired and mud-spattered soldiers who would pour out upon them all the dank bitterness of their life at the front."

VIII

THE GENERAL STOOD IN the opening of his tent and gazed at the grey horizon. Sheets of mist alternately rose and fell across the steep slopes opposite, perpetually blotting out one area only to reveal another.

The cemetery had no clear-cut boundaries. The streams winding around it had gnawed away the earth, one on each side, and washed it away, down the slope into the valley.

Little flags marked the places to be dug out. From time to time a group of men would form at one particular spot, and the general knew that another soldier's remains had been unearthed. The youngest workman would bring over the disinfectant canisters. Now, he sensed, they were disinfecting the recovered bones, and the expert was bending down to measure the skeleton's length, while the priest, standing at the expert's side, was marking a name with a cross, and also, if the height failed to correspond to that given on the list, with a question mark.

When the group took a long time to break up, the general said to himself: They're measuring him again. That means another question mark on the list, I suppose.

The young workman, the one in the pullover, would hurry over to his tent and come back with a nylon bag, a pretty blue bag, made to order, with two white stripes across it, black binding around the edges, and the discreet trademark "Olympia". The expert would take up the medallion with tweezers held between those long thin fingers, then drop it into a metal box.

One day there was an inspection to make sure we all still had our medallions. Someone had reported my mate for having chucked his away. "What have you done with your medallion?" the lieutenant asked him when he'd made him undo his battledress. "I don't know, I must have lost it." "Lost it? You know as well as I do that you threw it away. You useless idiot! Now you'll die like a dog and no one will be able to recognize that carcass of yours. And then we'll come in for it again, as usual! This man, take him to the guardhouse!" And two days later they brought him another medallion.

But when the group dispersed, on the other hand, it meant that the remains had been duly inserted into their nylon bag, then a label attached to it inscribed with the soldier's service number and the number on their list. Then the same workman would carry the bag back to the lorry, and the heavy, rhythmic blows of the picks in the damp ground would begin again.

The general was dropping with fatigue. Who is it they've found now? he wondered as he watched the little group form yet again in the middle of the cemetery. And with every fresh body disinterred he saw once again, in his mind's eye, that crowd of silent and sombre faces in his drawing-room, so far away, in his home, during those wet and stormy days when he had just come back from the seaside. All those who had come to see him talked about the relatives they had lost. Some seemed to never stop, others were less talkative, still others brought photographs with them, useless for the most part: as children, betrothal pictures, or sitting at a table with their friends. Others brought thick bundles of letters, while some carried nothing at all, except their brief telegram from the War Office.

The general huddled down inside his greatcoat and glanced towards the north-east.

It's over there, their memorial, he thought to himself, at the crossroads, just where you hear the splashing of the mill-race running down to that deserted mill.

As the veils of mist slid across the slopes he expected to see it emerging from them at any moment, that tall, very tall, slender monument with its facing of white stone, and then, beyond it, the ruined arches of an old house, piles of rubble, heaps of scorched stone, and further away still, just outside the village, the burnt-out and deserted mill with the water babbling down on its way, the only thing that had not been burned or destroyed. On the face of the monument, in clumsy capitals, were carved the words: *Here passed the infamous Blue Battalion that burned and massacred this village, killed our women and children, and hanged our men from these poles. To the memory of its dead the people of this place have raised this monument.* The village had now been moved to a spot lower down, near the bottom of the valley, and only the telephone poles, their bases thickly tarred, with an oblique supporting strut here and there, remained. The same poles from which, the story went, Colonel Z. had hanged men with his own hands. Their height varied according to the contours of the ground, their wires
still stretched taut through space.

But today even the telegraph poles were swathed in the deep mist, and from where he stood the general could see nothing. It was as though an immense white sheet had been spread over everything below, over the memorial, over the poles, over the old mill and the crumbling arches, as though in readiness for some grand inauguration.

"You'll catch cold," the priest said as he passed the general and entered the tent. "It's very damp."

The general followed him inside. It was lunchtime.

"Well, how did things go?"

"Quite well," the priest said. "If the people from the

co-operative come out to help us tomorrow on the far side of the stream, we shall be able to move on in four days."

"I think the men will come. But the women may not. They feel that it's an act of desecration to open up graves."

"I should say that the women will probably come too. I rather suspect they derive a sort of secret satisfaction from the work."

"You amaze me," the general said. "Is it possible to derive satisfaction from opening up graves?"

"For them it's a sort of belated vengeance."

The general shrugged his shoulders.

"And as a bonus it is also very remunerative work," the priest continued. "We pay them well enough for it to be worth their while to drop everything else. With what they earn working just a few days for us they can buy themselves a nice little radio. They're very fond of radios."

"I've noticed," the general said, yawning. "I'm beginning to be sick of living under canvas."

"And the weather is getting steadily colder every day. Let's hope this is the last camp we shall have to make in this area."

"As I recall there's still one more place in this direction we have to investigate. Somewhere up in the actual mountains, near a disused military supply route."

"Oh?"

"Yes, the dead men were manning a checkpoint on the road. I'm in two minds: why not leave it for next year? It can't be much fun clambering about up there in this weather."

There was the sound of an engine outside. The priest went out to investigate.

"What is it?" the general asked when he reappeared.

"Nothing," the priest said. "Just the new stock of disinfectant sprays arriving."

The general took out their thermos flasks. They lunched

79

frugally and silently on dry rations. Then the general lay down on his camp bed. The priest took up a book and began reading.

A book, the general mused as though he had just noticed the most absurd object imaginable. He too had tried reading but had not succeeded . . . Take a few books with you, his wife had said the day before he left. Only, no glum stories. Soothing books. Love stories, maybe? he had asked her with a chuckle. Why not, she'd replied. As for crime novels, you'll probably get all you need!

What did the priest get up to with the colonel's widow, the general wondered, his eyes fixed on the sloping tent-canvas. How charming she was! he thought, his hands clasped behind his head, eyes fixed on the canvas quivering gently above him. The rain had started to fall again. The sky was blue, totally blue, he thought to himself as he gazed at the slope of mauve canvas above his head. And that woman, under that sky, she was so pretty you'd have sworn there could be nothing in the whole world as graceful as her.

He had the feeling that the vision he was seeing must come from much further back in his past, that he couldn't have been seeing it as recently as last August, on that flaming late afternoon with the sun going down red like a huge tired eye, and here and there on the horizon, still pale and uncertain, the first glimmering of evening. The promenade along the sea front was always full at that hour, and they had been sitting with all their usual companions on the terrace of their hotel to watch the sunset, and the boats, and the gulls out to sea. They came there every day, to admire the evening sky, and they always waited until the sun had sunk finally into the sea and the big hotel signs had lit up, interspersed with the small, vertical ones of the night clubs, all around the bay, before they left their chairs to walk with the children on the beach.

That afternoon the terrace was packed, and the beams of the westering sun struck red-tinged reflections from the glasses on the tables. What did they talk about? He found it difficult to remember. It was one of those trivial conversations that fade with the daylight itself, and leave nothing behind but empty bottles on the tables.

Then suddenly he had the feeling that he was being stared at insistently from a nearby table. He turned slowly round and his eyes met that woman's gaze for the first time, then that of an old lady, then the eyes of a man, and lastly those of a second man. Clearly these people were talking about him. After exchanging a few nods of the head they began staring at him again, with the same insistence. And it was then that the young woman began to smile. After a moment one of the men suddenly stood up, walked over, and said with a slightly embarrassed air: "General, sir!"

That was how he had come to make the acquaintance of Colonel Z.'s family. They had all come to that resort for the sole purpose of meeting him: that pretty woman, the colonel's still young widow, the old lady, his mother, and his two first cousins.

"We were informed that you had been charged with this holy and sublime mission," the old lady said, "and we are happy to know you."

"Indeed, that was our reason for coming here."

"We tried endlessly to have him found, right up till the end of the war," the old lady went on. "Three times I sent people to look for him and all three drew a complete blank. The fourth man I sent was a con man. He pocketed the money and disappeared. When we heard that you were going out to that country our hopes were renewed. Oh yes, my child, we have placed all our hopes, all our great hopes, in you now!"

"I shall do my best, madame. I shall spare no effort, I assure you."

"He was so young, you know. And he had every virtue!" the old woman went on, her eyes filling with tears. "Everyone thought he had the makings of a military genius. Those were the words the Minister of War used himself, when he came to offer us his condolences. It is a great loss, a very cruel loss for us all, he said. But he was my son, and so the loss naturally hits me the hardest. Oh, you too, Betty, of course, I'm sorry, my dear. Do you remember that last time he came back from Albania? For those two weeks of leave? Only two weeks and we had to celebrate your marriage in such a rush, because time was so precious. His duties were so important he couldn't stay away from that accursed country anylonger. Do you remember, Betty?"

"Yes, mother, how could I forget?"

"Do you remember how you cried and cried up on the landing while he was putting on his uniform, how I tried to comfort you and keep myself calm, and then suddenly there was that telephone call? It was from the War Minister. The plane had to take off in half an hour. Our poor darling hurtled down those stairs, barely touching them, kissed us both, and left. Oh, do forgive me," the old lady said, "I do beg your pardon for pouring it all out like this, but I do feel things so, I always have."

During the days that followed they became even better acquainted, and the colonel's family became part of their group. They played tennis, swam, took boat trips, and went dancing together in the night clubs along the front. The general's wife didn't find this new friendship very much to her taste, but as was her custom she kept the fact to herself. Inwardly, however, she was decidedly chagrined to see her husband walking so often with Betty along the water's edge, and his whole attitude to this woman vexed her.

"I should very much like to know what you two find to talk about all the time you're together," she remarked one day.

"About the colonel," he answered. "What else?"

"Oh, come! I'm prepared to accept that his old mother talks about him non-stop all day, but that his widow has no other subject of conversation either, well . . ."

"That's not very nice of you," he interrupted her. "These people are in distress and they've asked me to help them. And after all, it's the least I can do to show willing."

"Show willing!"

"I don't follow your sarcasm. Indeed I find it quite out of order, in the circumstances, with death stalking the whole time."

"All right, all right. Such exaggerated attachment to a husband who's been dead twenty years, and with whom she lived for only two weeks, can be explained in only one way."

"Oh, I know what you're going to tell me: the old countess and her fortune, what she has to leave. Well, that's enough. I don't want to listen to gossip of this kind. It is my duty to bring back the colonel's remains. And that's all there is to be said about it."

Then Betty suddenly disappeared for two days, and when she returned the general noticed a certain coldness towards him combined with a great lassitude.

"Where have you been?" he asked her when he met her outside the hotel.

She was in a bathing costume and wearing sunglasses that masked her face. He could not prevent himself noticing that she had blushed under her tan as she spoke the name of the chaplain.

She told him that her mother-in-law had begged her to go immediately to the priest, on her behalf, and ask him to do his best in helping to find her son, that she had finally succeeded in locating him, that her mother-in-law's mind was now at rest, etc. . .

But he wasn't listening to her. He was gazing in a sensual stupor at her scantily covered body, and it was then that he wondered for the first time what her relationship with the priest really was.

Then the days sped by, soaked with sunlight. The colonel's old mother continued to hold forth on the virtues of her son – who according to her had been the entire War Office's blue-eyed boy – and on the antiquity of her family. Betty, meanwhile, would disappear from the beach from time to time; and when she came back – always with that same tired and distant air – the general always asked himself the same question.

Their group would spend the whole afternoon on the hotel's main terrace. A film star, the group's latest addition, said to him:

"You know, general, there is no one on this beach quite so strange as you. There is a veil of mystery all around you, and when I think that after these splendid days spent here basking in the sun you are going off to hunt for dead bodies over there, in Albania, I feel a shiver of horror. You remind me of the hero in that ballad by the German poet – his name escapes me at the moment but we had to study him at school. Yes, you're just like him, the hero who rose up out of his tomb to ride through the moonlight. I feel sometimes that you are going to come knocking at my window in the night. Oh! What a terrifying thought!"

The general laughed obediently, his mind not really there, while his companions all gazed in silent wonder at the setting sun. Except for the colonel's mother, who must needs refer everything to her son and therefore remarked:

"Oh, how he would have loved this. He was so sensitive to beauty of every kind!" And she wiped away a tear with her handkerchief.

Betty was still as seductive and as enigmatic as ever, the sky still as blue – only, from time to time, here and there, the horizon

84

was beginning to be darkened by black clouds, heavy with rain, sailing slowly eastwards, towards the Albanian coast . . . .

The general got to his feet. There was no one else in the tent. The noise of rain on canvas had stopped. Presumably work had begun again. He stepped outside. The mist, still as thick as ever, lay in a blanket over the scree. For a moment he followed the low flight of the sparrows, then it seemed to him that the blanket of mist was moving north-east, towards where the monument should be rising, and the telephone poles, with their wires stretched taut in space.

IX

THE PRIEST LIT THE paraffin lamp and placed it on the small table. His shadow and that of his companion wavered, bent in the middle, against the sloping sides of the tent.

"Brrr! How cold it is!" the general said. "With this damned humidity it soaks right into your bones."

The priest began opening a tin.

"We shall last out till tomorrow, I expect."

"Well, I wish I was already in tomorrow, that's all I can say. So that we could get the hell out of here. I've had enough of living like a savage. And I need a bath."

"It might be bearable without the cold."

"It's a job that should have been done in summer," the general said. Though in fact, he thought to himself, there was no possibility of that: in spite of everything he found some relief in venting his ill-temper, so it seemed to him.

"It's true it's hardly the best of weather for such an undertaking," the priest said. "The negotiations went on too long at the time. The government always has its reasons . . ."

"Needs must when the devil drives would be nearer the mark, I'd say!"

The general had unfolded their large-scale map of the cemetery and was pencilling in marks of some sort on it.

"And those other two, where are they, I wonder?"

"Perhaps they're still back there digging up that football field where we last saw them."

86

"Well, their task is no easier than ours. And they do seem to be very badly organized."

"Whereas with us everything goes like clockwork. We are the most up-to-date grave-diggers in the world."

The priest didn't reply.

"Though admittedly we are also very dirty ones," the general added.

Outside there came the sound of a song through the darkness. Beginning quietly, supported by deep, dark-toned voices, it rose steadily in pitch, increased in volume, and finally hurled itself against their tent in a fierce onslaught, just as the rain and the wind were perpetually doing all through those autumn nights. And it was almost as though the canvas, physically affected by the weight of sound, had quivered as the song struck.

"The workmen are singing," the general said, raising his eyes from the map.

They both listened for a moment.

"It is a very common custom among the Albanians of certain regions," the priest said. "As soon as there are three or four of them together like that they begin singing together. It's a very old tradition."

"Perhaps they're singing because it's Saturday evening."

"It's quite possible. They were paid today of course, and they must certainly have brought a bottle of raki from some passing villager."

"I'd noticed they like a drink or two now and then," the general said. "I suppose they find this work depressing too. They've been away from their homes a long time!"

"When they drink they generally start telling one another stories," the priest said. "The oldest one tells them stories about the war."

"Was he a partisan?"

"I think so, yes."

"So this job must bring back a lot of wartime memories for him."

"It's bound to," the priest said. "And at moments like this singing is a spiritual need for these men. Can you conceive of any greater satisfaction for an old soldier than that of pulling his old enemies back up out of their graves? It's like a sort of extension of the war."

The melody of the song was drawing itself out, languishing, and the accompanying chorus seemed to be winding round and round it, like a soft, warm, outer garment protecting it from the dark and the wet of the night outside. Then the chorus faded, and from its quiet heart a single voice sprang up in isolated song.

"That's him," the general said. "Do you hear him? But what is he singing?"

"It is an old song of war," the priest answered.

"It's a sad song. Can you make out the words?"

"Yes, quite clearly. It's about an Albanian soldier who has been wounded in the Arabian desert. When their country was under Turkish rule, you know, the Albanians had to do military service all over the Ottoman empire."

"Ah, yes, I remember your telling me about it."

"If you like I could try to translate it for you."

"Please do."

The priest listened attentively for a while.

"It is difficult to render it faithfully, but the meaning is more or less: 'I have fallen struck to death, my comrades, I have fallen in the depths of Arabia.'"

"So it is a song that takes place against the desert," the general said as though in a dream, and in his memory, like a dazzling carpet, the desert unfurled itself to infinity. He tried to walk on that carpet as he had done a quarter of a century before, in his lieutenant's uniform.

The priest continued to translate:

" 'Go and see my mother on my behalf and tell her to sell our bullock with the black coat.' "

Outside the song was being drawn finer, finer, as though it was about to snap, then suddenly recovered itself, was wrapped once more in the thick texture of the accompanying chorus, and finally flung itself again at the sloping walls of their tent.

" 'If my mother asks you about me . . .' "

"Yes, what will they say to that mother?" the general said.

The priest listened again for a moment.

"It goes more or less like this," he continued, " 'If my mother asks for news of me, say that her son took three wives' and 'that many guests attended the wedding'; in other words he was struck by three bullets and the crows and rooks came to prey on his corpse."

"But it is horrible!" the general said.

"Didn't I warn you?" the priest answered.

Outside, like a spring being stretched, the song was drawn out finer and finer until it finally snapped.

"They are sure to begin another in a moment," the priest said. "Once they begin singing it takes a lot to stop them."

And before long, as he had predicted, the chanting did begin again in the other tent. First of all they heard only the high, heart-piercing voice of the old workman, then another joined in to repeat a phrase, and finally the chorus enveloped the song in its folds and sent it soaring up, proud and harmonious, into the night.

They listened for a long while without comment.

"And this one," the general asked at last, "what is this about?"

"The last war," the priest said.

"The war generally?"

89

"As far as I can make out it's about a Communist soldier who was finally killed after being surrounded by our troops. And the song is dedicated to him."

"It wouldn't by any chance be that boy who hurled himself onto a tank, the one whose bust we've seen in various places?"

"I don't think so. The song would mention it."

In the other tent the singing had begun again.

"There is something heartrending in the way they draw those phrases out and out till you think they'll never end," the general said.

"Yes, really heartrending. It is the primitive voice of their ancestors still."

"I feel shudders up my spine listening to them. They frighten me."

"All their epic folk traditions are the same," the priest said.

"The devil alone could tell us what these people are expressing in their songs," the general said. "It's easy enough to dig holes in their land, but as for getting into their souls, no, never."

The priest did not reply and a long silence filled the tent. Outside, the song continued to unfurl slowly like the previous ones and the general had the feeling that the sounds were surrounding him, creeping up on him. "Will they go on much longer?" he asked.

"How can I say? Till daybreak perhaps."

"Listen carefully," the general told him, "and if they ever allude to us in their songs, make a note of it."

"Of course," the priest said. Then he glanced down at his watch. "It's late," he added.

"I don't feel like sleep. Let's have a drink. Then perhaps we'll feel like singing too."

The priest shrugged, as much as to say he didn't drink.

The general shook his head sorrowfully.

"You'll never get a better opportunity to learn. Winter, a tent on a mountain, alone in the wilds . . ."

Outside the song rose and fell, rose and fell. The general produced a flask from his grip. "Well, I'm sorry," he said, "I shall have to drink alone," and as he filled his glass his giant's shadow moved across the inside of the tent.

The priest had got into bed.

The general drank two glasses of brandy one after the other, then lit the paraffin burner and put a coffee pot to heat. He had long been accustomed to making his own coffee when alone. The coffee he made seemed to him to have a bitter taste.

He stood for a few moments with his hands clasped behind his back, his mind elsewhere, then walked out of the tent and stationed himself just outside the entrance. A fine rain was still falling, and the night was so silent and so black that he had the feeling that he was nowhere. There had been no singing from the nearby tent for several minutes now.

Perhaps they're just having a rest. They're sure to start up again, he feared.

And a second later, like an arrow, the singing did sail up once more into the night. The old roadmender's voice, leaving those of his companions behind, rose higher and higher, stopped at last, remained hanging for an instant, then broke off suddenly to fall back and mingle once more with the others, like a spark falling back into a bed of glowing embers.

Somewhere in the distance lightning flashed, momentarily lighting up the slope below, the workmen's white tent, and the lorry parked beside it, apparently on the verge of hurtling down into the valley. Then everything was cloaked in darkness again.

The general listened to the song and tried to sense what its meaning was. Like all the others it was a sad and solemn song. Adieu, adieu.

Perhaps he is singing about his dead comrades, the general thought. One of the visitors who had come to see him before his departure had told him that the Albanians often made up songs about comrades killed in battle. Who knows what goes on in that old workman's head, he said to himself. He goes all over his country finding graves and digging memories of the war up out of them. He must certainly hate me. I can see hatred in his eyes. Not that it could be any different. We are mortal enemies, yoked together to the same task, like a pair of oxen. One black, the other no less so. The joy of the one made the grief of the other. A grave-digger who digs up graves six days a week and sings on the seventh. A general who did likewise six days a week, but neither could nor would sing on the seventh. And if I were to begin singing, if I were to sing my song about the dead I collect, who knows what horrors would come pouring out then?

X

THE GENERAL SLEPT ONLY fitfully for the few hours that remained before morning.

He was wakened by the voices of the workmen as they wrenched the pegs of their tent out of the frozen ground. Then they threw it, soaking wet, into the lorry, on top of the big packing cases, beside their shovels and picks.

The two drivers had started their engines and were running them to warm them up.

The priest was already up and making coffee. He sat listening to the pleasant murmur of the burner as the little flickering flame threw its uncertain glow up into his face. The pale light of dawn was visible through the open flap of the tent.

The general felt a wave of homesickness.

He wished the priest good morning.

"Good morning," the priest replied. "Did you sleep well?"

"No, not well. It was very cold. Especially from midnight on."

"I was shivering too. Would you like some coffee?"

"Please."

The priest poured the coffee into the cups.

A little later they had left their tent and the workmen were busy striking it. The rain had stopped, but the ground was still sodden, and the opened graves down in the big cemetery half filled with water.

To the east, behind the high clouds, the sun was rising above the horizon, an alternately wan and dazzling blur of light.

In the car it was warm and the general fell into a doze.

They had been driving for more than two hours when the driver braked suddenly.

The general wiped the mist from his window and looked out. Right in the middle of the road, looking very small in his tight black jacket, stood a peasant boy signalling to them to stop. The lorry squealed to a halt only a few yards behind the car.

The driver stuck his head out of the window.

"We haven't any room. Sorry, lad!" he shouted.

But the boy gabbled something in reply and indicated the side of the road with one hand.

"Who is that man?" the priest asked.

The general wound down his window to see better. On the side of the road, a black cape over his shoulders, an old peasant was seated on a big stone. He had a big handkerchief spread out on his knees and was eating a breakfast of maize bread, cheese, and onions. In front of him, on the side of the road, lay a coffin. A little way away a mud-caked donkey was standing motionless on the verge.

"What's happening?" the general asked.

"How do I know?" the priest answered. "We shall find out eventually."

The expert had got out of the car and was talking to the two peasants. The old man shook the crumbs from his handkerchief and pulled himself to his feet. The expert came over to the car.

"Well?" the general asked.

"They have the remains of a soldier."

"One of ours?"

"Yes," the expert said. And then, gesturing towards the coffin: "He was working for this peasant when he was killed."

The general opened his door and got out of the car. The priest followed and went over to the old peasant.

"I didn't quite follow," he said.

"The soldier was working for this old man," the expert repeated. "He's a miller, and the soldier was employed in his mill. That's where he was killed."

"Ah!" the priest said. "Was he a deserter?"

The expert questioned the peasant anew, then came back:

"Apparently he was a deserter."

The general, who had missed these last exchanges, now joined them, walking very slowly and wearing a grave expression. It was the attitude he always adopted when in the presence of the Albanian peasants.

"Now what is all this about?" he asked.

Those cold, depressing days were behind him, the tent pitched among the mountains was a thing of the past, and now that he had a clean uniform on he had regained a sense of his own importance.

The old man's face was cadaverous, his eyes grey and tired. Unhurriedly, he took out his tobacco pouch, filled his pipe, then lit it from his lighter. The general let his eyes rest on the old man's fingers, as brown and dry as tinder, and his big, still-powerful hands. The boy just stood there staring, eyes wide with wonder at the sight of the general in uniform.

"We have waited here three hours," the old man said. "We set out before dawn. They told me yesterday you would come this way, so I decided to come here with my grandson and wait. We stopped many cars and lorries before yours came; but all the men in them said they weren't carrying any dead men. Two of them even thought I was mad."

"Was it you who buried him?" the general asked.

"Yes," the old man said. "Who else could have done? He lived with us."

95

"Ah, so he lived with you. But I should like to know, if possible, what sort of agreement you had come to with him. What could this soldier from a great regular army be doing with you, I mean how was it possible that he remained in your house of his own free will and found the life acceptable? You are a peasant, are you not?"

The expert translated, simplifying the general's words.

The peasant removed the pipe from between his lips and looked the general in the eyes.

"He was my labourer. Everyone will tell you that."

The general scowled and reddened at this insult. It was only now that he understood what had happened all those years ago. He gave the miller a sidelong glance as though to say: "Ah yes, it's easy for you to talk like that now, old peasant!" and nervously lit a cigarette, snapping two or three matches in the process.

"The man was one of those deserters who worked on Albanian farms," the priest explained.

The general grimaced.

"What was his name?" the expert asked the miller.

"I've no idea," came the answer. "We all just called him 'Soldier'. And that was all the name he ever had here."

"When did you dig him up?" the expert asked.

"The day before yesterday," the old man answered. "I heard that someone was coming round to collect them all so I decided to dig him up and deliver him to you. Better the poor fellow should rest his bones at home, I said to myself."

"Did you find a medallion with the body?"

"A medal?" the old miller asked in astonishment. "Oh, he wasn't the kind for winning medals. Work now, there he hadn't his equal. But war, no, that wasn't something he was good at."

"No, grandad, not a medal," the expert interrupted him with

a smile, "a medallion! Something that looks like a coin, but with the image of the Virgin Mary on it."

The peasant shrugged.

"No, I didn't find anything. I picked up his bones one by one, but I didn't find anything like that."

"You did well," the priest told him. "You did your duty as a good Christian."

"And who else was there to do it?" the old man said. "Of course it was my duty to do it."

"And we thank you for it," the priest said, "in the name of the soldier's mother."

The old man moved closer to the priest, who seemed to him to be an affable and kindly person, and began talking to him directly, gesturing from time to time towards the crudely fashioned coffin of unseasoned oak.

"I made it yesterday," he said, "and this morning, before dawn, the boy and I started out. We had a bad time of it getting from the mill to the main road. There was mud up to our knees. The donkey fell twice. Just look at the mess he's got himself in! And it wasn't easy to get him on his feet again."

The priest listened to him attentively.

"And the soldier, was it you who killed him?" he asked suddenly in a quiet voice, fixing him with his eyes.

The old peasant made a gesture of stupefaction and removed his pipe from his mouth as if to clear it. Then he began to laugh.

"Are you quite right in the head? Why ever should I have killed him?"

The priest smiled too, with the air of someone saying: "These things can happen, you know."

The miller, addressing nobody in particular, gave a brief account of how the deserter had been killed by soldiers of the "Blue Battalion", the punishment battalion, that unforgettable autumn.

Then, presumably still thinking of the priest's questions, he grew pensive.

"Why do they talk to me like that?" he asked the expert in a low voice.

"They are foreigners, grandad, they have different ways from us."

"You go to so much trouble, you come so far, and . . ."

"Now, now, old father, don't you let them upset you," said one of the workmen who had climbed down to load the coffin onto the lorry. "We're going to have to say goodbye to you now. We have to be on our way."

As the old man was talking to the expert and the workmen were lifting the coffin onto the lorry, the general, who was just about to climb back into the car, suddenly turned back.

"Is he claiming compensation?" he asked the expert.

The expert blushed.

"No!"

"He has a perfect right to do so. We are prepared to pay him what he asks."

"But he hasn't asked for anything!"

The general, thinking he had found a way of avenging himself to some extent for the affront he had received from the old peasant, insisted.

"All the same, tell him that we intend to remunerate him."

The expert hesitated.

"We should like to compensate you for your trouble," the priest told the miller in silky tones. "What sum would satisfy you?"

The miller scowled and lifted his head.

"I don't want anything," he said curtly.

"But after all, you have gone to a fair amount of trouble, taken up valuable time, used a certain amount of raw material . . ."

"Nothing," the peasant said again.

"But you provided this soldier with board and lodging for a considerable period. Perhaps we could make out a bill."

The old man shook out his pipe.

"I too am in his debt," he said. "I didn't pay him his last wages. Perhaps you would like me to give them to you!"

And, turning his back on them, the old miller walked back to his donkey.

As the car was about to move off the boy murmured something in the old man's ear and the latter began waving his hand towards them.

"Wait, devils, I nearly forgot! I have something else for you." And he thrust his hand under his cloak.

"He's going to ask for money after all," the general said when he saw the old man wave. "You see! I knew it!"

"What is it?" the expert asked, as he got out of the car.

"A book," the old man said. "He wrote in it sometimes. Here, take it!"

The expert stretched out his hand and took the book. It was an ordinary school exercise book filled with small, neat writing.

"His last wishes, no doubt," the old man said, "otherwise I wouldn't have taken the trouble to bring it to you. Who knows what the poor fellow scribbled in it. Perhaps he has left his goats and sheep to someone. I didn't like to ask him about that. But even if he'd had any animals, the wolves will certainly have eaten them all by now."

"Thank you," the expert said. "It will almost certainly give us his name."

"We all called him 'Soldier'," the old man said. "No one ever thought to ask him what his name was. Farewell. God be with you on your journey."

"Another diary!" the general said, flicking through the exercise book the expert had handed to him. "How many is that we've found?"

"This is the sixth," the priest said.

The car moved off, followed by the lorry, and the general, turning round, saw the old countryman stand for a moment without moving, looking after them, then turn in the opposite direction, driving his donkey before him, and set off home again with his grandson by his side.

XI

THE GENERAL, HAVING NOTHING better to do once he had sunk back into his corner of the car, opened the exercise book. The first page was missing – the first pages of most of the diaries they had found were missing – but once he had started to read he realized that probably no more than the first two or three sentences had gone. Probably the writer had filled most of the first page with his particulars and then, changing his mind later on, had ripped the whole page out.

The general continued reading:

The important thing is that no one should find this diary. Here the risk is not great; firstly because no one in the miller's family knows how to read, and secondly because they don't know our language.

Yesterday evening, when the miller saw me with my exercise book on my knee, he asked:

"What are you writing there, Soldier?"

Everyone here calls me "Soldier". No one has ever thought to ask my name. The miller's wife addresses me like that, and so does Christine, their only daughter. In fact I think she was the first to call me by that name. It happened the day our battalion was forced to retreat by the partisans. After throwing my rifle into a clump of bushes I ran off as fast as I could through the forest. I kept to a water channel, because I knew that such channels must always lead eventually to human habitations. I wasn't wrong. It turned out to be the mill-race for this mill. As I walked up to the door a young Albanian girl who was trying to calm down a big dog exclaimed with a surprised look: "Papa! There's a soldier coming here!"

And that was how my life as a mill-hand began that day. Sometimes I just can't understand myself, how a soldier like me, from the Iron Division, could be reduced to being a servant in an Albanian miller's house and wearing one of these white caps the peasants round here all wear.

"If you can help me in my work," the miller told me, "you shall have board and lodging here, and my protection as well. I am getting old and I'm no longer able to do a lot with my hands. My only son has gone into the mountains with the partisans. Only I warn you: no monkey tricks or I shall hang you from one of the beams in my loft."

And that was our contract.

It's more than a month since all that, and now I am responsible for a whole heap of jobs; I cut wood in the forest, I keep the mill-race clear, I fix back tiles when they fall off the roof, I fill and empty the sacks.

My mates in the battalion and all my family must certainly think I'm dead. If they could see me as I am now, an ex "Iron" soldier, covered all over in flour, with this cap on my head, they would be flabbergasted I should think and certainly end up bursting out laughing.

25 February

It's very cold. The wind has blown so violently all day that I feel it's going to rip up the mill by its foundations. Not much work. The winter is such a hard one that there are very few villagers prepared to risk the journey to the mill to have a sack of maize or wheat milled. The fields are deserted this year. The few peasants who do come tell the most terrible stories.

The howling wind. Day and night. I have the feeling that the wind is howling over the whole world.

March 1943

The miller treats me quite well. Yesterday I repaired a section of the roof that had been damaged by the wind. The miller was very pleased with my work. He said:

"Well, soldier, you're very good with your hands." Then after having looked me up and down for a moment he added in a bantering tone: "It's only war you don't go for much, I take it."

I blushed up to my ears. It was the first time anything had been said about my desertion.

He slapped me on the shoulder then.

"I wasn't trying to needle you," he said with a smile. "It just came out without my thinking."

His words have haunted my mind all day. I've noticed that the Albanians all have a profound respect for bravery. They despise cowards, and apparently I have given him the impression that I am one. A hulking great fellow like me, six foot one!

I would really be sorry to be thought of as a coward here. I'd be ashamed in front of Christine especially. She's not yet seventeen, and every time I see her I feel my heart emptying suddenly, like a burst bladder. Just like that!

Afternoon

Today something extraordinary happened. I'd gone to cut wood in the forest and when I came back I saw a man sitting on the step, outside the mill. I paused and listened, absolutely stunned. The man was whistling a tune from home. I went closer, and then I saw that the rags he was wearing were the remains of one of our uniforms. I shouted:

"Hey! Friend! Welcome!"

We threw ourselves into one another's arms, then we sat down together on the step.

In no time we told each other our stories: the units we'd deserted from, what became of us, the work we were now doing. He had come with his boss, a local peasant, to have some sacks of maize milled. He told me that from all accounts the "show" – in other words the war – was coming to a close, that nobody would go so far as to ask us why we had fled, rather the opposite, it would be us calling to account those who had despatched us to this "show". Then he told me confidentially that there were lots of soldiers like us working for the Albanian peasants. We both burst out laughing when he told me what he did: anything from taking the cows to pasture to rocking the babies like a nanny.

"It's only with the women that you have to pull your belt in," he said. "The Albanians are touchy about their honour. Run after a woman and they'll cut yours off, mark my word! But you, my friend, I have the impression you're onto a cushy number," he added with a mischievous wink. "I caught a glimpse of your boss's daughter just now. Fantastic!"

"You're mad! I wouldn't even dare think about it. You just told me yourself what the risks are."

"Yes, yes, I did, I agree. But I have the feeling that here it's different. It's a beautiful spot, so peaceful. Like I said, you'd think you were in Switzerland."

From inside the mill we could hear the monotonous rumble of the stones milling the maize.

He took out his tobacco tin and rolled himself a cigarette the way the peasants do round here.

"Listen," he said, his eyes half-closed, very thoughtful. "You haven't heard anything about the 'Blue Battalion'?"

I shuddered.

"No," I answered quietly. "Why?"

The mention of this name was enough to snuff out all my cheerfulness. "I see you're scowling. But don't worry. They're patrolling central Albania, slaughtering all and sundry, but you're not to let it bother you . . ."

"Will they have another go back here?"

"Who knows . . . what they're after in particular are the deserters."

"Shush!"

I stood up to avoid hearing any more of his soothing remarks that he kept larding so gaily with grisly details.

My miller and the farmer were engaged in a long discussion inside. When the maize was finally milled the two visitors each threw a bag over one shoulder and set off home, the farmer in front, the soldier bringing up the rear.

Sunday 2 April

Every time I hear the little bells tinkling on a bridle I am delighted at the thought of company, because the loneliness here is beginning to get me down.

The miller is a good, just man, but he has the drawback of being a man of few words. I have noticed that Albanians are generally far from talkative, and especially the men. All he does all day is suck at his pipe, and God alone knows what thoughts he is turning over behind those clouds of smoke. I have more conversations with his wife, "Aunt Frosa" as I call her. She's forever asking me questions, about my parents, my relatives, my home. When I confess to her how much I long to see them again she looks at me with a sympathetic air and shakes her head.

"Poor boy," she says quietly, and then she goes off to knead her bread or wash up.

"And while you're away," she asked me one day, "who is looking after your animals?"

I laughed.

"We don't have any animals."

"Not even any cows?"

"No, not even any cows. We live in town."

"And besides, even if you did have any, with you being away the wolves would have eaten them all by now. Ah, my boy, these days men themselves are tearing one another to pieces like wild beasts, we don't need to talk of wolves."

I could think of nothing to say to that.

Another day she asked me about my medallion.

"What is that you wear round your neck, my boy? It looks like a big Turkish penny."

I laughed.

"It's a sort of sign we soldiers wear, so that we can be recognized if we're killed in battle. Look, just below the image of the Virgin there's a number. Do you see it?"

Aunt Frosa put on her spectacles. They are rather absurd-looking spectacles with one lens cracked.

"And who gave you this?"

"Our leaders."

"May the lightning strike them!" she said, and walked away still muttering.

Those are the sort of things Aunt Frosa and I talk about. As for Christine, I see her very rarely and actually speak to her even less often. She's the one I'd really like to talk to, of course. Especially since I can get along fairly well now in Albanian. But we never see her at the mill. She's busy all day with her house-work, and the rest of the time she spends knitting. Even when she comes to tell us that our meal is ready she only stays at the door for an instant. She throws me an evasive glance from those dark, gentle eyes of hers, then she quickly turns her head away.

Sometimes she calls to me from a window without even bothering to come downstairs:

"Soldier, tell papa food is on the table!"

The fact is I think about her, come evening time; sometimes I play with Djouvi, the big dog. Sometimes I let my eyes wander across the sky as I listen to the brook splashing; then I go off into my daydreams again.

April

Today Christine smiled at me.

Last night some bandits tried to break into the mill. They wounded Djouvi. He is badly hurt. The miller and his family are very upset.

May, about 3 o'clock

A villager came by with a Turkish watch hanging from his neck. It's a long time since I last saw a watch.

I dream about masses of things, but it's Christine above all that I have on my mind. All sorts of crazy thoughts go through my head. I know that they're crazy of course; but all the same I enjoy letting them run on and seeing where they lead.

Yesterday, round about noon, I was stretched out near the race and having nothing better to do I was throwing pebbles into the water. The poplars were rustling all around me and I let myself be lulled into a doze.

Suddenly I heard a terrific noise: footsteps, voices, whistles, horses' hoofs. I jumped to my feet and what did I see? A long column of our soldiers had almost reached the mill. I wanted to run away, but, I don't know why, I did the opposite, I ran towards them.

"Is that the mill?" one of them asked, making a sign to me that the others couldn't see.

"Yes," I answered in terror.

"Right! Burn it down, men!" he cried, and led off at a run.

The other soldiers followed him. I joined their ranks. I don't know how or why but my legs were suddenly free again, and I felt light and strong as though my body had been freed from a spell. I was suddenly filled with the same fever, the same ferocity

I had felt the year before, when we burned those six villages one after another during the winter campaign.

We all rushed forward bellowing like crazed, stampeding animals. Two men set fire to the mill. Another group had seized the miller and were dragging him outside. They took him out into the yard and shot him.

I thought of Christine. I leaped up the stairs of the house two by two. There were soldiers coming down dragging Aunt Frosa bound hand and foot. When she saw me she spat in my face and cried:

"Filth! Spy!"

But I didn't care. All I could think of was Christine. I ran into her room and threw myself on her bed. She was trembling all over.

"No! Soldier! No!"

But the blood was pounding in my head. I had to be quick about it. There was so little time.

I pulled off the counterpane, frenziedly ripped off her thin nightdress in my impatience, and threw myself on top of her.

"Soldier! Soldier!"

I woke with a start. It was Christine's voice calling me. Beside me, as before, the quiet water lapped, and there was the smell of hay. I had fallen asleep briefly.

"Soldier! Soldier!"

I walked towards the house with heavy steps. Christine had appeared at the middle window.

"My mother wants you," she said.

I was still rubbing my eyes.

If she knew the nightmare I'd just had!

24 June 1943

The inhabitants of Gjirokastër are evacuating the town. They are passing all the time, exhausted, carrying their belongings bundled on their backs. The women carry their children in their arms and the old people drag themselves along behind as best they can. The place is in panic. They say that the town is going to be burned down. Some claim that it has been mined and is going to be blown up.

The fugitives are taking refuge out in the country.

Gjirokastër itself is being bombed every day. I sometimes climb up into the poplar growing beside the brook and look across at the town. I was stationed there for over a year with my regiment so I know every street and alley, all the café-keepers and the *gofté* sellers. I also know two tarts in Varosh, one of the poorer districts.

The planes are punctual. They come from the north, so they usually appear through the Tepelene gorge. The anti-aircraft battery at Grihoti is the first to open fire. The noise of the shells bursting doesn't reach as far as here though; we can only see the white puffs of smoke they make. Then the guns on the *teqe* hill go into action; but the planes seem just as unconcerned by those as by the first ones. They float on tranquilly towards the town, and then I begin to imagine the wailing of the sirens down there in Gjirokastër, and all the people rushing helter-skelter down into the cellars. It seems unbelievable that all the fear and horror battening on that town can be caused just by those three tiny objects flying overhead, glinting in the sun like silver coins tossed up in the sky.

The last anti-aircraft gun to open fire is the old one roosting up in the citadel, an old blunderbuss that everyone makes fun of. From here it's easy to follow the manoeuvres of the planes as the pilots come in, gradually losing height, then suddenly dive onto the military airfield, then make off, placid and gleaming, as if the columns of black smoke that rise at once over the town are nothing to do with them.

All that is in the daytime. At night the town ceases to exist beneath its blackout. First the darkness swallows up the streets and low houses, the bridge straddling the river, then it blots out the various quarters, one story at a time, starting from the ground floor, and the bridges over the streams, until at last it reaches the citadel, the steeples, and the minarets with their untidy stork's-nest hats.

Yesterday evening, as I watched the town being enveloped in the darkness and disappear, I remembered a similar night, almost three years ago now, when our company, on its way south, marched into Gjirokastër for the first time.

It was a stifling night, there was rain in the air, as soon as we arrived in the Grihoti barracks, even though we were whacked, covered in mud and feeling depressed as hell, we asked to be taken to the brothel. Our commanding officer gave permission for us to go, and immediately, as though by enchantment, all our vitality came flooding back, and just as we were, covered in mud, with several days' growth of beard, without even having unslung our rifles from our shoulders, we fell in again and marched back out through the main gate of the barracks. The brothel was in the very centre of the town and we had another kilometre to march in order to reach it. But now our legs were no longer heavy. We made silly jokes and teased one another as we marched along the dark road; and we were in our seventh heaven. We had heard a lot about this brothel and couldn't wait to be there. A prince's palace would not have been more enticing.

We were stopped at our checkpoint on the bridge over the river, then when the sentries had passed us through we left the high-road and took a short cut.

Our heavy army boots clattered on the cobbles, and the inhab-itants behind their shutters and their heavy doors must surely have been trembling with fright at the thought that yet another massacre might be about to take place. If only they had known where we were going!

At last we reached the "house". It was a very dark night and the muggy air made it almost impossible to breathe. We halted outside the entrance. The officer acting as our guide pushed it open and vanished inside.

The house was dark and silent. There didn't seem to be any other clients in there.

"Perhaps they're asleep," one of us said in a worried voice.

"Even if they have got their heads down, they'd better get them up again, and quick about it," someone else said.

"Hear, hear!" another joined in. "We're in uniform and they've got to respect us. Especially since we're only passing through."

"Here today, but where will we be tomorrow, eh?" a small voice added.

But just then the door opened, the officer re-emerged, and we rushed over to cluster round him.

"Now listen," the officer said. "You can go in straight away, but no noise, you hear! Any rowdiness and it's back to barracks right away! Right, fall in again!"

We arranged ourselves as best we could in two ranks, God knows how. We were just rearing to get in there.

"Now pay attention to me," the officer said. "It's very dark in there, but all the windows are open because it's so stifling hot, so we don't want any light. If any of you men takes it into his head to strike a match or use a lighter he'll live to regret it. There's a checkpoint not far from here with a machine-gun nest."

"No problem, sir," two or three voices murmured in assent.

"We don't need light. We'll get by without . . ."

"Yeah, it's not light we need, it's . . ."

"Quiet, you damned idiot!" the officer grunted. "Now, silence! The first five or six, forward!"

There was a scuffle, and they disappeared into the darkness of the courtyard beyond the door.

"Don't get your rifles mixed up!" the officer cried to them as they vanished. Then turning back to us:

"Six more follow me!"

I was one of those six. We crossed the flagged courtyard as though we were drunk, then went up the stairs and ended up on a landing with a long passage leading off it. It was dark along the passage and so stuffy you could hardly breathe. A pause, then I realized that all the others had melted away into the blackness and that I was all alone in the passage. I felt my way along it in the darkness, I heard a raucous gasp, then another, the blood rushed to my head, I dived through the first open door and heard a sound of violent panting. I rushed out again and found myself in front of another open door. In the shadowy darkness I could vaguely make out a white form in one corner of the room. I went in, took two more steps, then stopped.

"Come on," a soft voice said.

Shyly, I moved forward a few more steps, then stretched out my arms and touched her. She was completely naked. Her body was so moist with sweat that my hands slid over it. I felt my eyelids drooping and couldn't find the bed.

"Take off your rifle," she said gently.

I unslung my rifle and leaned it up against the wall. Then she lay down.

I couldn't make out her face in the dark, but to judge by her voice and her breasts she must have been very young.

"I'm sorry," I said a few minutes later as I lay briefly relaxed in her arms, "I'm sorry for being so dirty."

"Oh that doesn't matter," she said, and her listless tone made it clear that she had got used to soldiers' sweat a long long time ago.

"Where are you going?" she asked.

"South, to the front."

She didn't comment. And those were the only words we exchanged. I tried to make out her features, but it was no good: they just merged into an indistinguishable blur. I got up slowly, picked up my rifle, slung it over my shoulder, then turned back once more toward the pale form stretched out in the corner.

"Good night," I said.

"Good night," she answered with total indifference.

I left the room, groped my way back to the top of the stairs and went down them. The others who had finished were already outside. They were sitting on the stone seats on either side of the door, their rifles between their knees, smoking.

An hour later we were making our way back along the main road; but now we weren't talking or joking – just listening to the ragged clumping of our boots on the asphalt, once again in the dumps, weary to the bone, splattered from head to foot with every kind of muck.

"Damned darkness!" someone exclaimed as though in a dream; but no one answered and we continued on our silent way toward Grihoti.

A long time afterwards we happened to pass through Gjirokastër again, and naturally asked permission to visit the "house". We were told that it had been closed. I'm not quite sure why but apparently there was some sort of rumpus. One of the girls in the place had been killed and they'd had to evacuate the rest. It made me think of that girl I'd spent those few moments with in the darkness, on that muggy, suffocating night, and I thought to myself that it might quite possibly have been her. But it could just as well have been one of the others. There were five or six I think. Seven at most.

July, noon

Christine's eyes – hieroglyphs. Like the eyes of all Albanian girls. Love? On my side, yes. On hers, nothing.

Djouvi isn't getting any better.

July

Last night troops went by along the Gjirokastër road. They were moving north. We could see the beams of their headlights from up here. Presumably a regiment moving to a new posting.

21 July

The village near us is crawling with *ballistes*. They spend the evening singing old songs. Who knows what's going to happen?

But the miller has told me, just in case, that if I see any men coming in white caps with big eagles on the front, then I'm to hide straight away. He's told Christine the same thing.

Sunday

Christine is getting married in a week's time. I found it out quite by chance. I didn't know it but she's been engaged for a long time now, and yesterday, as Aunt Frosa was filling a pail with water at the race, I said to her, just for the sake of talking to someone:

"You've been stuck at that loom of yours weaving away for days and days now. Why is that?"

"Because the day's nearly on us, my lad, the day's nearly on us."

"What day?"

"What day? What day? We're marrying our daughter next week. Surely you know that?"

"No," I said, "I didn't know."

But my voice came out so faint as I said it that Aunt Frosa looked up and stared at me for a moment. My first thought was to try as hard as I could to control my feelings. But then I thought: The hell with it, why should I have to hide the pain I feel?

I honestly don't know whether she knew or not what a shock her words had given me, but she gave me another of her stares and said:

"Why yes, my son! Time passes, and girls grow up and have to be married. You too, boy, when you're home again, as soon as

114

this war is over, your mother will marry you to some pretty young girl, yes, as pretty as the flowers in May!"

When she said that I almost broke down altogether, because I felt she was trying to console me, and that just made the pain worse.

I went out and sat beside the brook. And I said out loud, just for myself: "Christine, you're going to be married!" That was all.

August

Monotony!

Christine is married. Last Sunday the bridegroom's relatives came to fetch her. Six men on horseback, all armed. The roads are very dangerous. There was no wedding feast. The men just sat down round the low table as a token, but they had a long journey back ahead of them and scarcely touched the raki. I was invited too, but I might as well not have been there for all the notice that was taken of me.

Two days ago I wanted to give Christine a little present. But what? I don't have anything! Then I thought of giving her my medallion. I'd seen her glancing at it two or three times with an intrigued look in her eye.

"Here, take this to remind you of me."

She took it and gazed at it with delight.

"It's the Holy Virgin!"

"Yes."

"Who gave it to you? Your mother?"

"No, the army."

"Why?"

"So that I can be identified when I'm dead."

She burst out laughing.

"And how do you know you're going to be killed?"

"Well, if I ever am!"

"Christine!" Aunt Frosa called from the yard.

Christine thanked me and fled away.

115

That was how I gave her the only thing I still possessed. And what good was it to me? Whatever happens I am lost. I am living, but lost, and what's the good of being found once you're dead!

At about noon the groom's men got up from the table, slung their guns over their shoulders and jumped up onto their horses. Christine's horse was white. She was crying. Aunt Frosa too. The miller kept his tears back. Then they kissed their daughter goodbye. I wanted to say goodbye to her as well, but I didn't have the courage to go over to the horses, because of the distant attitude of the men on their backs. I kept in the background. Djouvi, their big dog, staggered slowly about among them, his neck stretched out. I envied him. Christine bent down and kissed him. No one thought of me.

They set off. The horses disappeared from our view first, then the black caped coats, and lastly the long barrels of their guns.

August

For several nights now there has been a continual coming and going of troops along the Gjirokastër road. I can only suppose that something important is going to happen quite soon. The peasants coming to the mill say that the countryside is filling up again with people who have fled from the towns. They also say that the "Blue Battalion" has moved into the district. The nights have become gloomy again. I sleep badly and am constantly getting up to make sure everything is all right.

The longing to see Christine again obsesses me.

September

An autumn wind is blowing. I am often overcome by a profound feeling of sadness and I begin to be very afraid I shall never be able to leave here.

I sometimes sit on the bank of the canal, the canal feeding the race. It's my favourite spot. I watch the water flowing past, so smooth and tranquil, sometimes carrying a leaf on its surface, sometimes a twig, sometimes nothing but reflections.

I think back to the time when I was still with my division, advancing across the Albanian countryside. I remember the canals we came across then. I don't know why they disturbed me so, those still canals in those Albanian villages, dug out by the peasants with just pick-axes. I know that nothing else ever evoked for me in quite such a clear and concentrated way what the flavour of peacetime had been like. I walked along their banks, rifle slung on my back, with a feeling of unease. Something was stirring deep inside me. I felt they were awakening some atavistic instinct in me, that they were urging me on to something. They were calling me. I felt their eternal murmuring was coming from inside me as well – and certainly it was while walking along a canal that I first began to have the idea, very vaguely at first then more and more clearly, of becoming a deserter.

Afternoon

Djouvi is dead. We are all genuinely heart-broken. The miller's eyes are red. He must have been weeping in secret.

5 September

Calm. The leaves have begun to turn yellow. This morning, very high in the sky, hundreds of planes flew over us towards the north-west.

Who knows what part of the world they've come from and what other part they're on their way to bomb? There are no barriers in the sky.

XII

THE NOTES STOPPED THERE. The date 7 September 1943 had been written after the last entry, but then crossed out. Apparently he had decided not to continue the diary. Perhaps he had nothing in particular to say, or had simply grown tired of it.

The general tossed the exercise book onto the seat with a grimace of distaste.

"Anything interesting in it?" the priest asked.

"The diary of a sentimental idiot, and a self-pitying one to boot."

The priest picked up the exercise book and opened it at the first page.

"You won't find his name in it," the general said. "Only his height: six foot one."

"Really? Exactly Colonel Z.'s height!" the priest said.

Their eyes met for a moment then disengaged.

"No other indication," the general added. "He wrote down the dog's name, but not his own."

"Strange!"

"And there are one or two mentions of the 'Blue Battalion' too. But nothing about Colonel Z."

The priest began reading the diary.

The general, remembering the old miller's story, sat trying to imagine how the story in the diary might have ended. The "Blue Battalion" had passed through the district, raging under the sting of defeat; some of them had suddenly appeared at the mill one afternoon, having no doubt been informed that there was a deserter hiding there, and they'd searched until they found him, hidden under the sacks, white under his white covering of flour, as though already wrapped in a shroud. They had taken him outside, pushing him ahead of them with the barrels of their sten-guns, and like that, backing, backing, he had reached the mill-stream. He would have fallen backwards into it, but when he was two steps from the edge someone fired: he had fallen backwards, and only his head had slumped backwards into the water. Then a little eddy had formed around it, as though it was a big stone, and the gentle current had spread his hair downstream, waving like strange black weed.

And that must have been that, the general said to himself, drawing on his cigarette.

"Well?" the general asked about an hour later, as the priest closed the book in his turn.

The priest shrugged.

"A diary no different from a hundred others," he said.

Although each of them was conscious that the other was turning over in his mind what he had just been reading, they both kept silent for a good while.

"Have you read what he said about the canals?" the general eventually asked. "He was looking to them for safety though it was death that was stalking him there."

The priest did not answer.

The driver sounded his horn vociferously. A long flock of sheep was crossing the road in front of them. Two shepherds armed with long crooks were trying to make an opening to let the two vehicles through.

"They've brought them down from the mountains for the winter," the priest said.

The general looked out at the tall mountain men with the hoods of their thick, black, sheepskin cloaks pulled up over their heads.

"Do you remember those two lieutenants who were reduced to looking after sheep in that Albanian village? What division were they from? Weren't they from one of the alpine regiments?"

"I don't remember," the priest said.

"What an odd phenomenon that was," the general mused. "And it happened right through our forces in Albania. Really curious. Or rather shameful, I should say!"

"Absolutely," agreed the priest. "Some ridiculous things happened."

"We ourselves have come across instances of this kind. The times we've blushed for shame as we heard stories of our troops being reduced to washing clothes or minding the poultry for Albanian peasants. Just two hours ago some shepherd or miller, I can't recall, had my blood boiling . . ."

The priest once more nodded assent.

"You say ridiculous things happened. But they are worse than ridiculous, these incidents, they are worrying."

"In war it is always difficult to say exactly what is tragic and what is grotesque, what is heroic and what is worrying."

"Some people try to explain such things away," the general said. "They try to justify the attitude of our troops when they were left behind here, marooned after the capitulation. 'There were no ships,' they say, 'there was no way of crossing the sea. What were the unfortunate fellows to do? After all, they had to survive somehow.' Survive, yes! But surely they could have done that without dragging the dignity of their country in the mud!" the general cried angrily. "An officer in a great army like ours, even in defeat, agreeing to look after chickens! It's unheard of!"

"In the beginning many of them sold their weapons," the priest said. "They sold them or sometimes bartered them for a little sack of maize or beans."

"Were you here then?"

"No. But I've been told all about it. Apparently revolvers were given away for just a hunk of bread and a little wine, because the Albanians set much less store by pistols than by rifles. The rifles fetched much more – sometimes as much as a whole sack of bread. As for machine-guns, sten-guns, grenades, they were given away almost for nothing – for an egg, a pair of torn *opingas*, a couple of onions, or if they were lucky a pound or so of curd cheese."

"How contemptible!" the general said.

The priest was about to go on, but the general spoke again:

"And it's the reason the Albanians are so ready to jeer at us. You saw how that shepherd or miller, whatever he was, insulted me."

"They worship weapons. They can't conceive how anyone can sell his rifle for a piece of bread."

"And the heavy weapons?"

"The heavy weapons were not all that easy to put to use, they were picked up wherever they were left lying. At the time nobody was surprised at the sight of an anti-aircraft gun being towed by a donkey."

"Contemptible!" repeated the general.

"And you know there were more really appalling accidents in Albania that year than ever in the past," the priest went on. "The children were using real weapons as toys, and sometimes, after a quarrel, they would blow their brains out with a grenade. Sometimes the women in a street would squabble during the day and end up abusing one another from their windows, the way women do, but then at night the men would get up into the windows or the lofts with their machine-guns and there would be a blood bath."

"You must be exaggerating."

"Not in the slightest. Everyone here was in the grip of a terrible psychosis. The Albanians behaved as though they were drunk in some way; all their ancestral instincts were allowed to run completely wild, and they became more dangerous than ever."

"Perhaps because they were caught in the crossfire of battle, and wounded what's more," the general said. "Tigers go crazy like that as soon as the first bullet hits them. And besides, at that time the Albanians were presumably very much on the alert for new dangers. Their neighbours could perfectly well have rushed in and overrun them at any moment."

"The Albanians always exaggerate the dangers that are threatening them," the priest said.

"There's one thing I really don't understand though," the general said, "and that is why they didn't just tear us to pieces after the capitulation. Because in fact they did the exact opposite; they protected our wretched troops against our former allies, who were shooting our men on the spot whenever they could lay their hands on them. Do you remember?"

"Yes, I remember," the priest said.

"What a deplorable epilogue to our army's period of occupation in Albania," the general went on. "All those soldiers in uniform, with their weapons, their badges of rank, their braid and medals, transformed into domestic servants, menials, farm labourers. I feel myself blushing when I think of the tasks they were reduced to doing. Do you remember how they even told us in one place about that colonel who did laundry and knitted socks for an Albanian family?"

"Yes," the priest said. "I have sometimes wondered whether perhaps Colonel Z. too didn't go into service with a peasant family somewhere. Perhaps he is still with them, guarding a flock of goats somewhere."

The general could not believe his ears. The priest, who up till then had been exasperating him with his moderation, no longer concealed his own exasperation at the thought of the dead man.

"I wonder what Betty's reaction would be, seeing him like that," the general persisted. He expected the priest to weigh in further against his rival but, no doubt regretting his sally, he held his peace.

Most of their journey was passed in silence. The roads were strewn with yellow or rotting leaves. The yellow ones flew up, fluttering to and fro in the wind of their passing, but the others stirred only sluggishly then sank back into inertia, weighed down presumably by their burden of water and mud, scattered over the road, withered, as though waiting patiently for death.

Chapter without a Number

THE CAR AND the lorry were nearing the outskirts of the capital. Modern farm buildings began to appear now and then on the sides of the road, then a small aerodrome with a few helicopters standing on its tarmac, then the aerials of a radio transmitting station.

Suddenly the two vehicles turned off the main road and continued more slowly along a muddy secondary road to the right. The landscape changed dramatically. They were crossing an area of flat, waterlogged waste land sparsely dotted with bushes. Sticking up out of this bare expanse stood a long shed roofed with grey asbestos tiles. The two vehicles drew up outside it. A long-haired dog outside the door began barking.

The door slowly opened and a tall man dressed in a long threadbare overcoat emerged coughing. He was the storekeeper.

The workmen unloaded the big crates from the lorry. The

expert walked inside the shed with the storekeeper. The general and the priest climbed out of the car and followed them.

It was cold in the shed. The feeble light that did manage to find its way in through the windows fell on the rows of plastic bags arranged on the long wooden shelves.

The workmen carried the crates into the shed. The storekeeper began removing and counting the nylon bags from the crates. Then he laid them out along the shelves, muttering their numbers to himself as he did so.

"Not that one," he said when the workmen brought him the heavy coffin the miller had handed over to them on the road. The expert tried hard to make him change his mind. "No," the storekeeper said. "It is against the clauses in the contract."

The workmen carried the coffin out and loaded it back onto the lorry.

When it was all finished the storekeeper opened a drawer and produced from it a thick ledger with a dirty cover. He opened this book, blew on his fingers, then began clumsily leafing through it.

"Here's the place," the expert said.

He wrote something then put his signature underneath. Delivery had been completed.

XIII

SEVERAL DAYS LATER THE priest and the general were once more facing one another across a table in the Hotel Dajti lounge. The strains of dance music were still rising from the floor below, and the general was aware of the presence, diffused all around them, of foreign life being lived. His features were drawn and his eyes had a wilder look than usual.

"I slept very badly last night," he said, "I had a strange dream. I saw that prostitute, the one whose story the café-owner told us, you remember?"

"Yes," the priest said.

"Yes, it was definitely her in my dream. She was dead, laid out in a coffin. And outside the door of the house, all in their coffins too, there was a whole crowd of soldiers waiting their turn with her."

"What a terrible dream!"

"And yet it all seemed perfectly natural to me. As I was walking past I asked someone: 'Those soldiers waiting there, are they moving up to the front or coming back from it?' And the answer was that some were moving up and some were coming back. So then I said: 'Tell those on their way to the front not to wait; let them go and fight first, then they will have the right to some relaxation, but not till then. Tell those who have just come back from the front to stay in line.'"

"A nightmare," the priest said.

"Another night I saw Colonel Z. in a dream. He looked at me with an ironical smile and said: 'Do you really think my height is six foot one? Well I feel bound to tell you, my good sir, that you are mistaken. That is not my height.' – 'How tall are you then?' I asked him. He laughed in my face at that. But then, in a sullen voice, he said: 'I shan't tell you!'"

The general took a packet of cigarettes from his pocket and added:

"I have nightmares almost every night."

"It's a sign of overwork."

"Yes of course. That last tour was a backbreaking business. Worse than the others."

"There's no help for it, though," the priest said. "And we're not at the end of our troubles even yet."

"We've become like pilgrims in the Middle Ages. We keep on and on while the rest of them" – he pointed away towards where he reckoned the men's families should be – "imagine we just press a button and the bones come popping up out of the ground. They just have no idea what it's like."

"It's not their fault," the priest said.

The general sat tapping his fingers on the table.

"I suppose you've read a lot of ancient history and that sort of thing," the general said. "Have you ever come across cases of people in a situation like ours?"

"No," the priest answered – though without making it clear whether it was a knowledge of ancient history he was denying or the existence of parallel cases.

"So history is mute on the subject then."

"Would you like to go for a stroll?" the priest suggested. "It's quite fine this evening."

They walked down the hotel entrance steps and set off in the direction of the main university building. There was an unusually large flow of traffic along the boulevard. As the stream of head-lights emerged from the bridge, at the corner of the boulevard and the avenue Marcel-Cachin, it divided as some of the cars turned left – up towards the residential district where most of the embassies were to be found – while the rest kept going straight on towards Skanderburg Square.

The general and the priest walked as far as the Presidency then turned back. On both sides of the boulevard workmen were in the process of tearing up the mimosas and replacing them with pine trees deeply planted in freshly dug trenches.

"Preparations for the festivities," the priest commented. "That's why they're working so late."

Outside the hotel entrance they encountered the mayor, on his own.

"Where's my colleague got to?" asked the general.

"He is in central Albania at the moment. We are investigating some sites in the lowlands there just at present. And you?"

"We are taking a few days' rest."

As they walked they arrived at the top of the entrance steps. The mayor said good night to them and moved off towards the lift. They returned to the lounge and sat down again.

The general ordered brandy and lit a cigarette. A bottle of brandy was brought to him. He filled his glass and drank. The contours of the Albanian earth began an obsessive dance before his eyes, and above them, the rows of graves.

I don't see why our comrades' remains should be restored to their families. I don't believe that was their last wish, as some people claim. To us, to all old soldiers, such displays of sentimentality seem very puerile. A soldier, living or dead, never feels at ease except among his comrades. So leave them together. Don't split them up. Let their serried graves keep the old warlike spirit of yesterday still alive in us. Don't listen to those chicken-hearted people always ready to yell at the sight of a drop of blood. Listen to us, we fought here and we know.

The general felt the alcohol going to his head.

I have a whole army of dead men under my command now, he thought. Only instead of uniforms they are all wearing nylon bags. Blue bags with two white stripes and a black edging, made to order by the firm of "Olympia". And those bags will now be inserted into their coffins, tiny coffins of precisely determined dimensions, of a size stipulated in the contract signed with the local governments' association. At first there had been just a few sections of coffins, then, gradually, companies and battalions were formed, and now we are on our way to completing regiments and divisions. An entire army clothed in nylon.

"And what shall I do with it, my army?" he said between his teeth.

"You don't seem quite yourself," the priest commented. "Perhaps you have a fever coming on."

"No, it's nothing," the general answered, though he could feel the alcohol taking its effect much more rapidly than usual, perhaps because of his excessive fatigue. "It's really nothing," he repeated. "I just feel like drinking. But you, priest, colonel, whatever you are, you want to stop me. What is it you want with me, eh?"

The general was suddenly overwhelmed by a feeling of aggression.

"I cannot tolerate this supervision. What is it you want of me? Speak!" the general almost shouted.

The thin man who was sitting writing, as usual, at the table near the television, turned his head.

"Nothing at all, I assure you, general. There is nothing I am preventing you from doing and there is nothing I want of you. The idea of either had not crossed my mind," the priest said curtly.

"In that case you can just sit there and watch me drink."

"There is no point in making a scene," the priest said.

The general raised his glass again. The priest wouldn't bother him any more now. When it came to the crunch, he was still the boss.

He began thinking about his army. His blue army, with its two white stripes and its black edging. What shall I do with my soldiers? he thought. There are a lot of them now, such a lot of them, and they must be feeling the cold in those thin nylon coats. Those idiot generals of theirs have just abandoned them and left the burden on my shoulders. When I think of all the battles I could have won with them.

He tried to recall the battles he had studied at the Academy so that he could decide which ones he could have won with the forces he now had under his command. He began making tiny sketch-plans on his cigarette packet, marking the positions of the troops, his lines of attack, the points where the decisive assaults would occur. The priest sat silently drinking his chocolate and watching him scribble away. The general began with ancient history. First he surrounded Caesar, then he cut off Charlemagne's supplies, and after that he staged a whirlwind confrontation with Napoleon and forced him to retreat. But he was not satisfied. He was worried by the fact that he might be winning all these historical battles solely because of the superiority of the modern weapons at his disposal and not as a result of his talent as a general. So he relived the battles of more recent wars. He landed on half the world's coasts and advanced on capital after capital. His soldiers moved in one bound from the beaches of Normandy to the 38th parallel in Korea. He ordered them into the terrible jungle of Vietnam and led them out again safe and sound. He won many battles that history says were lost. And if he did emerge the victor it was because he led his troops with skill and never abandoned them to their fate. He was a general who knew what it meant to command. And at the moment he was in the throes of a study of warfare in mountainous terrain. And besides, he had brave soldiers under him, oh yes, very brave soldiers. But the reason they're such daredevils, he thought, is that they've nothing left to lose. And he took another drink. The cigarette packet was black with his scribbles, but another battle suddenly came to him. At first he was obliged to fall back, but then, having reinforced his army with dead men not yet inscribed on the lists (and they were the most savage fighters of all when it came to it), he won again.

"And there it is," he murmured with satisfaction. "Who would dare stand up to my Nylon Army?"

He was dead drunk.

XIV

THE GENERAL WOKE UP stiff all over. He got up and opened the shutters. It was a cold morning. The clouds stood high and motionless in the grey sky. He leaned against the glass, seized by a slight dizziness. Something not right, he thought. Is it starting up again?

He looked out. The autumn was almost over. The trees in the park facing the hotel were completely bare. It was undoubtedly many weeks since anyone had sat on those green benches. Apart from the dead leaves. But even they were rotting now. The general had been familiar for years with the uniforms of all the various N.A.T.O. forces, but he had never noticed before how their colours echoed the changing tints of the autumn leaves. Green first, then turning to a pale brown, and later a coppery yellow; then when they rotted they turned black.

In the middle of the park, beside the circular dance-floor, the rusty chairs had been stacked in piles for the winter, and the cleared and deserted dance-floor looked very large and sad. The platform for the band and the floor itself were littered with dead leaves, which the sweepers were even now gathering together into big piles.

Yes, there's something wrong with me, the general said to himself as he walked downstairs to breakfast.

"You look unwell," the priest said to him when they had sat down at their table. "Perhaps you need a little rest."

"I don't know myself what's wrong with me," the general said, "but it's true I don't really feel at all well. I seem to remember being rather offensive to you yesterday evening. I apologize. I had drunk rather too much."

"Oh please," the priest said affably.

"What appalling weather they have in this damned country!"

"It would perhaps be best if you didn't come with us tomorrow. I imagine our investigations will be much less arduous in the coastal districts than up in the mountains," the priest said.

"Yes, I had been assuming so myself."

"Rest a little. And one evening you ought to go to the theatre, or the opera."

"I am sleeping badly. I ought to take a sleeping pill."

They went out for another stroll along the boulevard after breakfast, walking up and down the wide pavement with its edging of tall pines. Groups of young men and girls passed from time to time – presumably students hurrying to lectures.

"What is this loathsome task we have been burdened with?" the general suddenly said, as though he were continuing some interrupted discussion. "I feel it would be easier to dig out the pharaohs still buried in the depths of their great pyramids than to excavate a mere two feet of earth in order to retrieve these soldiers of ours."

"You can't tear your mind away from that subject, can you? Perhaps that is why you are feeling unwell."

"The war here wasn't like other wars," the general went on. "There were no proper fronts, no direct confrontations. The war simply insinuated itself all over the country, like a breeding worm burrowing into the country's every cell. That's why it was so different from the sort of war that's fought elsewhere."

"That is because the Albanians are given to war by their very nature," the priest said. "They hurl themselves into it with all their hearts and with eyes wide open. Once they've been given a shot of it they become intoxicated with it the way other peoples do with alcohol. Their psychological conditioning . . ."

"Yes, you said something of the sort once before," the general said.

"Yes, I remember. Maybe I've bored you."

"No, please don't think that. I enjoy listening to you. You were speaking of the Albanians' warlike nature."

"Yes," the priest said. "It is a state of mind that goes back a long way. All through their history the Albanians have gone everywhere with weapons slung over their shoulders. The mountain people who lived a patriarchal existence may have been still living in the stone age until a few years ago, but that didn't stop them being equipped with the most modern of guns. Just think of the contrast! I have told you as much before: deprived of war and weapons this people would wither away, its roots would dry up and it would eventually just disappear."

"Whereas with war and weapons it will always regenerate itself?"

"So they believe. Though in fact weapons will reduce them to non-existence even more rapidly."

"According to you then, war is a sort of sport for them, an exercise they need in order to keep their circulation going and stay fit?"

"That is its effect for a while, yes," the priest said.

"In other words, with weapons or without, they are a people doomed to annihilation."

"It would seem so, yes. Their government has raised the nation's ancient propensity for war to the status of a political principle and embodied it in their policies. It is fortunate for their neighbours that the Albanians number only a few million."

The general lit a cigarette but did not speak.

"Do you remember the songs our workmen sang those nights

133

we were under canvas?" the priest went on. "Do you remember the melancholy, the depression we felt as we listened to them?"

"I remember," the general said. "There are some things not easily forgotten."

"The predominant themes of their songs are destruction and death. That is characteristic of all their art. You find it in their songs, in their dress, in the whole of their existence. It is a characteristic common to all Balkan peoples of course; but it is even more pronounced in the Albanians than anywhere else. Look at their national flag: simply a symbol of blood and mourning."

"You speak with great passion on the subject," the general observed.

"I have given a great deal of thought to these matters," the priest answered. "Oscar Wilde said that people of the lower classes feel a need to commit crimes in order to experience the strong emotions that we can derive from art. His epigram might well be applied to the Albanians, if one were to substitute the words "war" or "vengeance" for "crime". For if we are to be objective we must admit that the Albanians are not criminals in the common law sense. The murders they commit are always done in conformity with rules laid down by age-old customs. Their vendetta is like a play composed in accordance with all the laws of tragedy, with a prologue, continually growing dramatic tension, and an epilogue that inevitably entails a death. The vendetta could be likened to a raging bull let loose in the hills and laying waste everything in its path. And yet they have hung around the beast's neck a quantity of ornaments and decorations that correspond to their conception of beauty, so that when the beast is loosed, and even while it is spreading death on every side, they can derive aesthetic satisfactions from those events at the same time."

The general listened attentively.

"The life of the Albanian," the priest continued, "is like a theatrical performance governed by age-old customs. The Albanian lives and dies as though he were interpreting a role in a play, with the one great difference that the scenery is provided by the plateaux or the mountains where he and his kind pass their lives in such harsh penury. And when he dies, it is often because certain customs must be respected, not for objectively valid reasons. The life that succeeds in subsisting on these rocks amid so many ordeals and privations, a life that has never succeeded in eliminating either cold, or hunger, or the avalanche, is snuffed out suddenly as the result of an imprudent remark, a joke that went a little too far, or a covetous glance at a woman. The vendetta is often set in motion without the slightest passion behind it, solely in order to conform with tradition. And even when the avenger kills his victim he is doing no more than obeying a clause of unwritten law. And so these time-honoured and unspoken rules go on twisting themselves around these people's legs throughout their lives, until the day comes when they inevitably trip them up. And once they are down they never rise again. So that it is true to say that for centuries now the Albanians have been acting out a blood-thirsty and tragic play."

They heard footsteps behind them. It was the expert.

"I went looking for you at the hotel," he said.

"Why, is something the matter?"

"No, but tomorrow we have to go through some reports with the representatives of the local government association."

The priest was observing the expert closely, trying to decide whether or not he had overheard the end of their exchange.

"We were talking about your national customs," he said. "They are so interesting."

The expert smiled to himself.

"He was telling me about the vendetta," the general added. "It seems to be of great psychological interest."

"Nonsense, it is of no psychological interest at all," the expert contradicted. "I know there are some foreigners who have the idea that our vendetta and various other pernicious customs are to be explained by the so-called Albanian psychology, but the whole notion is too absurd."

"Ah!" the priest said.

"Yes. There are certain foreigners who come here and study our vendetta with what appears to be enormous enthusiasm; but they do so with a predetermined intention."

"They study it because the question is one of scientific interest, surely," the priest put in.

"I disagree. Their real aim is to spread the notion that the Albanian people is doomed to annihilation, to make people familiar with it and accept it."

"Oh, I hardly think so, I hardly think so," the priest said with a forced smile.

The expert walked a few more steps with them, but then took his leave of them.

"Just listen to that!" the priest remarked.

The general resumed their discussion.

"You explain the matter of their customs solely on psychological grounds," he said, "but I think that one cannot altogether exclude certain other motives from any such explanation, objective motives of an historical and military order for example. Do you know what the Albanian people remind me of? They remind me of the sort of wild beast that at the approach of any danger, before leaping or charging, freezes into immobility in a state of extreme tension, muscles coiled, every sense on the alert. This country, I feel, has been exposed to so many perils for so long that a state of alert like that has become second nature to it."

"Yes, that is precisely what they mean by their much vaunted vigilance," the priest said.

He continued with the subject, but the general was no longer listening to him. After a while he broke in:

"Have you noticed how much we talk about them? After all, what do we really care about their affairs? All we ask is that they should exterminate themselves. And the quicker the better."

The priest gestured his agreement with spread fingers and a shrug.

"We would do better to put our minds to our labours," the general went on, "our wretched labours that have exhausted us and that we cannot seem to bring to any successful conclusion. There is even a sort of evil spell, something sinister anyway, dogging this work of ours."

"I cannot agree," the priest rejoined. "I am aware of nothing of the sort. Our mission is a sublime one."

"I have the feeling that we wander across this country like an ambulatory tumour. We just get under the feet of all the inhabitants and hinder them in their work."

"You are referring, I take it, to the incident when the work on the aqueduct was delayed a few days on our account?"

"No," the general said. "I am not thinking only of that. There is something queer and maleficent in our work altogether."

"There is nothing of the kind," the priest said.

"Has it ever occurred to you that the unhappy creatures we are hunting out so zealously might prefer to be left in peace where they are?"

"That is absurd," the priest said. "Our mission is a noble and humane one. Anyone would be proud to be entrusted with it."

The general thought that the other was going to bring up the purification of the spirit, the light of the afterlife that enlightens the kingdom of the departed. But his interlocutor's expression was rather sombre.

"And yet there's something not quite right about it, a certain irony, however slight."

"I do not accept that," the priest said. "There is no such element in our mission. But perhaps there are other motives that affect your emotion, motives concerned with your profession as a soldier."

"What motives of that sort could I have?"

"Perhaps it would be better not to talk about them. It may be that you do not even wish to admit them to yourself."

The general produced a forced smile.

"More psychology?" he said. "Apparently you are a devotee of psychoanalysis. It is something I have heard a great deal of talk about but that I don't, to be honest, really understand. We soldiers do not go in much for that brand of hair-splitting."

"Yes, I realize that," the priest said, obviously meaning "everyone to his taste".

"But leaving that aside, what is this explanation of yours of my uneasiness about this mission of ours? I should like to hear your arguments; it's always a pleasure to hear you talk. And I promise you not to take umbrage at whatever you say."

"Very well, since you insist, I will give you my opinion," the priest said with the greatest possible calm. "The reason you are suffering from this sense of oppression is that in the depths of your soul you regret not having led our divisions in Albania yourself. And you tell yourself that under your leadership everything might perhaps have gone differently, that instead of leading our troops to defeat and destruction you would have ensured that they emerged with honour from that great test. That is why you are constantly spreading out those maps of yours, hunching over them for hours on end, scribbling battle plans on your cigarette packets. You lament over every failure, you relive every setback as though they were realities, and you see yourself retrospectively in the place of those ill-starred officers who commanded our troops then; and you have begun to entertain an utterly irrational dream: that of transforming our defeats into victories . . ."

"That is enough," the general said. "Am I a psychopath that you should start burrowing into the secrets of my soul like this?"

The priest simply smiled.

The general's face had clouded over.

"No," he said slowly, "there is no secret reason. I am not an ignorant young girl, after all, imagining that a search for the bones of soldiers fallen in battle could even remotely resemble a sentimental journey. I had always assumed that the task ahead was an arduous and sinister one."

He spoke truly. He had a sense from the start that this task awaiting him was quite unusual. He knew, as the Minister said, that he would be helped by love and hate. As he was returning home from the War Office, that day when he was first entrusted with this mission, he felt music echoing in his heart. Solemn, funeral music. And then, when he began opening the files and looking through them, and he felt that those interminable lists were breathing out great gusts of vengeance, he had gone to the globe and looked for Albania. And when he had his finger on it he felt a sadistic satisfaction at seeing just how small it was – no bigger than a dot. But then he had felt the hatred flood through him again. This pinprick on the map had filled the mouths of his country's brave, beautiful children with dust. He felt he wanted to get to this savage, backward country (as the geography text books all called it) as soon as he possibly could. He wanted to walk proudly among these people that he envisaged as a wild barbarian tribe, looking down at them with hatred and contempt as if to say: "Savages, look what you've done!" He pictured to himself the solemn ceremonial as the remains were borne away, the troubled and bewildered look in the Albanians' eyes – the guilty look of the lumbering lout who has smashed a priceless vase and stands there feeling dumbly sorry, looking askance at the fragments.

"And yet," the general resumed wearily as he pursued his thought, "I felt proud. We would bear our soldiers' coffins proudly through their midst, demonstrating to them that even our deaths are nobler than their lives. But when we got here it all turned out differently. I don't need to tell you that. Our pride was the first thing to go; then before long it was clear there was nothing solemn left in the whole business, my last illusions gradually faded, and now we have to keep on and on amid general indifference, observed by mocking, enigmatic eyes, pitiful clowns of war, more to be pitied in the event than those who once fought and were defeated in this country."

The priest made no answer, and the general was sorry he had spoken.

They walked on a short way in silence. The last leaves continued to fall onto the pavement. They passed other pedestrians. The general was aware of distress and loneliness inside him. He found it distasteful talking about such subjects. Better to walk on and recall those dark days they had spent on the road and in their tent, when the rain soaked them daily and they shivered in the wind, those enigmatic looks cast at them by the sombrely clad peasants in their coarse woollen clothes, that night when the priest – trapped in God knows what nightmare – shrieked with terror in the dark; the battlefield now drowned beneath the artificial lake of a hydroelectric dam; the graveyards lying beneath the deep waters, and the red, bright red reflections from their surface as the sun sank; and that skull too, its golden teeth all gleaming in the sun as the workmen unearthed it, seeming to cast a sarcastic smile at everything around it.

On both sides of the path the ditches were full of dead leaves, and the statues in the great park seemed to be shivering beneath the stripped trees.

Having reached the summit they were able to look down the far slope to the artificial lake lying at its foot, surrounded by small hills and insinuating its variously shaped inlets among them. On the curving brow of the hill itself there stood a church, and beside it an open-air café. All around the café's dance-floor, tall cypresses quivered in the keen wind. In one corner, apparently abandoned, stood a big pile of crates with the words *Birra Korça* printed on them in black.

They turned their backs on the lake and gazed out across the city. The general's raincoat flapped loudly in the wind.

Their eyes came naturally to rest on the line of the main boulevard that bisected the city. A poplar swaying in the wind would conceal now the Presidency building from their view, now that of the Central Committee. When there was a particularly strong gust, a branch would move across in front of the tall clock tower apparently stuck to the minaret of the mosque, then conceal a portion of Skanderburg Square, stretch across the façade of the Executive Committee building, and just manage to brush the State Bank.

"In my book on Albania it said that the buildings along the last section of the main boulevard, when viewed as a whole, form what looks like a giant Fascist axe," the general said, extending his arm in the direction of the buildings in question.

"Look more closely," the priest said, stretching out an arm in his turn. "The boulevard is the handle of the axe, that big building there, the Rectorate, is the head of the handle protruding beyond the blade itself, the opera house is the back of the axe, and the stadium" – and here the priest made a sweep of the hand to the right – "represents the curved cutting edge."

"In a word, one could make a sort of gigantic brand burned into the very heart of their capital."

"It was after the war, when they flew over the city for the first time, that the Communists noticed the effect. And they immediately gave orders that the image of the axe must be removed in some way."

They continued along the wide asphalt path beside the church. A young man and a girl were sitting side by side on one of the benches spaced along it. The girl, a dreamy look in her eyes, had lain her head on her companion's shoulder while he gently stroked her knees.

"Shall we go down again," the general said. "The wind is cold up here."

XV

HAVING LEFT THE ROAD and advanced for a while through fields the two vehicles were now skirting vineyards. The general, map spread on his knees, glanced out occasionally through the window, knowing that at the same moment, in the cabin of the lorry behind with his copy of the self-same map also spread on his knees, the expert was probably glancing out of his window in exactly the same way, thus ensuring that there was no chance of their missing the precise spot at which they were supposed to stop.

On the right there is a line of tall poplars. Looking towards them you see the farm buildings beyond, and then further on still, a mill. The place is at the foot of the trees. So as to be able to locate the graves again more easily later we dug them in a V formation, the point towards the sea. Five on one side, five on the other, then the lieutenant at their head.

"Tell him to drive towards the poplars," the general said. The priest translated the order to the driver.

As they stepped out of the car the tops of the tall trees were quivering in the wind. The priest set off towards the site of the graves slightly ahead of the rest of the group, and uttered a cry of surprise.

"What is it?" the general asked as he caught up with him.

"Look," the priest said, "look over there."

The general turned his eyes in the direction indicated.

"What does it mean?" he said angrily.

At the foot of the poplars were two rows of opened graves forming a V. The trenches had presumably been dug some ten or fifteen days before, since the recent rains had half filled them with water.

"I just can't understand it," the priest said.

"Someone has come and opened these graves before us," the general said. His voice quivered as he spoke.

"Here is the expert," the priest said. "We shall see what he has to say."

"What is it?" the expert asked in his turn as he approached.

Without a word the general gestured with one hand towards the trenches. The expert looked at them for a moment then shrugged his shoulders.

"That's strange!" he said in a low voice.

"These graves have been opened without our authorization, without our knowledge," the priest said. "What have you to say?"

Once more the expert shrugged.

"When will these provocations end I should like to know?" the general cried. "I shall take the matter to the highest authority immediately."

"At the moment I can give you no explanation," the expert said, "but I hope to be able to clear the matter up without delay. If you will only have a little patience."

"Of course, of course," the general said, fuming with fury.

The workmen and the two drivers had by now caught up and were also staring stupefied at the graves.

"Nothing like this has ever happened to us before," the oldest one said.

The expert counted the graves for the second time as he rolled up his map.

"Listen," he said turning to the lorry driver. "Drive over to that farm and bring someone back with you. Anyone you can find.

144

Tell them we're from the government and that it's an urgent matter." Turning back to his interlocutors, he added, "I can't offer you any explanation for the moment. I can only assure you that if someone did in fact commit such an action as a deliberate and calculated outrage, then he will be punished in accordance with our own laws."

"Whatever the intention," the priest said, "it is still a serious profanation."

Meanwhile, standing looking down at the graves the workmen were expressing astonishment at their odd arrangement.

"It's the first time we've come across a cemetery like this. In a V."

"It's strange!"

"That's how the storks fly," the old workman said. "Haven't you ever seen them in the autumn?"

The sound of the returning lorry's engine could be heard in the distance. There was someone sitting up in the cab beside the driver.

"I hope that everything will be cleared up now," the expert said.

The driver got down then went round and opened the other door for the newcomer. The latter, having clambered down, stared at them all attentively one by one.

"Do you work on this farm?" the expert asked him.

"Yes."

"Do you know anything about these military graves?"

The man glanced over at the trenches.

"Only what everyone else round here knows," he said.

"Which is?"

"Well, they're the graves of foreign soldiers, aren't they? And they've been there over twenty years now."

"Then how do you explain . . ."

"And ten days ago they were opened up again."

"Ah, now that's just what we want to know about," the expert said. "Who was it who opened them up again ten days ago?"

The man stared round once more at the workmen, the general, the priest, then the two vehicles.

"Did you see them with your own eyes, the people who opened these graves?" the expert tried again.

The man seemed reluctant to reply. Then he suddenly burst out:

"Are you trying to make a fool of me?"

"What? What do you mean?"

"You know the answer as well as I do."

The expert was visibly taken aback. They all stood around in silence, obviously dazed.

"Please. Can you tell us quite simply who opened these graves ten days ago?"

The man from the farm glared at the expert angrily.

"You opened them, you know that," he said curtly. "All of you," the man went on, and his pointing finger swung round to include the workmen, the general, the priest, and the two drivers.

They all stared at one another in bewilderment.

"Where did you manage to find this one?" someone muttered to the lorry driver.

"Listen," the expert said to the man, "it is really not in very good taste for you to . . ."

"I don't want to hear any more!" the man interrupted him, his eyes flashing with anger. "If you think you can get me all tied up with your clever talk you're wrong! You think just because you're educated you can just laugh up your sleeves at ordinary people, don't you?"

He gave the expert a last scornful glare then turned his back on him and set off back towards the farm.

The old workman shouted after him:

"Hey, wait a moment, comrade!"

"Hey you, stop! Come back!" the lorry driver called after him.

"You ought to be ashamed of yourselves," the man grumbled as he halted and turned back. "Do you take people for idiots? Do you think no one saw you or something, when you were here ten days ago? You must have known someone was bound to see you, you were all day digging away here."

"This is the last straw," the priest murmured.

"Us? You're talking about us?"

"Yes, who else? You were here with that same green car and that lorry with the cover over the back."

"Ah, now wait a minute," the expert said suddenly. "Were you actually here, on this spot, when the graves were being opened?"

"No, but we could see you from a distance."

The expert nodded.

"I think I understand now," he said. "There isn't much doubt, it must be those others. What a mess-up!"

"What do you mean? What happened?"

"That one-armed general and his companion must have got here before us."

"And you think they did this?"

"I'm quite certain they did, for my part. What other explanation can there possibly be?"

The man from the farm was explaining something to the workmen and the drivers that involved a great deal of gesticulation.

"How is it possible?" the general said.

"They have no maps. Nor any detailed information about their graves. They may perhaps have taken these to be some of theirs!"

"But they could have questioned the people who live nearby. And besides, there are the medallions," the priest protested.

"Yes, that's what puzzles me," the expert said, biting his lower lip.

"It is a serious profanation," the general mumbled.

"It isn't the first time they've been involved in something like this," the expert went on. "Somewhere in the south, so I was told in Tirana, they opened the graves of two *ballistes* by mistake. And in another place they began excavating in an old Moslem cemetery."

"And did they remove the remains?"

"Oh yes, it appears so."

"It's fantastic," the general said. "Are they in their right minds, those two? What could have got into them to behave in such a way?"

"Perhaps they had a motive," the expert said musingly. "And I suspect I know what it was."

"What? What motive?"

The expert was obviously unwilling to reply.

"I can't say any more. Please excuse me."

"Perhaps they've found their work so difficult without maps and so on that they've just taken to robbing any graves they happen to come across."

"They said themselves that they were hunting in the dark."

"And the worst part of it is that the remains they collect are despatched overseas immediately," the expert said.

"That's the limit!" grumbled the general.

"You mean we shan't be able to get these eleven back from them?"

"It will be difficult – if the remains have already left the country."

"In other words, our soldiers' remains are going to be handed over to families in some other country instead of their own!" the general cried. "It is enough to drive one mad!"

"One can only assume that they had entered into some kind of contract," the priest said. "How else is one to explain their hurry to send off the remains they find?"

"Yes, and when they can't find any of their own they just make off with any that happen to be around. A pretty way to carry on!"

The general was beside himself with fury.

"Let's get on!" he said suddenly. "There's nothing we can do here now."

They climbed back into their two vehicles and set off towards the sea, in the direction the little V-shaped cemetery was pointing.

XVI

THE SHORE LAY DISMAL and deserted. Small concrete look-out forts jutted up from the damp sand, most of them ravaged by time or human activity. Rusty iron struts stuck out through cracks, like ribs.

There was a cold wind blowing off the sea.

The general turned his eyes to the north, where beyond the forts there lay the first of the villas fringing the resort, then the little stations of the narrow-gauge railway for the summer visitors, the row of rest homes and the big hotels, most of them closed at this time of year.

The priest and he had come here looking for the remains of their country's soldiers who had lost their lives on the first day of the war. All that week they had done nothing but rush up and down the coast pausing briefly at all the landing sites, each of which had its own little cemetery.

He could remember it well, that first day of war in the spring of 1939.[2] He had been in Africa then. That evening the news had come over the wireless: the Fascist army, it said, had landed in Albania, and the Albanian people had greeted the glorious divisions bringing them civilization and happiness with peaceful waves and even flowers.

Then the first newspapers had arrived, followed by magazines crammed with pictures and on-the-spot-reports of the landings.

2 Mussolini's troops invaded Albania on 7 April 1939.

There were descriptions of how wonderful the spring was that year, of Albania's dazzling sea and sky, its beaches, its healthy air, its beautiful and amorous girls, its colourful costumes and graceful popular dances. Not a day went by without some kind of story appearing in at least one paper or magazine, and at night all the soldiers dreamed of being posted to Albania, to that pretty seaside paradise nestling in the shade of its eternal olive trees.

The general remembered that he too, at the time, had felt the desire for an Albanian posting, for later on. And it is now that I have been called upon to fight it, over this difficult terrain, at a time when all the rest of the world is at peace.

He had never been able to decide whether it had worked out in his favour or to his detriment.

After throwing their tools onto the crates, the workmen climbed into the lorry.

The two vehicles moved off.

They drove past the villas which lined the beach, cold and dismal looking with their blank shutters, then on in front of the new hotels and summer restaurants, all long closed now. The terraces of the bathing establishments jutted out towards the sea, their tables and chairs stacked up in big piles in one corner, abandoned vestiges of summer pleasures.

"Blockhouses everywhere," said the general.

"The Albanians are always only too eager to tell one that their country is a citadel perched on the shores of the Adriatic," the priest said.

The general turned to look at the shore.

"You once told me the sea has brought the Albanians nothing but misfortunes. That they hate it because of that."

"Yes, it's true," the priest said. "The Albanians are like animals that are afraid of water. They like clinging to rocks and mountains. They feel secure then."

The line of the road was moving further and further from that of the shore, and now the little narrow-gauge stations and the scattered white villas were concealed from their sight.

"Of the soldiers killed that first day of the war only one now remains to be found on the coast, the last," the general observed. "If the very first grave is along here, as I think it is, then it must be that poor wretch, the one mentioned by the old men on the corner, who dragged all the rest after him by the leg . . ."

"A soldier of the very first day," repeated the priest. "After that, if I'm not mistaken, we'll still be left with another difficult trip in an area in the foothills."

"Quite right," the general agreed. "Then there'll be two more. Then the penultimate. Then the last . . ." He gave a deep sigh. "It's much too early to think of going home. Yes, just too soon."

The priest nodded his agreement.

You just can't wait, the general thought. Because there's someone waiting for you.

"It's a long time since we last saw those two," he went on aloud.

"Heaven alone knows where they're excavating now."

"In another football stadium I should think. Unless they've decided to dig up a main street somewhere."

"They're making heavy weather of it, poor things!"

"That's their affair," the general said. "All that concerns us is making sure they don't pinch any more of ours."

They remained silent for the rest of the journey.

The monastery where they were going in order to look for the isolated soldier's grave stood on top of a small hill overlooking a fork in the road.

They began climbing the hill. The general walked at the head of the little group, followed first by the priest and the expert, then by the workmen, their tools on their shoulders.

Outside the monastery stood a few isolated and impressive

tombs, obviously ancient, topped with great crosses and carved with Latin inscriptions. The gate, obviously very old too, was closed. In a stone embedded in the arch above it were carved the words *Societas Jesus*.

The expert knocked several times. Eventually answering steps were heard from the other side. A white-haired monk in a black habit appeared on the threshold.

It took them some time to explain what they were after.

"We have written authority from the government and from the archbishop," the expert added, and began producing some papers from his wallet.

The monk lowered his grey eyes with their lower lids puckered into tiny pouches, and began to read the documents, moving his lips all the while as though chewing something.

"Good," he said. "Follow me. I'll take you there at once."

They walked after him along the inside of the monastery wall and eventually arrived at the back of the main building where the church stood.

"There it is," the monk said. "It's that grave there."

It was a very modest grave. At its head, a stone cross and a helmet. The varnish on the helmet had long since worn off, the two sides were embedded in the earth and, when the grass began to sprout in spring, it must certainly be hidden by the green blades.

One of the workmen ripped it out of the ground with his shovel. Two more began removing the cross, and the remaining two prepared to dig.

"Why is this grave on its own like this, so far from all the others?" the general asked.

"It's because this soldier was killed in extraordinary circumstances," the old monk said in a deep, muffled voice, "by a man called Nik Martini."

At the name, the general glanced over questioningly at the priest.

"A peasant from the mountains," the latter explained.

"I saw this soldier hit with my own eyes. Nik was firing from that outcrop up there," the monk said. With a shaky hand he indicated the outcrop where the peasant was supposed to have fired from.

They all turned and looked up at the mass of rock rising sheer above the road like a castle keep.

"Was there a battle near here then?" the general asked.

"Oh no," the monk answered. "This whole area, from here down to the sea, is uninhabited. No one ever expected any troops to land here. Nik Martini, the son of Martin Nik, he knew!" The way he spoke, he assumed that they knew all about it.

"When I saw him walking with such a brisk step, even though he had a rifle over his shoulder, it never occurred to me he was going to shoot. The mountain folk always go about like that, and one can never guess from their demeanour whether they're off to do some shopping in the local market or commit murder."

Noticing that the others were all hanging on his words, the monk rehearsed his meeting with Nik Martini, the words he had spoken: "Where are you off to, Nik?" I called. "I'm off to fight" he answered. Then the two of them climbed to the top of the bell-tower, from where one could see the hillside swarming with troops. Then what he said to him was: "Nik, you can't shoot from God's house." Then Nik's anger, the threat of excommunication that he the monk had uttered, the way Nik climbed down from the bell-tower and set off up the hill where he could observe the entire shore.

"And then? He really fought?" the general asked.

"Yes. He kept sniping for ages, until a mortar got the range of him."

"And that's when he was killed?"

"No, that's what we thought at first, when we didn't hear his gun again. But later on we learned that he had appeared again, further off, on top of another outcrop, and that's where this poor unfortunate was gunned down," and he indicated the trench.

"And the mountain fellow, he got out of it alive?" the general asked.

"Nik Martini?" The old monk lifted his grey eyes with their veiled gaze up to the hills. "No," he answered, "he is dead. He fought in four different places that day, until he had no strength in him left to fight. They say that when all his bullets were gone, and he could see the lorryloads of soldiers still driving past towards Tirana, he began to howl with grief, as our mountain people do when they are mourning the loss of someone near to them. So then they surrounded him. They tore him to pieces with their daggers."

There was a silence lasting several seconds.

"But Nik Martini has no grave," the old monk added, perhaps under the impression that his visitors were also seeking the hillman's remains. "No remains, no cross. There is only a song to keep his memory alive. It's often sung, especially in those two villages, out there on the horizon." And the monk pointed towards the north-west with a shaky hand. "Last year a mission from the Folklore Institute came this way and, if I'm not mistaken, they collected this song along with others. Then the members of the mission were at sixes and sevens. Some said it was a great deal older and was being erroneously attributed to Nik Martini's prowess. Others asserted that with this type of song it's always the same: the trunk goes back a long way but the branches and leaves are of recent date."

The old monk rambled on but it was some while since anyone had been listening to him.

"It's astounding," the general said half an hour later, as they were driving back towards Tirana, "that a single man could have dreamed of fighting an entire army."

"They cling to the honour of solitary combat," the priest said. "It is an ancient tradition among them."

The general lit a cigarette and sighed:

"Another day of war lived through!"

The priest said nothing. He looked out at the fields stretching away on either side of the road. The winter winds were already sweeping across them. A few miles further on the Adriatic re-appeared, on their right now, imposing in its immensity.

Small hills with rounded summits overlooked the shore; on their slopes they bore the scattered graves of the Albanians killed on that first day of the war.

In fragments, and from varying sources, the general had grad-ually pieced together a picture of what had happened during those days along Albania's two sea-coasts. He had been told how the news had spread through all the regions of the country, and how from all its four corners men set out in groups of five, or ten, or twenty, guns over their shoulders, on their way to fight. They came from considerable distances, without anyone having organized them, crossing mountains and valleys, with a hint of something ancient in their progress, something very ancient that had perhaps been handed on to them like an instinct, from generation to generation, since the legendary times of Gjergj Elez Alika, when evil, like a monster, always emerged from the sea, and had to be exterminated on the very seashore itself if it was to be prevented from insinuating itself inland. It was a very old sensation of alarm that had awakened in them, an ancient apprehension aroused by the sight of blue waters, and more generally by the sight of all flat country, since it was from such country that evil had always sprung. As soon as they sniffed the air from the sea and then saw it lying there so vast before them, these men, coming down from their mountains to join the remnants of the royal army then still fighting on, experienced a sense of awful peril and supposed that what they heard thundering in those waves was the sound of martial music summoning them on to war.

And so it was that on that day, drawn by tradition, many scores of guerrillas came down from the mountains. Among them there were men in felt hats and glasses mingling with tall mountain-dwellers from the far *bayraks*, with those mountain people who still led a patriarchal existence, many of whom were not even concerned to know what country it was now assailing them, or what enemy they were going to fight, since that was a matter of little importance to them. The important thing was that the evil was rising once again from the sea and must be driven back into it. Many had never seen the sea before in their lives, and when the Adriatic appeared before them they must no doubt have cried: "Ah, but how beautiful it is!" And perhaps they could no longer believe it possible that this was the source of the evil. But then they looked out with indifference at the teeming war ships standing off the shore, at the gigantic gun barrels trained on the coast, at the skimming planes, at the landing barges, and without further ado they began the fight, as tradition prescribed. And so they fell, some almost at once, some after a short while.

And then, when the sun was about to set, the latecomers arrived, those who had come from the furthest reaches of the mountains. And without waiting, worn out as they were, dropping from their long journey, they hurled themselves into the battle in their turn, as the sun sank, as the invaders started up their great pumps to wash the streets of Durrës clean of the blood that was making them flame in the westering light.

The mountain men had continued to flow shorewards until

night fell. Some had come alone, and they could be seen silhou- etted at the summits of the hills, the barrels of their guns pointing skywards above them. Then, as the searchlights revealed their ambushes, so the machine-guns mowed them down, and they lay there on their bellies until the morning, their hair wetted by the dew.

Next day they were buried where they had fallen, and their graves that spring were to be seen all over the slopes that face out to sea, scattered like innumerable grazing sheep. No one knew their names, or even the districts from which they had come. Only the mountain people could tell that from their clothes. Some of them had come from the distant *bayraks* far to the north, from those districts where the whole family dresses in black when a relation dies, and where they stretch a covering of black cloth even over the dead man's cold, sad *kulla* of stone before they dedicate a song to his memory. And the songs they sang for those who died that day must surely have spoken of the distant and treacherous sea.

PART TWO

PART TWO

SPRING RETURNED, THEN passed. The grass began to grow again in that foreign land. It covered the valleys, it sprouted on the slopes of the valleys, and persistently it invaded the narrow strips of gritty earth along the sides of the roads.

As summer came the general, the priest with their expert and their band of navvies rushed up hill and down dale, from region to region across Albania. Despite their efforts they were unable to dig up all those they were looking for. The good weather stole up on them, but they allowed themselves no more than a fortnight's rest, for they did not seem to be progressing as fast as they wanted.

At the press conference he had given in his own country, just before he returned to Albania, the general did not conceal his irritation. Yes, it's true, he had requested an extension from the Albanian government beyond the deadline to complete his search. It was perfectly true that the search was taking longer than anticipated. Unexpected difficulties had cropped up. No, they weren't ones created by the local authorities. Nor was it to do with administrative delays nor with budgetary cuts effected by his own government.

The journalists' questions were as usual hair-raising and verging on the cynical. He said nothing to them about the coldness of the locals, nor about the sombreness of their songs, nor about the incomprehension with which they kept meeting. But he did not spare them a description of other difficulties they ran up against: the rugged terrain, the biting winters in the mountains,

161

the drainage canals which, in Communist countries, as everyone surely knows, are excessively large, the previous year's earthquake which had ravaged some of the graveyards.

As he touched upon this last item, silence descended on the hall for the first time, a silence so deep that, for a moment, he had the impression that a complete severance had come between himself and his audience – they were no longer listening to each other.

He had already had this impression of deafness in the Albanian archives, when he had come across the description of the earthquake. As if dealing a final blow, it had shaken up the dead a year before he had landed in Albania himself. It was as though he had shaken them in their sleep to warn them of his arrival.

This press conference, like the many vexations of these final days – hordes of visitors, correspondence, telegrams, phone calls – lodged in his mind like a distant hum as he boarded the aircraft, with the priest, at the end of August for Albania.

The background was the same as for his last visit, neither more nor less hostile; on the deserted tarmac the same folk as before, the same words, the same frosty smiles, the same mispronunciations as the year before.

XVII

THE GENERAL'S EYE STOPPED on one sentence: "Usually we spent the entire day smoking, leaning against the bridge parapet." He almost crossed it out, but his hand hovered over the sheet of paper. He chewed his lips, like one who concedes defeat, and, without touching the sentence, continued to the end of the letter he was writing to his wife.

Since he had noticed that, not only in his conversation but in every episode of his life, alien elements were creeping in little by little, the words of visitors he had received, fragments of letters or diaries of dead soldiers, he had tried to dam up this flow. But this had proved so powerful that the words and phrases, sometimes entire narratives by the dead men, kept invading his mind. They trampled on all else and each day reinforced their tenure.

Sometimes he would comfort himself with the thought that it was something he was bound to expect. And his fear that if he kept making use of sentences or words deriving from people in the kingdom of the dead, he would fetch up there himself, this fear did finally pass. He had in effect joined up with them; day after day, season upon season, he had entered this universe and, never mind what he did now, there was no escaping it any more.

Henceforth he had grown accustomed to it, and there were even days when, in place of his earlier torment, he felt a kind of serenity. And with this feeling came the cold satisfaction that this universe had accepted him.

*

Usually we spent the entire day smoking, leaning against the bridge parapet or sitting in the little hut with its notice over the door: "Cofee – Orangeade", printed all lopsided by the fellow who ran it. There were six of us guarding the bridge. The road over it was a strategic route opened up by the Austrians in the First World War and allowed to fall into disuse soon after it. We'd arrived only a few days after the refurbishing of the bridge and the road was finished. The soldiers who'd repaired them had also built a blockhouse and a small block for living-quarters at the same time. So everything was ready for us when we got there. We set up our heavy machine-gun in the block-house and kept a light one in the barrack block – for emergencies.

The country all round was dreary and empty. Just uncultivated land with a few little rocks and trees scattered about. And the village was tiny – ten houses at most. Strange stone houses they were, with tiny little slits for windows, just like the slits in our blockhouse.

At first we nearly went mad with boredom. There were only very occasional army vehicles going by, and the villagers made it quite clear they didn't want anything to do with us. All day long we just walked to and fro beside that parapet and threw stones in the stream. Then at night we took turns on guard duty.

But then, one fine day, down the path from the mountain we saw a man approaching leading three mules loaded with planks, crates, and rolls of tarred paper. He was a trader from the nearby town. In two days he had put up a hut just by the bridge and painted up in black paint, above the entrance, the words: "Cofee – Orangeade".

From that day onwards we became assiduous customers. Although he had only painted cofee and orangeade over the door he did in fact sell raki and a horrible sort of local wine. From time to time soldiers from a passing lorry would draw up outside and get out for a drink; it was as though his bar had managed to whip up a little life in that dismal spot. Sometimes even the villagers came for a drink. But it wasn't the trader's raki that attracted them, and his rotgut wine even less. They had other things on their minds. They'd come to exchange their eggs for our cartridges. It was strictly forbidden, of course, but we did it all the same. At night, during our guard duty, we'd fire a salvo or two of rifle shots, then ask for twice as many replacements next day as we'd actually shot. And the ammunition we managed to hoard in that way we swapped for eggs.

But those fusillades into the dark were ill-omened. It was as though they were a signal we had ourselves sent to ill fortune; because after a while the partisans did begin to worry us in good earnest. If it hadn't been for the blockhouse they'd have wiped us out in no time.

The first of us was killed on the bridge, while he was on guard duty one night. Apparently the partisans had made an attempt to blow the bridge up, but our sentry had prevented them by giving the alarm. In the morning we found him dead beside the parapet. He was lying in a very strange position, with his mouth open. Did you ever see that film Death of a Cyclist? Well when I went to see it I almost yelled out right in the middle of it. The body, on the screen, was so much like that vision I still have engraved in my mind.

Scarcely two weeks went by before it was the second one's turn. The circumstances were identical you might say. We were pretty sure the village people were shooting at us themselves, but we had no proof. We'd stopped bartering our cartridges with them by now of course. But it was too late.

After a third of our number had been killed we decided not to keep watch out on the bridge any more. With the replacements for our casualties we had also been sent a search light, which was now set up inside the blockhouse and used to sweep the bridge at irregular intervals. With its hundreds of black, interlacing girders, which gave it a spooky, insect-like look, it had an altogether sinister and frightening appearance. Sometimes, in the middle of the night, I would look out at it outlined in that harsh, white light and feel a presentiment that it was going to swallow us all up, one after another.

And the partisans were not about to give up.

The fourth of our men was killed the same night I was wounded. That's all I know about it though, because I was hit in the first few seconds of the attack. When I came to again I realized I'd been hoisted up onto a mule that was now walking slowly across the bridge. The planks made strange cracking noises under its shoes. It was morning, a grey winter morning. My eyes just stared numbly at the innumerable bolts filing past so close to them. Then I felt my heart contract as something heavy and cold pushed down on it, and that one moment left a scar on me for ever.

As the mule left the bridge and set off slowly along the road I managed to twist my head round a bit and look back for the last time at the blockhouse, at the dismal houses of the peasants scattered over the plateau, at our men's graves at the foot of the bridge (the last one still to be dug) and at the wooden hut, passing quite close at that moment, with its squalid sign: "Cofee – Orangeade".

The general sat on a block of concrete smoking. Below him, at the foot of the bridge, the workmen were searching and digging in the spaces left by the huge shattered blocks scattered on all sides among the twisted pieces of rusty ironwork. The new bridge had been built a few hundred yards further downstream, where the new road emerged from its cutting near an oil-store. What had been the mountain road was now overgrown with bushes and brush.

The explosion must have been terrible, the general thought to himself. The bridge had been sliced in two, the great concrete tiers had been shattered into fragments and sent soaring as far as the blockhouse – some even farther – along the disused road. Near the bridge there still stood an old wooden hut, and over the door it was still possible to make out the words: *Cofee – Orangeade*.

When they had arrived, a week before, the hut, like the bridge, the blockhouse and part of the road, was half destroyed. The tarred paper with which it had been roofed was ripped in places, a number of boards had been torn away, and a good many of those remaining were rotten. But two days later a travelling licensee of the local catering union turned up. He had brought cigarettes, brandy, and a stove to make coffee on. It was like manna from heaven for everyone, because apart from the five full-time workmen they had taken on another seven on a temporary basis, and the whole lot of them – to say nothing of the drivers, the expert, the priest and the general – were doomed to two long and wearisome weeks in the spot. So, after he had nailed up some new planks in one or two places and weighted the torn strips of tarred paper down with big stones so that the wind couldn't lift them, their state victualler had duly set up shop in the old hut.

His bar whipped up a little life in the place. In the morning the workers would take their coffee or a small glass of brandy there before starting work. During the day the villagers would loiter outside for hours on end, watching the workmen dig.

Two of them, the general happened to notice just then, seemed to be in the process of explaining something to the old foreman, gesturing with their hands towards a spot somewhere down at the foot of the bridge.

Who knows which of them fired at the sentries? the general would think every time he saw the villagers coming down to mingle with the workmen or buy cigarettes at the hut. It was now a week since they had arrived and by now he was able to recognize some of them by sight.

The priest and the expert were clambering along the embankment towards him. The gorges in the mountains all around them were deep in mist.

"Foul weather," the general said.

The priest nodded.

"The Albanians have a proverb," he said: "'Bad weather is forgotten in a friendly house'."

"Then we certainly haven't much hope of forgetting it," the general said. "No one in this country would even open their front door to us."

"Quite so," murmured the priest. "We're fastened to this bridge and can't pull ourselves free."

"I can't stand this place, with those peasants prowling about and watching us dig up our dead."

"It's true, they do prowl," the priest said. "I think they must be deriving some sort of satisfaction from our work."

"Those men guarding the bridge, they knew them. They lived with them as neighbours for quite a long while, they bartered their eggs with them for bullets, and yet it was one of them for sure who shot those men."

"They hang around our excavations as though they were waiting for a chance to boast to our workmen and our drivers that they were the ones who actually killed the sentries," the priest said. "Have you noticed one old man in particular? He has a long moustache, a big revolver stuck in his belt, and he comes here every morning, very stately and solemn, strolling around among the workmen."

The general scowled. "The one with two or three medals stuck on his chest who walks with his head up in the air? The expert told me that his son was killed by our troops."

"Oh, is that so?"

"Apparently he pinned the medals on as soon as he heard we were here, then came straight down to parade himself with his revolver in his belt. And he's done it every day since."

"Even the Albanian workmen don't escape his contemptuous looks. Yesterday, when the expert asked him about something, the old fellow didn't even deign to reply."

"He's an old fanatic. Presumably he feels the expert and the workmen are in some way our allies. What I do know," the general continued as though imparting a confidence, "is that we must be prepared for anything. I distrust that kind of psychopath. You never know, he could go crazy one day, pull out his gun, and just shoot at us in broad daylight!"

"It's very possible," the priest said. "Anything could happen with a crack-brained old fellow like that about. One must be careful."

They heard the thunder rumbling again in the gorges of the mountains all around.

The general lit a cigarette.

"I find the interest these villagers are showing in our excavations more or less understandable," he said. "A soldier who used to be one of the detachment guarding this bridge came to me before we left home and described what life was like here in wartime. When I was sitting over there just now I was thinking over what he had told me – for perhaps the tenth time."

"We remind them of those war years."

"Yes, it's quite natural. During the war they found their whole destiny suddenly linked with that of the bridge. Its proximity proved fatal. As soon as the bridge had been destroyed, our troops swept in, intent on reprisal, and massacred them. Without this bridge, life in a village so cut off from the rest of the world would just have gone flowing calmly on, and the currents of war would never have reached it. But the bridge was there, and it was the cause of everything. And now, out of the blue, we have appeared and started looking for our soldiers' remains. This stirs up their memories and makes them restless. They come and go, buy cigarettes at the hut which maybe more than anything else reminds them of the climate of those days."

The priest listened carefully.

"Dwelling on the past. Nothing can be more dangerous."

The general had the impression that the other was not anxious to pursue that line of thought.

After lunch the general settled down to work on his lists for a while. They now had all sorts of notes scattered down their margins. Not identified. Reference 1184. See report of exhumation. Head missing. Not identified. See report of exhumation. Head missing. Not identified. See report of exhumation. Right arm shorter than left. Reference 1099. Number 19301. Listed as killed twice. Dentition does not correspond. Not identified . . .

That afternoon it began to rain. The workmen gathered in the cold, smoky hut and watched the fine rain falling outside.

XVIII

THAT EVENING THE OLD workman became ill. He had begun to feel slightly unwell during the afternoon, but he had decided it wasn't important. By evening he was looking pale and felt he needed to lie down. Everyone simply assumed he'd caught a chill. He was taken to one of the village houses and settled down in front of a big fire to keep warm. But as night drew on, his condition grew even worse.

It was still not dawn when the expert woke the general as he needed to borrow the car.

"The foreman is in a pretty bad state. We must get him to the nearest hospital urgently."

The priest had woken in his turn.

"What is the matter with him?" he asked. "He looked perfectly well yesterday afternoon."

"I can't tell you exactly," the expert said. "I'm afraid it's an infection. He has a scratch on his right hand."

"An infection?" the general broke in, lifting his head in surprise.

The expert left.

"What's really wrong with him, I wonder," the general said.

"I think it probably is an infection," the priest said. "His face was quite grey yesterday evening."

"What rotten luck!"

"Perhaps a rusty greatcoat button, or a broken bone. They opened a whole lot of graves yesterday."

"Yes, but he knows what he's about. He's the one who always shows the others how to go about it."

"Obviously he won't have noticed," the priest said. "Perhaps he had mud on his hands and just didn't know he'd scratched himself."

"He should really have been taken into the town yesterday evening."

"The road is bad; it's a long time since it was last used. It isn't an easy journey even in daytime."

"But all the same . . ."

"They'll be in time, even setting out now. I don't think he's in any great danger. Modern drugs can usually cope with infections of this sort."

The general buried himself again beneath his thick woollen blanket.

"What's the weather like?" he asked.

"Cloudy," the priest replied.

When they emerged from their tent a few of the workmen were already at work. The others were standing outside the hut drinking their morning coffee.

"The expert being away is going to hold up the work," the priest said. "The workmen don't really know where to dig."

"Do you think there may be other infected remains?"

"Why shouldn't there be?"

"Perhaps we should throw quicklime in the graves already opened," the general said.

"We must ask the expert. He's the one who knows all about these things."

They reached the hut and ordered a coffee each.

"The germ can stay buried there for twenty years, then suddenly jump out as virulent as ever. It's strange," the general said.

"But true," the priest added. "At the first contact with air and sunlight it returns to life."

"Like a wild animal coming out of hibernation."

The priest sipped slowly at his coffee.

"I think it's going to rain this afternoon."

And it proved a gloomy day indeed. They wandered about all morning not knowing what to do with themselves. Then in the afternoon the rain began to fall again.

"If anything happens to him we shall have to indemnify his family," the general said.

"A life pension?"

"Yes, it's stipulated in the contract. Section 4, Paragraph 11, if I remember rightly."

The priest entered the tent and re-emerged with a sheaf of papers in his hand. "Yes, that's it," he said. "It's stipulated in Section 4, Paragraph 11. In the event of a fatal accident, the family is entitled to a life pension."

"Maybe he'll pull through," said the general.

"Pray God!"

The expert returned next morning. The lorry driver was the first to see the car as it toiled its way towards them along the mountain road.

"Here they are!" he shouted. "They're back!"

The general, the priest, and the workmen, who were all huddled in the hut sheltering from the rain, immediately came out to see.

Still a long way off, picking its way among the big stones scattered across the roadway, the green car was climbing slowly upwards.

"He must be better," someone said.

As the car got closer they saw that it was spattered all over with mud.

The expert was the first to emerge. His face was pale, his features drawn, his expression tired and haggard. He pushed out one leg first, then the other, and glanced around him with an indifferent, absent air.

"Well? What happened?" someone asked, breaking the silence. "What've you done with Gjoleka?"

The expert turned to look at the speaker as though amazed by such a question.

"Gjoleka? He is dead," he answered, articulating each word.

"Dead! You're not saying . . ."

The driver, who got out of the car after the expert, came forward reeling like a drunkard. His eyes were red, his hands mud-caked.

"What? Don't you believe us?" he shouted huskily. "Run along to the hospital morgue if you want to make sure."

It took them a little while to get over the shock and express their thoughts.

"When?" another voice asked.

"About midnight."

"It was a terrible infection he had," the expert said, as though to himself.

The little group made its way in silence back to the hut.

"Make them some coffee, can't you see they're all in!" someone shouted at the licensee.

"Have a brandy too. That will make you feel better."

"Right, a brandy I certainly wouldn't say no to!"

"Now then, tell us a bit about it, if you can."

The driver downed the brandy in one gulp.

"Fill that up again for me," he told the licensee. "What a night! During the whole drive he didn't once open his mouth. Sometimes he shivered till his teeth chattered, sometimes he seemed to be on fire. Then he began getting dizzy spells. We told him to lie down, and he stretched out as best he could on the back seat, but it didn't seem to help him at all. You can imagine I had my foot down as much as I dared. God knows how we didn't end up in a ravine! We kept on asking him 'How are you feeling?', but he never opened his mouth, not once. He just stared back at us as though he was saying 'Bad, chum, bad!' Well we got to the town at last and they took him straight into the hospital. We went every half hour to ask how he was. We could tell from the nurses' faces he wasn't doing too well. One of them told us: 'You should have brought him in earlier.' That was when we really realized how bad it was. We asked to see him. They wouldn't let us. By that time it was dark. We just went from café to café. We were too worried to go to a hotel and get some rest. About eleven we went back to the hospital again to see how he was. We were pretty surprised when they told us we could go straight in and see him. We asked how he was. 'Very ill,' the nurse told us, 'he won't last the night.' That was why they'd let us go straight in. You could see he wasn't going to last much longer. His face was lead-coloured, he'd tremble all over for a moment then go stiff, just as though he was made of stone. He looked up at us sort of nodding his head. Then he began staring and staring at the scratch on his hand as though he was saying: 'You're what did for me, you rotten bastard!' About midnight he had some sort of terrible fit, then a little while after that when the agony was over, he just faded away. And that's all there is to tell. Just fill that glass again will you, for the love of heaven! What a business!"

There was silence in the hut, except for the sound of a torn strip of tarred paper flapping on the dilapidated roof.

"I just can't believe it," someone said. "To think he was here with us only a few hours ago, and now we shan't ever see him again."

"Yes, poor old Gjoleka has left us. Just whisked away without us even realizing."

"He was a good fellow," someone else put in, "always kind to everyone, and not proud."

"Who's going to tell his wife?"

"That won't be an easy task!"

"Poor woman, she didn't like him doing this job anyway. It was as though she had a presentiment of this. She used to write in every letter: 'When are you going to finish with those graves?' And he'd answer: 'Just a little while now and it will all be over.'"

"Poor woman," the driver said. "Once when I delivered a letter from him to their home, in Tirana, she even complained to me about it. She worried about him constantly. She had waited for him so many years during the war, and now she felt somehow that he was away fighting again."

"He was always saying much the same thing himself: 'The Fascists kept me busy while they were alive, and now that they're dead I'm still having to hunt for them, they're still keeping me busy!'"

"Yes! He fought against them so many years, and he beat them. But it was them that got him in the end. What pig luck!"

"Like a revenge after death."

"They waited twenty years for it too. But all the same, when he fought them he fought them fairly, in open war, whereas they killed him with a rusty button like filthy cowards."

"The enemy is always the same, even when he's dead."

"They stand up there, not talking, like two crows," the driver said in a hoarse voice, casting a look of hate at the priest and the general standing wrapped in their long capes by the ruins of the bridge. "Well, are you satisfied now?"

"Hush!" someone said. "Be sensible, Lilo!"

A heavy silence descended once more in the hut. There was just the sound of the wind flattening the strip of tarred paper on the roof, then lifting it up again.

"They've killed him and we shan't see him again," someone said through a sob. "They've taken him away from us!"

*

Night fell, gloomier than ever. The general could not get to sleep and twice had to take a sleeping pill. He slipped into a disturbed sleep interspersed with wakeful periods.

The death had quite unsettled him. Sometimes, in his dismay, he exaggerated the degree of adversity he had to cope with.

It was quite a new death and thus seemed both unacceptable and a promise of further ills. In this realm of silica grown cold over twenty years, such a death seemed as alien as could be.

The general felt panic-stricken without knowing why. As he tossed and turned on his camp bed, he thought he heard the priest praying.

Chapter without a Number

NOTHING. BEFORE THE expert said a word, the priest had already understood.

"No, nothing," the expert answered in a tired voice as he picked his way carefully over the great gouts of slippery clay.

"It's very odd," the priest said.

"We're going to dig in two more places, one on each side of the spot marked on your map. He must be somewhere round here after all."

The general came over. His boots were caked with mud and he was having difficulty unsticking them from the ground at every step.

"Well?" he asked the expert.

"Still no luck."

"We shall have to give this one up," the general said. "What was his rank?"

"Lieutenant."

"He could have dragged himself a long way from here, after he was wounded."

A few scattered drops of rain fell onto the red mud heaped up on both sides of the trench. They hunted till about noon, when suddenly they heard a cry from one of the workmen further off:

"Here! Here! We've found him!"

The expert, taking his time in case he should slip, made his way over to the freshly dug trench. The priest followed.

They hovered for a long while beside the opened grave, and finally the priest returned with a crestfallen air.

"We might have saved our trouble," he said wearily. "It wasn't one of ours."

"Who was it then?" the general asked.

"According to the expert it must be a British pilot."

The expert came over to them again.

"I'm afraid we've gone to all this trouble for nothing," he told them.

"What do we do now?" one of the workmen called over as he walked towards them.

"We're going. There's nothing more we can do here."

"And the Englishman?" the workman asked.

"Bury him again," the priest said. "There's nothing we can do for him."

"Nothing we can do. Re-bury him," the general concurred.

The expert turned towards the grave.

"Bury him again," he told the workmen.

Two of them threw the bones back into the trench and began filling it in as the little group moved off. When the general turned back, after a moment or two, the two men were still at work and he could see their shovels moving up and down in time with one another. A little later, when he turned to look again, he supposed they must have finished, since he could see them walking back down the hill, their tools over their shoulders, and there didn't even seem to be a mark on the earth where the grave had been filled in.

"A day wasted," the general said, "totally wasted."

Another Chapter without a Number

BONE BY BONE, vertebra by vertebra, the skeleton of the great reptile reached completion. Here and there the odd gap subsisted. And there were not a few uncertainties. Just as he heard the remains of the last bugler being dug out from the common grave, the general fancied he heard the solitary sound of his instrument.

These common graves had become his terror. Luckily they were only three in number; in two the identification of the skeletons was finally completed. The work still remained to be carried out in the third, the hardest – it lay at the bottom of a stony ravine.

Some months earlier they had wasted several days hereabouts, on the false indications of a peasant who had claimed that he had seen with his own eyes a great mass of bones in the cellars of a ruined fort. Even though every weapon lying about them had been collected up previously, it was clear from the first glance that the bones belonged to soldiers of an earlier age. It took the expert no time to convince the general to stop searching here. There were no medallions struck with the picture of the Virgin anywhere near any skeleton, so it had been pointed out to him by someone handing him a metal disc in the shape of a many-pointed star.

This symbol was the only one turned up and, so far as the expert knew, it belonged to the *munadjim*, the Ottoman army's astrologer.

The general held the metal star for a while in the palm of his hand, but came nowhere close to understanding just what the astrologer in question was hoping to find in these trench bottoms – the worst place in the world to find any part in the things of Heaven.

Another Chapter without a Number

THE THIRD COMMON grave was to be found at a place known as Wind Ridge. This was the one that gave them the most trouble, and it was clear that it had cost the general a great deal of sleep three months earlier, when they were not yet anywhere near it. Then it had disturbed his nights again two weeks ago, as they were approaching the region in which it lay. And of course the last week, while they were striving to glean some information about it. He had a chronic headache. The skein that appeared at the last moment to be on the point of coming untangled in fact was getting into only a worse tangle, as in a nightmare. All they had gathered with regard to this grave pointed in totally opposing directions: the notes from his Ministry, depositions by other soldiers, letters that had a bearing on it, a telephone conversation of twenty years back, an article in the local press about flooding that had ravaged the area, accounts by elderly villagers, the deposition of a Greek soldier taken prisoner in Albania, who had noted things told him by a cell-mate, gypsies' tales, a police report, another by a schizophrenic – so many elements combined together, it seemed, only the better to contradict each other.

Occasionally he would console himself with the thought that, in the end, among all these endless catacombs this one grave constituted only a tiny detail. But the next day he remained persuaded that until he had dug out this grave right to the bottom he could not consider his mission accomplished. He had the feeling that everything was tied to this excavation, as by a double knot: his sleep, Colonel Z., the misfortunes that kept up their latest barrage . . .

Some of the locals maintained that the grave went back to the first winter of the war, while others said it was more recent. Some maintained that it had first been dug by gypsies looking for dead men's medallions, imagining that the metal had some value, and then they had hastily piled the bodies in a heap. There were also different versions of the story of the flooding. Of course it had caused problems, but it had affected every burial ground in the region. There were still lawsuits pending that arose out of it. As for the Bohemians, it was common knowledge that with any disaster of this kind it was always at them that people threw stones. Thank God at least they didn't single out the Jews in these parts! Believe me, no one tells the truth, everyone's frightened. This common grave has been here forever. Only it's normally been emptier rather than fuller. And thus will it always remain, like the roadside inn. As for me, I make no mystery about it. Know it's where we'll all fetch up . . . But why waste your time listening to him, sir, don't you believe he's a lunatic? You should rather be asking old Hil, he's the village memory . . . Thank you, my child, I'm an old man, but I couldn't tell a lie even if I wanted to. I address more words to the earth than to men. The earth – the earth never lies. The grass grows up on it each year and it will be our lodging, for all of us, that is its promise . . . As for the grave at the place they call Wind Ridge, you'll not find an ounce of truth if you look for it there. Only silence, shadows. Or rather something that you living folk, you'll never be able to grasp. Better to ask me no questions. My tongue would refuse to answer you even if I wanted it to . . . Which is just as well for you! . . .

181

Another Chapter without a Number

ONCE UPON A time a general and a priest set off on an adventure together. They were going to collect together all the remains of their soldiers who had been killed in a big war. They walked and walked, they crossed lots of mountains and lots of plains, always hunting for those bones and collecting them up. The country was nasty and rough. But they didn't turn back, they kept on further and further. They collected as many bones as they could and then they came back to count them. But they realized that there were still a lot they hadn't found. So they pulled on their boots and their raincoats and they set off on their search again. They walked and they walked, they crossed a lot more mountains and a lot more plains. They were quite exhausted; they felt they were being crushed into the ground by their task. Neither the wind nor the rain would tell them where to look for the soldiers they were seeking. But they collected as many as they could and came back once again to count them. Many of the ones they had been looking for still hadn't been found. So at the end of their tethers, quite tired out, they set out on another long journey. They walked and they walked, on and on and on. It was winter and it was snowing.

"What about the bear?"

"Then they met a bear . . ."

The story the general told himself every evening, and intended to tell one of his grand-daughters as soon as he got back, invariably ended with the question: "What about the bear?", simply because his grand-daughter always asked that question, sooner or later, when listening to a story.

XIX

A T LAST, ON THE tenth day, they began to come down again.
The road was sinking lower and lower and the mountain
peaks were rising higher and higher behind them.

They were coming to the end of their last and most arduous
tour. Because of the bad weather at this season the remoter regions
were even harder to reach. Here and there small villages cropped
up, perished with cold; they seemed impatiently waiting to crouch
down again in the mist.

The high mountains carried tragic scars whose menace the snow,
rather than attenuating, only served to accentuate; the mountains
pretended to withdraw only to rear up again a little further on. In
spite of everything, they were becoming less steep. Crags ever more
spaced out were coming away from the main summits. At the foot
of these crags boys and girls were clearing the ground for planting.
Here and there the snow cleared only to reappear further down; it
looked bland enough but still flashed wickedly.

The Alpine troops who had gone looking for death amid familiar snows had found it. The snow was not the way it looked at first
sight: noble, easy on the shovel, no – the snow proved every whit
as intransigent as the terrain. Just as it had tormented the last
hours of the victims, twenty years before, it was now tormenting
those who had come seeking them out, just as badly if not worse.
It had carefully covered everything up, as though refusing to let
anyone seize what it protected in its bosom. The general found
this more and more natural, accustomed as he was by now to this

mute resistance. What did not, in his view, conform to a natural order was his stubborn purpose in wresting from the earth or from the snow these remains with which they were by now familiar.

Let's be gone, dear Lord, before we're landed in some nasty surprise, he would sometimes pray inwardly. He had come from afar to disturb the sleep of an entire army. Equipped with map and lists, he had used metal tools to strike the ground that covered them, and had no idea whether they themselves actually wished to be disturbed.

The road snaked and twisted, coiled round each hilltop and dropped down again; he had the impression of going round in circles. It seemed to the general that he was going along exactly the same stretch of road as he had the day before, he had the feeling sometimes that this road was unfailingly going to bring them back to where they started, without ever letting them come out. He began to distrust the figures he read on the milestones – some of these were truncated, others had been pulled out and stuck back in any old how, even upside down. Indeed, just as his mission was nearing its end, the general sometimes, especially at dusk, had the feeling that he was never going to get out of these mountains again.

They had spent the last two nights in villages swarming with dogs who kept howling. Then came the day when they were to exhume the very last soldier. The general was filled with a sombre premonition. He wondered whether they were not in duty bound to leave this one at least in the ground. He had almost persuaded himself that after all the snags and reverses he'd been obliged to endure these last two years, this much compensation was due.

He was so far persuaded that had he not felt a bit embarrassed by the priest and the Albanian expert, he would have dreamed up some pretext to cut and run without opening up this Alpine soldier's grave.

With drawn features he watched the workmen breaking open the frozen earth with their pick-axes. He kept rubbing his hands and took note of the fact that it was with these hands and these tools that they had unearthed an entire army.

The final stroke of the pick-axe sounded in his ear like a detonation. A moment later the expert shouted from a distance: "Five foot three! Exactly as listed!"

His regret at not having shown himself better disposed towards the earth was tempered by the idea that, after all, it was a kindness that the earth could maybe do without. The earth still kept back dozens of soldiers who had never been found and, whatever happened, even if several further missions were to be despatched, it would nonetheless keep hold of its share.

Thus he strove to set his mind at rest, but all it took was a panel at the roadside with the words "Caution: Rockfalls" to remind him of his fear. Neither the music nor the news broadcast from the car radio managed to stir him to the point of banishing the most far-fetched of these imaginings. Of these the worst was the thought of being required to hand back this entire army that he had assembled at so great a cost. Then he and his priest would have to resume their journey from hill to hill, from one ravine to the next, like sombre pilgrims, and replace each skeleton, one at a time, at the exact spot from which they had removed it.

He shook his head to free himself of this oppression. No, the story is absolutely at an end now, he told himself, almost out loud.

It was in fact their final day. They were coming down. The hard snow which hitherto had given no sign of softening was starting to give place to the softer snow of the lower slopes, and lower still, in the villages, they were awaited by their old acquaintance, the rain.

Before long he would be home again. Others would take charge of the remains and finish off the task. With this tour his whole mission was coming to its end. Now it was for representatives of the local government association and accountants from both countries to meet around a table and draw up their accounts of the work that had been done. They would start producing great heaps of complicated debit and credit sheets, there would be masses of bills and receipts to be dealt with, and lastly there would come the final, the ultimate report. After that a little banquet would be given, a few brief official speeches made, and after the banquet a solemn Mass for the Dead would be celebrated for the souls of all those dead soldiers. The press agencies would announce that his mission had been brought to a successful conclusion, and once again he would be obliged to answer the questions of a multitude of infuriating journalists at a variety of press conferences.

Meanwhile, unnamed carpenters would have finished making up the thousands of tiny coffins to the precise dimensions stipulated in the contract. Clause 17 a and b: Coffins in half-inch ply, $70 \times 40 \times 30$ cm. White-painted and numbered in black.

In the shed, in the midst of that waste land on the fringes of Tirana, Charon in his long, threadbare overcoat would blow on his fingers and open his thick ledger for the last time. The big dog would stand truculently outside the door while the workmen carefully placed the appropriate blue bag in each coffin. Companies, battalions, regiments, divisions, and all such categories would blur and melt away in that multitude of coffins. And even the solitary woman would merge indistinguishably into that mass of soldiers, for she was to be treated as a "soldier" too with all the rest, since it takes an anatomist, after all, to distinguish between a woman's skeleton and a man's.

The convoy of lorries loaded with the coffins would rumble down towards Durrës. There they would all be loaded onto a big ship, and the ship would manoeuvre heavily out of the harbour, bearing home a whole army now reduced to no more than a few tons of phosphorus and calcium. Then, on the far shore, they would be unloaded, so that each coffin could be despatched to its given address. Some families would perhaps be waiting for their dear ones' remains on the dockside. But at all events, on that dock the army would finally be disbanded. The "Olympia" bags, loaded into postal delivery vans, into lorries, into buses, into big limousines or little cars, onto the racks of motor bikes or bicycles, or simply a man's back, would all departin various directions never to be assembled again.

As for those they had failed to find, they would remain in Albania. Later, perhaps, another expedition might come, with another general at its head, to search and excavate again. For there were still about two hundred to be found – with Colonel Z. still heading the list. The new expedition would make the circuit of these same dismal and interminable itineraries in its turn, until all the remains of those poor soldiers were collected one by one. And who knows what thoughts would go through the mind of the officer leading them? Would he cast indirect aspersions on him as people tend to do on their predecessors, or would he meekly bow his head? Listen, he would sometimes say inwardly to the colonel or captain in question (it certainly wouldn't be a general. They couldn't send a general for only forty-odd men, after all), listen, my boy, forty lost corpses are quite capable of achieving what proved too much for an army of 40,000 men!

The road was still descending, winding back down all the snaking curves around the mountains that he remembered from the ascent. But the bends were constantly growing wider, and the general had begun to feel that everything was finally untangling itself again, that calm was at last returning to his soul.

During the descent he turned to look back from time to time. The mountains were further away each time. Their jagged outlines were becoming blurred, their threat was fading. The general stared back at them as though to say: "It's finished, your

tyranny over me. I've escaped you, escaped you, do you hear?"
Then, as he dozed, he was suddenly gripped by a vague sensation
of alarm.

But he wouldn't be going up there again.

Never!

He felt his last moment of fear precisely at the point when
he thought they had finally reached the plain. The rumble of
the engine dragged him out of his torpor and he was horrified to
realize that instead of the plain he was expecting, a steep escarp-
ment stood in front of them. Instead of keeping on down, the car
was climbing painfully up to the gorge. He nearly shouted at the
driver: Stop! Where are you taking us, back up into the mountains? But he was dissuaded by the peaceful face of the priest
sitting beside him. Bewildered as he was, he could not take his
eyes off the steep valley slopes he was making for as for an egress.

Calm down! he told himself two or three times. On the roads of
Albania sudden climbs and abrupt drops are common currency.

As they penetrated this side-valley, he reckoned once again that
this is how it was. From above he noticed the houses of a large
village on the mountainside, and they were rapidly dropping
down towards it.

So the short interval since he woke had proved sufficient to
draw up before him the final torment of this pilgrimage, and it
had happened in a flash, the way nightmares come: after pretend-
ing to let him go, the mountains at the last moment, right on the
border of their territory, had sought to force him back. Perhaps
he had somehow wronged them while he was among them,
perhaps he had infringed some age-old ritual. Perhaps he now
had to do something by way of reparation. Like hand back a
part of the army that had been recovered? Or perhaps stay behind
as hostage himself to allow this army to . . .

My nerves are at breaking point, he told himself as he gazed at the village chimneys. He had the feeling that these chimneys would have the power to restore his serenity better than any tranquillizer.

"A village," observed the priest, who was also watching the scene attentively.

"A large village," the general corrected him. "My impression is it's where we're to spend the night."

They came upon a village as night fell. For the first time in ten days the general's face lit up with a smile. It was over, really over at last. They would sleep here this evening and leave next morning for Tirana. In a few days they would be home again. The general had regained his good humour. A warm tide of wellbeing, hesitant at first but rapidly becoming bolder, began to flow through him.

The lights were not on yet in the village. Escorted by a mob of children the car made a stately progress along the extremely muddy main street. He could see the little running legs in front of them, through the windscreen, and then, turning round, he saw the other children running after them, and he smiled again. As far as he could make out he seemed to be the one the children were most interested in, while the priest apparently left them fairly indifferent. He couldn't help feeling flattered at this, even though he knew perfectly well that he owed their interest solely to his uniform.

The desire for greatness and acclaim that had never quite died inside him was stirring weakly to life again.

Having traversed the village in this way, the noisy procession finally came to a halt outside the building occupied by the co-operative council. The expert and the driver disappeared briskly up the steps and into the entrance. A moment later the lorry drew up behind the car and the workmen began jumping down. Neither they nor the lorry seemed to excite much interest in the children however. Instead they were glueing their faces to the car windows in order to peer in at the two men sitting so calmly on the dark seats inside. One of them was smoking a cigarette. From outside that was all the children were able to make out, but they kept milling and circling around the vehicle, continuing to flatten their questing, wide-eyed little faces against the glass from time to time.

"It was probably in this village that Colonel Z. disappeared," the priest said.

"Quite possibly," the general replied.

"We must make enquiries," the priest said. "We must do our best to find out if anyone knows anything."

The general took two or three draws at his cigarette before saying slowly:

"To be honest, I'm not particularly anxious to find him. This evening I have no urge to find any dead men at all. For my part I just feel utterly delighted to have reached the end of our ordeal. And here you are wanting me to set off on some new quest."

"But it's our duty," the priest said.

"Oh yes, I know, I know, but just now I just don't want to have to think about it. This is a tremendous evening for us. I'm amazed you don't feel that too. It's an evening for celebration. All I want is peace and quiet. A good hot bath! That's my main concern this evening. My kingdom for a bath!" he added with a chuckle.

The general was in good humour, very good humour. The long and arduous pilgrimage that he saw in his mind as a vision of terror was at last at an end. But it wasn't a pilgrimage. It had been a march through the valley of the shadow of death. As the old song sung by the Swiss soldiers has it: "Our life is but a winter journey, a journey through the dark!"

The general rubbed his hands.

He was safe. He could look back at them in the distance now, those sheer and hateful peaks, with calm indifference.

"Like a tragic and lonely bird . . ." Was that it? Was that what she had said to him, that great lady wishing him good luck on his journey, so long ago now . . . ?

The expert re-emerged from the council building.

"You will be sleeping in that house over there," he said, and pointed to a bungalow with a verandah.

Ten minutes later the general emerged onto the verandah and leaned his elbows on its wooden balustrade. The priest was in the bedroom unpacking. There was a little garden all around the bungalow, and a view of a section of the village from the verandah. The general could hear the clinking of a bucket and women's voices from a nearby well, the lonely lowing of distant cattle, the sound of a radio that had just been switched on, and the cries of the children still at play, running to and fro across the square. The village lights had been switched on now, and the monotonous hum of the generator could be heard on the outskirts.

That night would have gone by like all the others, without leaving them any particular incident to remember, if the general had remained content just to stand there breathing in the characteristic Albanian village smell, the subtle, almost imperceptible aroma that had by now become so familiar to him that he could have picked it out unerringly from any number of others. The priest had gone out hunting for information about Colonel Z. and so the general just stayed there, leaning on the rail of the verandah, watching the women as they took their turn to draw up water from the well. It was a routine village evening, even though in the distance, from the centre of the village, there could be heard the beat of a drum and the song of a violin, combining to cast a further spell of mystery over the night.

The general recognized the drumbeats as being the usual prelude to a wedding feast in that district. Had it not been late autumn he would have found it out of place, jarring on the nerves.

But he had known in advance, from his book on Albania, that Albanian country folk almost always celebrate their marriages in autumn, after the work of harvest has been completed. This was the second year in succession that the priest and he had been going from village to village at precisely this time of year. But now it was the beginning of winter and only the very last marriages were being celebrated, those that for one reason or another had been put off, whereas at the start of their tour they had come across them almost every day.

Often, during the night, through the sound of the falling rain, the general had caught the sound of drum rolls and the song of a violin alternating between sprightly joy and soulful revelry. And listening to them, his head buried under the bed-clothes, his thoughts would go to the lorry that was always parked outside, standing all night with the rain falling onto its black canvas cover. He would muse on how very much one is a stranger in foreign lands. More of a stranger than the trees planted along the edges of the roads, he would think, and they, after all, are only trees. Certainly much more of a stranger than the sheep, or the sheep-dogs, or the calves whose bells you hear clinking as the evening falls.

And this particular evening too would have passed off like all those others, if the general, after having stood there thinking of all these things on the verandah, had not had to listen to the priest telling him about Colonel Z., about how he, the priest, had gone to the club and sat down at a table with some of the villagers, about what they had to say concerning the colonel's disappearance, and about the suspicions that their remarks had aroused in him. But the general's attention was not on what the priest was telling him. He was in a good mood.

"Enough," he said to the priest for the third time. "Enough of all that. What we need now is a little relaxation, a little entertainment. Don't you think?"

The priest did not reply.

"It's a beautiful evening. A little music, a little glass of brandy . . ."

"And where will we find them?" the priest said. "There is no café here, only the co-operative club. And you know what that will be like . . ."

But the general, without allowing him to finish, broke in with a proposal that left him dumbfounded. When he did regain his composure, however, the priest refused to subscribe to the idea. It was the first time that he had made such a formal show of opposition. But the general nevertheless pointed out to him point blank that he, the general, was the leader of the mission, and made it clear that if he was forced into it he would simply order the priest to accompany him.

"We are proud of our mission, aren't we? You have told me so often enough. And now we have concluded it, our glorious mission. So this evening I want to enjoy myself, listen to some music, see a play, anything! Wasn't it you who told me that the wedding feasts in this country are as good as an evening at the theatre? Or was it only funerals you were talking about? It doesn't matter anyway. The important thing is that I want to enjoy myself a little this evening. If there was a funeral going on then we'd go to that too, you understand? I'm not going to hold back out of some sort of respect for these peasants. And besides, it was you yourself who told me that the Albanians carry hospitality to almost absurd lengths. There is no risk of our not being well received."

The priest had riveted icy eyes upon him. The general talked on hoping to avoid a silence. But at last the silence came.

"No," the priest said then, extending an arm in the direction he presumed the marriage feast was to take place. "We must not go. We are in mourning. We must not desert them."

Don't desert us. The age-old cry. For a year and a half the general had been hearing it, sometimes weaker, sometimes stronger, from his army. They wanted him near them. For love of them he had renounced his own life. Each time he had tried to leave them, even if only for a few hours, he had heard their muffled murmurs of appeal. He was their general; but this evening he was rebelling.

This thought left him paralyzed – standing up to his whole army! Normally it was quite the opposite: the troops mutinied against their leader. But this general fatefulness left everything topsy-turvy.

The priest's arm was still extended.

"I'm not deserting anybody," the general said in a hoarse voice, "I simply want a little relaxation."

Without waiting for a reply he pulled on his waterproof and walked out.

The priest followed.

XX

THE WEDDING FEAST WAS being held in a house at the very centre of the village. Even from quite a distance away the general and the priest could see bright patches of light through which the rain seemed to be falling even more thickly. Despite the bad weather the big double door of the house was wide open and there was quite a crowd under the wide porch. There were people coming and going, and the little street in which the house stood was full of bustle and whispering and every kind of noise. The two men advanced towards the house, neither of them speaking, swathed in their long, black waterproof capes, and their footsteps echoed back from the narrow lane's stone walls – the heavy, thudding stride of the general, who splashed his way on through the puddles without even noticing them, and the lighter, livelier tread of the priest.

They paused for a moment beneath the porch, where a few young men in festive costume were smoking and talking quietly together, then went in through the doorway into the hall. The general entered first. The priest followed him inside. The passage was crammed with women and children making a tremendous din. The drum had fallen silent and they could hear the sound of men's voices from the main room. A little group formed out in the passage, a messenger was sent into the big room, and eventually an old man, looking surprised, emerged from it and came towards them. He placed a hand over his heart in traditional greeting as he approached, then helped them off with their capes, which he proceeded to hang up alongside the villagers' thick cloaks. He was the master of the house. He led them through into the main room, and at their appearance a general agitation became apparent; all those present seemed to begin murmuring, whispering, turning to one another, craning their necks, like a clump of multicoloured bushes suddenly stirred by a strong breeze.

The general had certainly not expected to be so troubled by the scene that presented itself to his eyes. At first, he was so put out of countenance that for a while after entering he was unable to perceive anything at all except a palette of living, moving patches of colour, just as though he had been given a hard blow on the head and was seeing stars.

Someone led him to a table, then someone else helped him off with his coat. He tried to speak, but all that came out was a few mumbled syllables, and eventually he gave way to his bewilderment, simply nodding and smiling at the moving splashes of colour around him.

It was not until the drum began to beat again, and the violin voiced its first piercing invitation to the guests to stand up and dance, that he was able to recover himself slightly. Through the crystalline tinkling of the glasses he heard a voice at his elbow say in his own language: "Will you raise your glass?" and did as he was asked. The same voice then continued to speak, as though it were explaining something to him, but he was still in no state to understand anything that was said, and was himself astonished at feeling so completely disoriented.

Now the feast seemed to him like a great organism, powerful and amorphous, breathing, moving, murmuring, dancing, and filling the whole atmosphere around him with its warm, disturbing, intoxicating breath.

It was some short while before the general had completely recovered himself. He could feel that the children were staring at him, their eyes bright with silent delight. Pushing their heads together, they were pointing fingers in his direction, as though counting the buttons on his uniform, or the circles of braid round his cuffs, for they then began discussing something and shaking their little heads in evident disagreement.

Then little by little the general became aware of everything else surrounding him. He gazed in turn at the old men with their long moustaches, sitting cross-legged on their benches and exchanging grave comments as they smoked their long Turkish pipes, at the bride in her white dress, so graceful in her shy excitement, at the groom, sweating profusely and hopping here and there the whole time looking after everyone, at the bunches of young girls, all laughing and whispering in the corners as though that was all they knew how to do, their attitude some-how a promise of hidden joys, even though it was never to be fully kept, at the disillusioned look of the young men smoking their cigarettes, at the swarthy musicians soaked in sweat, at all the women scurrying from one room to another with such a business-like air, and lastly at the old women, dressed in black, their faces marked by the years and their eyes heavy with emotion and affection, sitting along the wall like a row of pale icons.

Now he was following the agile movements of the dancing legs and the rhythmic tapping of heels on the floor, obedient to the vibrant orders of the drum, the rustling of the white fustanel-las, those fustanellas with their thousands of fine pleats as white as the snows of the mountains they had just returned from, the long and convoluted toasts that seemed to lose all meaning when translated, the rough songs of the men recalling the brief moun-tain twilights, and the trailing, pathetic songs of the women, songs that seemed to lean on the robuster shoulders of the men's songs and to make their way submissively, eternally, by their side.

The general allowed his gaze to wander all around him without managing to think of anything at all. He simply sat there drinking and smiling, without even knowing himself to whom his smiles were addressed.

I don't know what army you are part of, because I've never been able to recognize uniforms, and I'm too old now to start, but you are a foreigner and you belong to one of those armies that killed my family. That's clear enough. To judge by your insignia, invading people is your trade and you are one of those who broke my life, who turned me into the unhappy old woman I am, an old woman who has come to a wedding feast that is nothing to do with her and sits in a corner mumbling like this. No one can hear what I am saying because everyone here is merry and I don't want to spoil the joy of their feast. And it is precisely because I don't want to spoil anyone's joy that I am staying here in my corner cursing you between my teeth, quietly, oh very quietly, so that no one will hear. I should like to know what made you come here to this wedding feast, and why your legs did not give way under you before they brought you here. You are sitting there, at that table, and laughing like an idiot child. Get up, can't you, throw your coat over your shoulders, go back through the rain to where you came from! Can't you understand that you are not wanted here, accursed man?

The women were still singing. The general felt a warm breath of tender emotion flooding through his breast. He had the sensation of being laved in a delightful bath of sounds and light. And the waves of sound and light pouring over him like the waters of a healing spring were warming him, purifying his body of all that graveyard mud, that foul mud with its unmistakable odour of putrefaction and of death.

Now that his first dazed reaction had passed, the general had regained all his good humour. He felt he wanted to talk, to keep himself from thinking with a flow of words. He tried to catch the eye of the priest, who was sitting one place away down the table on the other side. He was obviously in a state of great unease.

The general leaned over to him.

"You see, it's all perfectly all right."

The priest didn't answer.

The general stiffened. He could feel the glances of the people around him falling on him like silent arrows. They were falling on his pockets, on his epaulettes, and occasionally, very occasionally, on his eyes; the dark, heavy arrows of the men, and the nimble, glittering, uncertain arrows of the young girls.

(Like a wounded but indomitable bird, you will fly on . . .)

"It's interesting, isn't it?" he said, addressing himself once again to the priest.

But the priest still did not reply. He merely looked at the general as though to say "Possibly", then turned his eyes away again.

"These people are showing us respect," the general said.

"Death commands respect everywhere."

"Death . . . ? I don't think it's written on our faces," the general retorted. He tried to smile, but failed. "It is a long time since the war was over. The past is forgotten. I am certain that no one at this wedding has a thought for past enmities."

The priest did not speak. The general decided to cease addressing him – and yet, somehow, a piece of his companion's cassock, a black patch, seemed to stay dancing in front of his eyes.

The priest obviously feels unwanted, he thought to himself. And wouldn't that mean that I was too? It's very difficult to say. But it's done now. Here we are. Wanted or not wanted, there is no way of leaving. It would be easier to retreat under machine-gun fire than to stand up now, throw our coats over our shoulders, and walk out into the rain.

You know quite well you're not wanted here. You can feel there's someone at this feast who is cursing you; and a mother's curse is never

199

voiced in vain. Despite the respect they are showing you, you know well enough that you should never have set foot in this place. You are trying to persuade yourself it isn't so, but it's no good, is it? Your hand trembles as you raise your glass, and the shadows that pass across your eyes betray the terror that you feel!

The drum was beating again. A clarinet began to lament, then several violins joined in. A fresh group of belated guests arrived, their cloaks dripping. They had been held up by the rising river and forced to wait for several hours before they could cross it. They went round the room formally greeting all those present, then took their places around the big table.

It's as though a wedding feast represents something really sacred for these people, the general mused, otherwise they would hardly take the trouble to travel on a night like this just for a little share of someone else's joy. It must be absolutely teeming. On such a night you couldn't even dig a grave: it would fill with water as you were digging it.

It seems you've come here to collect all the dead men who came from your country. Perhaps you've already dug up a great many, and perhaps you will find a lot more, perhaps you will collect them all, but I want you to know that one of them, yes one of them you'll never find, never till the end of time, just as I shall never find my little girl or my husband again in all the ages to come. How I should like to speak to you about the one you'll never find! And if I don't, it's because I don't want to bring back all their sad war memories to all these guests. She was my daughter, I was her mother. As our elders used to say: you've become a mother, evil has befallen you – and so it has, wretched as I am! How it rained that night! Harder even than tonight. The water was streaming everywhere. You couldn't dig a grave because it filled with water as you dug, with water as black as pitch that seemed to well up out of the darkness. And yet I did dig one, I did dig one! But I mustn't tell you about it because

I don't want to spoil other people's joy, not even yours, curses on you!

The general lit a cigarette, then felt in some strange way that it was too small, that it was pitifully impotent compared with the long, black pipes whose big boxwood bowls the old men were clasping in their brown hands, and on which they drew from time to time as they talked, as though to punctuate the rhythms of their conversation.

The master of the house, the same old man who had greeted them in the passage on their arrival, came and sat by him, his pipe in his fist just like the other old men and a medal on a yellow ribbon dangling from his thick, black homespun jacket. The general knew them well, those medals, from having seen them on the chests of so many other peasants, and it now seemed to him that each one of them bore on its reverse the pale face of a soldier from his dead army. He smiled at the old man's furrowed face. It made him think of a knotty, cracked tree-trunk but still full of sap. A man sitting beside him, the one who had urged him to drink earlier on, translated the old man's first words to him. The old man was apologizing to his guest for not having come to speak to him earlier, but the guests were still arriving and he must by custom be there to receive them all.

The general replied with a profusion of polite phrases and much deferential nodding of the head. The old man was silent for a while, then he puffed gently at his pipe and asked the general in calm tones:

"Where are you from?"

The general told him.

The old man shook his head in a wondering way that conveyed to the general that he had never heard of such a town – despite the fact that it was a large and very well known one.

"Have you a wife? And children?" the old man then asked.

The general nodded and the other said: "May they enjoy long life!"

The old man drew another puff of smoke from his pipe and the furrows on his brow visibly deepened. He seemed to want to speak, and the general sensed that he was about to say precisely what he was most apprehensive of hearing that evening.

"I know why you have come to our country," his host went on, still in the same perfectly even tone, and the general felt the words pierce his heart like a dagger.

Ever since the evening began he had been fearing a conversation of this sort, one that might develop into some kind of provocation, and he had studiously obliterated the reason for his presence in that place from his mind, under the illusion that his own forgetfulness would ensure that of others. That evening he would have liked to be nothing more than a simple tourist, taking an interest in the fascinating customs of a people with a long past so that he could talk about them later to his friends, back in his own country. And now at last the accursed subject of conversation had proved unavoidable and the general was sorry he had come.

"Yes," the old man said, "it is good that you should collect the remains of your dead soldiers the way you are doing. All God's creatures should rest in the earth from which they sprang."

The general expressed his acquiescence to this sentiment by bowing his head. The old man shook out his pipe, then rested his eyes on its embers.

"You had poor weather," he said.

Again the general nodded.

The other gave a deep sigh.

"As the saying goes: rain and death are met with the world over."

The general found the expression enigmatic, but dared not ask that it be interpreted for him.

After a moment more his host gravely rose and excused himself; he had to do the honours of his house to other newly arrived guests.

The general returned to his drink with relief. His good humour had returned once again. The danger of provocation seemed to have passed. He could now follow the development of the wedding feast without uneasiness and drink as much as he liked.

"You see?" he said once more to the priest (his words were already slightly slurred). "They respect us. I told you so. The past is forgotten. What do you say?"

"I have already said that on such occasions it is not easy to make out the exact dividing line between a respect for customs and a respect for persons," the priest replied.

"Generals always inspire respect."

The general finished off another glass.

"You know something?" he said, pushing his face nearer to the priest's and speaking with a certain hint of malice. "I've had an idea. I wouldn't mind getting up and dancing with them."

The priest looked dumbstruck. "You don't mean that seriously?"

"Yes, why shouldn't I?"

The priest gave a nervous shake of the head.

"I just can't understand what's got into you this evening."

The general was irritated by the remark.

"You've played the nanny long enough now. It's time you let me be, damn it all! I don't want anyone keeping tabs on me."

"Not so loud," the priest said. "There are people listening."

"When is it going to be abolished, I'd like to know, this loathsome practice of keeping generals under supervision?"

The priest rested his forehead in the palm of his hand as if to say: "This is all we needed!"

"I'm going to get up and dance, and that's all there is to it!"

"But you don't know the dance, you'll just make yourself ridiculous."

"Not in the slightest. The steps are extremely simple. And besides, who is it I'm going to make myself ridiculous to? These peasants?"

The priest rested his forehead on his hand again.

This evening it seems someone was asking in the club about him. I think you've been looking for him a long time, haven't you? And all in vain. But why should you want to find him, that horrible colonel? Was he a friend of yours? Yes, he must have been, because otherwise you wouldn't be so interested in him. Everyone was questioned in the village this evening. But it was no good: even though they know he is buried somewhere around here no one will ever guess the exact spot. You will leave without him, your friend, your wretched friend who turned my life to mourning. Go quickly, quickly, because you are as cursed as he was. Oh yes, now you're behaving as gentle as any lamb, and there is a smile on your lips as you watch them dancing, but I know what's going on in the back of that mind of yours! You're thinking that one fine day you will trample your way across this country with your troops so that you can burn our houses and massacre us just the way your comrades did. You should never have come to this feast. You should have felt your knees trembling under you when you decided to set out. Even if only out of regard for me, a poor bewildered old woman whose fate has been so cruel and black. But what is this? You are going to enter the circle! You have the gall to leave your chair? You even dare to smile! Yes, you are standing up! And they are breaking the circle to let you in! No, wait! What are you doing? This is too much! It is a profanation!

The drum beat out its summons yet again, like cannon firing. The clarinet resumed its lamentations, while the violins accompanied it with their slender, almost feminine voices. In the middle of the room the rudiments of a farandole were forming as two, then three, then a steadily increasing number of dancers took the floor.

The general looked at the circle. Then he looked back at the priest. Then at the circle. Then at the priest. At the circle. The priest. The circle . . .

He had risen from his place. What had to happen had happened. He was there, on his feet, swaying like one drunk, prepared to enter the circle of dancers that seemed to him now like a circle of fire. He stretched out his arms two or three times, then immediately withdrew them again as though his hands had been burned. The dancing circle span before him like a top, and the old man leading the dance bent his legs, squatted almost, then rose again, slapped his sole on the floor as though to say: "That's how it is and that's how it always will be!" whirled his white handkerchief, released his partner's hand in order to execute a pirouette, bent his knees again, seemed certain to collapse on the floor, his legs cut from under him as though by a sickle, then rose again and sank again, like one struck by lightning, only to spring to life again at the instant that the thunder rumbled out. The drum was beating with redoubled fury, the cries of the clarinet were pouring out in wilder and stronger waves, like sobs emerging from the throat of some Titan, and the violins' strings were vibrating like lost souls. The drum beat quicker and quicker, so that now, through the lament, it was as though great rocks could be heard thundering down from the mountains. The general, still on his feet, was seized by giddiness in the face of this frenetic and dazzling abandon. He had no idea how long it all took. For the space of a few seconds, as though through a veil, he stood there seeing the sweating faces of the musicians, the mouth of the clarinet swaying up and down like the barrel of an anti-aircraft gun following a moving target, the closed, ecstatic eyes of the dancers. Then the drum fell silent, the violins relaxed, and there followed an enchanted calm.

The feast gave promise of being a very successful one and of continuing far into the night. But just at the moment when the dancers were returning to their places a howl pierced the hubbub in the room. The general felt a sort of pinching inside his chest. The noise hadn't stopped and yet, strangely, everyone had heard the cry. No one would ever have thought old Nice could howl like that.

She sobbed as more tiny, high-pitched cries forced themselves from her throat. The silence that suddenly descended was so deep that you could hear the convulsive hiccups that were punctuating the old woman's moans. But the silence lasted only a second. The general saw people rush towards the old woman and fuss around her. Someone was called over, and the poor woman who was now weeping hot tears, though heaven knows why, was quietened down a little.

If the old woman had really quietened down, as the general and those who were not close to her supposed, everything would have settled down again and perhaps the general would have stayed there very late, until far into the night, but old Nice began to weep again. It was evident that nothing they did succeeded in calming her, quite the contrary in fact. She began howling again; other voices rose around her, but they were quickly subdued by the power of her lamentation, which sliced through the general joy like a sharp blade. More people hurried over to surround the old woman, and the general had the feeling that the more fuss they made over her the more ear-piercing her lament would become. The musicians started to play again, but when old Nice uttered a fresh cry even more strident than any of her previous ones the instruments fell silent, as though intimidated. The general saw the cluster of people around the old woman shift and stagger as though before some violent assault; then Nice, escaping at last from the grasp of those restraining her, burst through and hurled herself towards him. For the first time the general was able to take a close look at the pale, emaciated face, the staring eyes swollen with tears, and the tiny, frail body. "What has happened to her? What does she want? Why is she crying?" the general asked, suddenly sober again. But no one answered his questions. They rushed after the old woman; two women grasped her arms and tried to coax her away, but she simply began howling again and advanced till she was standing face to face with the general. He looked down at the hate in those twisted features, but had no idea what the cause of it could be. She managed to shout a few words at him, to wave her arms at him in fury, to shriek in his face; and he just stood there in front of her, pale as wax. It lasted only a few seconds, then they took the old woman away, dragging her backwards by her arms. Then, fighting free, she rushed over to the door and vanished.

The general stayed standing where he was, and no one attempted to explain what old Nice had said to him. No one knew that the priest could speak Albanian. Everyone had clustered now around the weeping bride and her mother, the mistress of the house, who was standing looking very pale and crossing herself.

"I warned you," the priest said. "We ought not to have come."

"What happened?" the general asked.

"This is hardly the moment to tell you. I'll explain later."

"You were right," the general said. "I went too far."

The groups of people who at the beginning of the evening had seemed to him like a rustling, multicoloured thicket were now transformed in his eyes into a dark winter forest. Heads, arms, hands, long fingers, were all waving, bending this way and that like branches and twigs stripped by the storm wind, and over their sombre agitation, with a dry croaking, anxiety hovered like a black bird.

"What right have they to come to our weddings?" one of the young men said.

"Hush! You mustn't say things like that."

"Why not?" another young man said. "They even have the gall to get up and want to dance."

"We couldn't turn them away, could we now? At a wedding all are welcome, it is the custom."

"What a custom! And what does poor old Nice say about a custom like that?"

"Hush! You don't want them to hear you."

"Don't worry," someone else put in, "there's far too much noise, they couldn't hear, even if they understood our language."

And it was true that the general and the priest were unable to hear anything that was being said. They simply stood looking round at the encircling faces, the general's eyes resting only briefly on those of the men and boys but dwelling longer on the women, who in their great black shawls had the air of a chorus in an ancient tragedy.

Then suddenly he was filled with alarm. Why had he come? What insane whim had brought him here? Up until now everything had gone off more or less smoothly. He had been escorted and protected by the laws everywhere he went. But this evening he had taken a great risk. Whatever could have got into his head to make him come to this wedding feast tonight, alone with just the priest? Here he was outside the protection of laws and regulations. Anything could happen to them here without anyone being held responsible.

"Let us go," he said abruptly. "Let us leave immediately."

"Yes," the priest said. "Yes, let us leave. We have been grossly insulted. That old woman made the most offensive allegations about us."

"Then we ought to refute them before we leave. But what did she say exactly, the old woman?"

The priest was about to tell him when the master of the house came over.

"Sit down again," he said, gesturing towards the big table. Then he made a sign to the women who were waiting on the guests and they brought raki and *meze*.[3]

The general and the priest exchanged glances then turned back to the master of the house.

"These things will happen," the old man said. "But please stay, I beg of you. Be seated again."

Embarrassed at standing there, feeling all eyes upon them, they both sat down again. They felt somehow that people would pay them less attention seated.

A certain order seemed to have returned to the big room now, and the guests had resettled themselves at the tables. The general found the same man beside him as before, the one who had attempted to translate the complicated toasts earlier, and this neighbour now explained to him that Nice was a slightly half-witted old woman who had been widowed during the last war, her husband having been hanged during the reprisal operation carried out by Colonel Z.'s "Blue Battalion". The general also learned that the colonel had subsequently ordered the wretched woman's daughter to be brought to his tent at night. She was scarcely fourteen, and at dawn, on her way home from his tent, she had thrown herself down a well. And it was in fact the very next night that the colonel had disappeared. Unaware of the girl's

3 A sort of hors-d'œuvre.

death, he had apparently gone to her home with the intention of seeing her again. He had left a soldier outside to guard the house and remained inside a long time – much longer than seemed necessary in fact, but the soldier had been given orders not to move till dawn. Next morning there was no one at all to be found inside the house and no one had any idea what had happened to the colonel. Some said that he had received an urgent summons to return to Tirana, others explained his absence in a variety of ways, but the officers of his own battalion were silent on the matter. Two days later the troops left the district.

All this information was conveyed in snatches, in broken and disconnected sentences that struck at his temples like hammer blows.

Meanwhile the music had begun again, though no one got up to dance for a while. Eventually, however, a few women decided to do so, and at last everyone began to feel that the incident with old Nice was over and done with, forgotten by all except the old woman herself. The general remained where he was, sitting at the table, in a state of stunned paralysis that prevented him from concentrating his thoughts on anything at all. Then his eyes met the priest's once more.

"I still want to know what the old woman said."

The priest's grey eyes stared into his, and the general felt uncomfortable.

"She thinks you are a friend of Colonel Z. And the mere sight of you puts her in a frenzy."

"Me, a friend of Colonel Z.?"

"Those were her words."

"And what put that idea into her head? Perhaps because we spent the evening enquiring about Colonel Z.," the general said musingly, as though talking to himself.

"Very possibly," the priest answered curtly.

The general's black mood grew still deeper. He no longer saw or heard anything that was going on around him.

"I shall stand up and tell them," he said suddenly. "I shall stand up and make a public statement here and now that I am not a friend of Colonel Z.'s, and that as a soldier I abhor his memory."

"Why ever should you want to do that? As an apology to these peasants?"

"No. For the good name and the honour of our army."

"And will the good name of our army be sullied because one old Albanian woman has insulted it?"

"I want to explain to them that all our officers did not stoop so low, to the point of getting themselves killed by a woman!"

The priest's eyebrows flicked.

"We are not here to pass judgements of that kind," he said slowly. "Judgement is the prerogative of Him who is above."

"They really look as though they do believe I was a friend of his," the general went on. "Can't you see how they're looking at me? Just look round you. Look at their eyes."

"Are you afraid?" the priest asked.

The general threw him a furious glance. He was on the point of making a savage reply, but then he felt the thunder of the drum against his temples, and the words were frozen on his lips.

The general was afraid in fact. He had gone too far that evening. He had yielded to impulse. Now what he must do was make a cautious retreat. He must immediately assert the gulf that lay between Colonel Z. and himself. He must somehow rid himself of the colonel, as he would of a lump of mud stuck to his boot.

The situation, it is true, now seemed to be settling down to normality again; but that was only on the surface. He sensed that inside this amorphous organism there was something still simmering. It could be seen from people's eyes, it could be sensed from the whispering that was going on. And then, behind the door, out in the passage, alongside the thick cloaks and the coats, hanging on a row of nails in the wall, were the guests' rifles. The priest had told him that murders frequently occurred at Albanian weddings.

They must act now, before it was too late. If they left too abruptly, then some drunken guest might very well shoot them in the back. Dogs always chase a fleeing quarry with redoubled fury. They must contrive some means of effecting a cautious retreat.

The general stared in a daze once more at the whirling, dancing, laughing crowd all around him; then his eyes came to rest on the line of old women who had not moved from their seats since the beginning of the evening, with their silent faces and their slightly bowed heads, eternal chorus on the sidelines of that eternal scene; and abruptly tired of it all he let his head sag forward and was silent.

The drum sent out its muffled thunder through the room again, the clarinet pierced the heart of the feast with its raucous and heart-rending cry. The men, sitting at their tables, had broken into a song, and the general was back in the mountains seeing the dusk creep down from the peaks; now he was listening to the piercing voices of the women as they sang with lowered heads; it was an oppressed song, cut into short phrases by the urgent interruptions of the male singers; like the panting of a woman in the embrace of the man she loves.

"I think it is high time we left," the general said.

The priest nodded.

"This is a good moment."

"We must get up quietly."

"Yes of course."

"The main thing is not to draw attention to ourselves."

"You get up first. I'll follow."

"The thing is to take it easy."

It was nearly midnight. The feast was at its height and everyone, or almost everyone, had totally forgotten old Nice when suddenly, just as the two foreigners were preparing to leave, she reappeared. It was perhaps the general who was the first to become aware of her return. He suddenly sensed her presence the way an old huntsman senses the approach of a jungle tiger. Seeing people beginning to buzz and whisper around the doorway he immediately heard a voice crying in the depths of his being: "She is there!", and felt himself go pale. This time the old woman was not weeping, nor could her voice even be heard; yet everyone could sense that she was there, at the centre of the group by the door. The band went on playing, but no one was listening to the music now. The group at the door increased in size. People were trying to puzzle out why old Nice had come back. And then, possibly influenced by her appearance, possibly by her supplications, the people by the door moved aside to let her pass, and she moved forward into the room amid general exclamations. She was drenched through, covered with mud, her face as pale as death; and she was carrying a sack on her back.

The general rose mechanically to his feet and moved to meet her. He did not need to be told that he was the person she had come to see. He walked towards her without being asked, like one of those animals that become spellbound by a predator's presence as soon as they scent it, and run towards their fate rather than attempting to flee from it.

The guests clustered around them. Everyone was tongue-tied. The old woman took her stand in front of the general, fixed him with a slightly uncertain gaze, as though it was not him she was seeing but his ghost, and in a cracked voice punctuated by coughs she delivered herself of a very short speech that was obviously intended for him but of which he understood only the one word *vdekje* – death.

"Tell me what she is saying!" the general cried, like a dying man calling for help.

His plea was met with silence. Whereupon he threw a glance around him and met the eyes of the priest. The priest came over.

"She claims that she once killed one of our officers and wishes to know whether or not you are the general who has come to collect the remains of the soldiers killed in the last war," the priest said.

"Yes, madame," the general said in a toneless voice, summoning up all his strength to hold his head high before this old woman who filled him with such terror.

The old woman then added a few words that the priest was unable to translate because they were half lost in a noisy murmur from the crowd, and before anyone could make a move to stop her she had pulled the sack from her back, amid terrified shrieks from the women, and thrown it on the floor at the general's feet. There was nothing left for the priest to translate; all translation had become superfluous, for everything now had been made clear, and nothing in fact could have been at once more meaningful or more horrible than the sack, covered with great gouts of still damp black mud, that had just thudded down on the floor. The women all drew back in violent alarm, covering their faces with their hands, or in the case of the older ones crossing themselves with horrified gasps.

"She had buried him under her doorstep!" someone cried.

"Oh, Nice! Nice!"

Suddenly the old woman turned her back on them all and left as she had come, drenched and mud-spattered, without it occurring to anyone to prevent her, for what was meant to happen had happened.

The general could not take his eyes from the floor. He felt dazed by the noise, the cries, the horror of the scene. All at once, without his being able to say how or why, a great silence enveloped him. Perhaps in reality there was no silence at all, but the general was nevertheless under the impression that there was. At his feet, as all the guests looked on, lay that sombre and silent shape, that old sack chequered with patches. Someone must attend to it! he thought. And then, in the silence, he slowly bent and grasped the sack by the neck with trembling hands, lifted it as it was, plastered with mud, and let it fall again. Then he put on his coat, took up the sack once more, hoisted it slowly up onto his shoulder, and left that place, bent beneath his burden, mortified, as though he were carrying all the shame and the weight of the earth on his back.

Behind him, somebody could not suppress a sob.

XXI

THE GENERAL KEPT WALKING straight ahead, splashing his way through the puddles. The priest followed him. They made their way back along the little street, emerged into the village square, turned along beside the old church, and then, in the darkness, realized they had lost their way. Without a word they retraced their steps, the general still leading the way. They passed the village well, then the club and the side of the church, but still without being able to locate the house where they were supposed to be staying. Twice they found themselves back in the same spot, as they could tell from the dark silhouette of the village bell-tower rising above their heads. And by now the force of the gale was such that they almost expected the wind and rain to set the bells ringing up there with their violence.

The hand clasping the sack was quite numb by now.

"How light you seem to me, Betty!" he said to me one evening in the park. We were out walking arm in arm, two nights before we were married. It was an autumn night, warm and exciting. That afternoon it had rained and the park walks were dotted with little puddles. So he carried me in his arms like a little girl, and he kept on saying: "Are you really so light, Betty? Or is it just my happiness that makes me think you are?" And as he splashed his way along the paths without looking, so his big soldier's boots sent the moons in all the puddles flying up around us in tiny silver drops. "I'd like to hold you in my arms like this all my life, Betty. Yes, just like this." And as he walked he kept kissing my

hair and saying over and over again: "Oh Betty, how light you are!"

And now it's your turn to be light, the general thought. There is nothing in the world as light as you are now. Six or seven oundsat the most. And yet you are breaking my back!

They continued their wandering for a long time, went all round the village several times, completely lost, like two drunks on their way home, constantly trying to keep as far as possible away from the church, which as constantly kept reappearing beside them, darkening the sky overhead; and they did not stop until they almost stumbled into the bonnet of their car, which was scarcely discernible in the darkness.

They remembered then that the car had been parked exactly in front of the house where they had been given rooms, and the general felt his way to the door, pushed it open and stepped through into the yard. The door banged to behind him; he advanced a few more steps, located and opened the inside door, and as soon as he was inside dropped the sack on the hall floor.

In the feeble glow from his lighter he trudged noisily up the stairs, walked into their bedroom, shed his wet coat onto the floor, then threw himself down fully clothed onto the bed. A moment later he heard the door open and close, then the sound of somebody lowering himself onto the other bed.

The priest, he told himself.

He tried to sleep, but in vain. Then he directed his efforts towards sorting out his jumbled thoughts, but with equal lack of success.

I must sleep, he thought. Sleep, sleep. Keep as still and as quiet as that lorry outside. I must sleep at all costs.

He closed his eyes very hard; but that didn't help at all. The tighter he squeezed his eyelids the less absolute the darkness under them became; it was invaded by blotches and ribbons of lights, sometimes interspersed with patches of sky or with an expanse of sea seen from a distant beach.

I must have darkness, he thought. I need total blackness, without so much as a speck of light, if I am to sleep.

But the blue and white and violet ribbons, the red and yellow patches refused to fade. They were there in front of him, just a few inches away, in whatever direction he turned his head, always glowing in the heart of the darkness.

He got up, took a Luminal capsule, and lay down again. He had barely begun to doze before he suddenly shot up once more. The drum had begun to beat again, over near the square.

Is that damned feast still going on? he wondered. What can be happening?

He buried his head under the bedclothes so as not to hear. But it did no good. He had a vision of a little gnome, a tiny figure out of a fairy tale, squatting on his brain and playing a little drum like the ones toy soldiers carry. It was no good stopping up his ears, the gnome was still there, sitting cross-legged somewhere inside his head drumming and drumming away, keeping up a relentless unchanging rhythm: boom, boom, tararaboom, boom, boom . . .

And he had the impression that the drum was beating time to a marching column of soldiers.

It is my victorious army on the march! he thought. Then he sat up abruptly on the bed and said out loud:

"That's enough!"

Then he lay down again and tried to settle his head on the pillow, but after a few moments he got up again and called over to the priest:

"Father! Hey, father! Colonel, wake up!"

The priest woke with a start.

"What's the matter?"

"We must leave this place as soon as possible, get up!"

"Leave? For where?"

"For Tirana."

"But it's still the middle of the night!"

"Never mind. We are leaving all the same."

"But why?"

The floorboards creaked beneath the general's boots.

"Can't you hear? Can't you hear the drum? They are still at it down there, and my mind is full of forebodings."

"Are you afraid?" the priest asked.

"Yes," the general admitted. "I have the feeling that at any moment they are going to come to this house and gather round it beating drums, the way they do in some countries to drive away evil spirits."

The general lit his lighter and began packing his case.

"Very well, let's go," the priest said.

The general closed his case.

"A dance," he murmured. "I simply wanted to dance one dance with them and it almost ended in disaster. Heavens above, what a country!"

We should never have gone, he mused. Never!

"Just one dance. And it nearly turned into a dance of death," he added out loud.

The priest muttered something incomprehensible in reply and they both left the room. The general's boots drew a variety of cracks and creaks from the wooden stairs. He walked straight out into the yard and over to the outer door. Realizing that the priest was no longer just behind him he turned and saw him emerging from the house carrying something on his back.

Of course, the general thought, the sack!

They walked out into the street. The rain had stopped and the darkness was less intense.

"What time is it?" the priest asked.

The general lit his lighter.

"Half-past four."

"It will soon be dawn."

Somewhere the first cocks began to crow. An icy wind was blowing down from the mountains all around. A little further on they could make out the black form of their lorry.

They halted beside the car and turned to look for the dawn. It was as though someone was brushing the eastern sky with layers of white paint, absorbent paint that was gradually soaking the darkness out of the sky and diluting it to a wash of cold, wet grey.

"That's where they said they'd be sleeping," the priest said with a nod towards the house opposite.

"Go and wake our driver up. Tell him I'm ill and we must leave for Tirana immediately."

The priest pushed open the house's outside door. As it opened it set a bell ringing, whereupon a dog began to bark in a yard nearby, then another in answer to the first, and within a few moments all the dogs in the village were in full cry.

But even the chorus of barking did not prevent the general from still being aware of the beating drum and the distant murmur from down by the square.

The yard door grated on its hinges again: it was the priest reappearing with his sack still over his shoulder.

You're really sticking to that sack, aren't you? the general found himself thinking.

"He's getting dressed," the priest said. "He'll be out directly."

"These dogs!" the general said.

"Yes, it's always the same in a village. One starts and they all have to join in."

"Let them bark away," the general said. "What does a little barking matter after all? If they knew what was in our lorry they'd

220

start up a death howl, and that, yes, that would really be horrible!"

"This accursed wind!" was the priest's only reply.

One by one the dogs ceased their barking.

In the distance a cow lowed as though still half asleep.

The yard door grated again and the driver appeared in the half-darkness. They exchanged good mornings. The driver unlocked the car doors, coughing as the cold night air got down into his lungs, and the general got in.

"Open the door in front," the priest requested.

The driver did as bidden.

"What's that?"

"A sack. It may come in handy."

The driver stowed the sack away beside him, pushing it firmly into the corner with his foot, and the priest took his place in the back.

They set off.

The headlight beams slithered along the dark hedges that bordered the road on either side, then fanned out ahead as they turned onto the main road. As soon as the car moved off the general turned up his greatcoat collar, huddled into his corner and closed his eyes. At last he could hear nothing but the gentle purring of the engine, and he had but one desire: to sleep. But he could not stop his brain playing back all that had happened at that feast, down to the last tiniest detail.

I simply must get some sleep, he told himself. I don't want to remember anything about it. I never want to set foot in that place again.

But in his mind he was still back at the feast. He was taking off his coat. He was sitting down at the table. Everybody was there, as though they had been expecting him. He felt as if this returning among them was the only way he had to be rid of them. For them too, perhaps, to be rid of him.

In a panic he opened his eyes before the dreadful old woman reappeared.

Outside it was still night.

The road, wakened by the sudden onslaught of their lights, was perpetually emerging for an instant from the chaos of night, pale and still half asleep, only to sink back into it as soon as they had passed. Every so often pairs of very white milestones flashed past on either side. Their whiteness was unpleasant. It sent a shiver up the spine. They made the general think of tombstones.

The priest, head lolling forward on his chest, was dozing in his corner.

The driver suddenly braked so hard that the priest was shocked into wakefulness by banging his head against the seat in front.

"What's happening?" he asked in a daze.

The general, still half asleep, looked out of the window. The car had stopped by the side of a bridge. He could hear the sound of water rushing beneath it.

"Why have you stopped?" the priest asked.

The driver said something about having to look at the engine, then got out and slammed his door behind him.

The beams of their headlights lay parallel between the sides of the bridge. The driver opened the bonnet, leaned in to peer at the engine, then came back to fetch some tool or other. He pushed at the sack, which was in his way, then pulled it out onto the road in order to lift up the seat.

The general opened the door on his side and got out too. He began pacing round and round the car. The priest hadn't moved. The driver mumbled a swear word and came back to look for something else. The general stumbled for the second time over the sack.

It's this sack, he thought suddenly. It's this sack that's the trouble. It's almost done for us once tonight. Up until now everything had been going perfectly, but now this sinister sack has forced its way into our lives and everything is going wrong!

"It's this sack that's put a jinx on us," he said out loud.

"What did you say?" the priest answered.

"I say that this sack is bringing us bad luck," the general repeated.

And as he spoke he gave it a vindictive push with his foot. The sack tumbled down the slope and fell with a resounding thwack into the water flowing at the bottom.

"What have you done?" the priest cried, as he scrambled out of the car.

"That sack had a curse on it," the general said, drawing in his breath with difficulty.

"Just when we'd found him! Two years! Two years we'd been looking for him!"

"Yes, but his bones nearly cost us our lives," said the general wearily.

"You don't seem to realize what you've done!" the priest cried as he switched on his pocket torch.

"I didn't mean to throw it out. All I did was give it a shove."

His voice betrayed lassitude and remorse.

They both went over to the roadside and looked down into the darkness from which the sound of the rushing water rose. But the two tiny beams threw no more than a pale glow on the steep embankment.

"It's too dark to see," the general said.

They joined the driver, and all three stood raking the river bed with their eyes for a few moments.

"It will have been carried away by the current," the general said.

The priest merely threw him a furious glance, then turned his torchbeam as though he were looking for a way down.

The general returned to the car. The priest stayed a moment or two leaning over the bridge parapet, then returned to the car as well.

They were on their way again.

He must be whirling round and round in that dark water now like someone caught in a nightmare, the general thought. Then he closed his eyes in order not to see the milestones and tried to sleep.

XXII

THE WEEK WAS DRAWING to an end. It was the last day of their stay in Albania. The general got up late. He opened his shutters. The morning was overcast.

It's nearly ten, he thought. The Mass, as I remember, is scheduled for eleven-fifteen, then the banquet at four-thirty.

His bedside table was covered by a big pile of letters, telegrams, newspapers, and magazines forwarded to him from his home.

But there were more letters than anything else. As before, they contained all manner of stories, place names, sometimes sketches of a hill or a copse. As for the articles, they were more or less summed up by their titles: "An Army Exhumed", "Imminent Return of the General of the Shades", "Government Promises to the Families of the Dead . . ."

He looked throught these papers without stopping at any one of them, then took a deep breath, got into his cape, and left. He took his time walking down the stairs, made his way across the deep-piled carpet of the main lobby. At the desk he asked for the head waiter, who arrived a moment later.

"Have you been told that we're having a small banquet later this afternoon?"

"Yes sir. All will be ready for seven o'clock in Room 3."

The general asked if anyone had seen the priest, and was told he had gone out.

There was a great deal of activity going on in the lobby and around the reception desk. There were two telephones that never seemed to stop ringing and several groups of guests waiting for the lifts with cases at their feet. A number of Negroes were sitting in some of the big armchairs, a group of Chinese escorted by two young girls walked past him into the main restaurant, and beside the telephone switchboard two very blonde young women, presumably Scandinavian, were waiting to be put through.

The general went through into the lounge where he usually took his coffee, but couldn't find a single empty table. It was the first time he had seen such an influx of foreigners in the hotel.

He retraced his steps with the intention of leaving the building and met yet another group of Africans walking in through the main door carrying their luggage.

Outside, beneath the tall pine trees, there were far more cars parked than was usual.

What is all the activity? he wondered to himself as he walked down the entrance steps. He turned right and began walking up the boulevard in the direction of the main government buildings.

When he reached Skanderburg Square he noticed that there were flags flapping in the wind all around the little park there. And between the flagpoles, as well as across the façades of the ministries and the big columns of the Palace of Culture, workmen were fixing up strings of lights and big banners with slogans on them.

Of course! he thought. The day after tomorrow is their national day of celebration.

The pavements were crammed with strollers. He gave barely a glance at the cinema posters, his mind was otherwise occupied, so much so that two steps beyond he had forgotten the titles of the films.

He looked at his watch. Eleven o'clock.

I'll collect my ticket after the service, he thought, and turned left. Outside the bank, just behind the *Studenti* café, there was a veritable horde of travellers by the bus stops. It was the terminus for the routes serving the suburbs. The church where the *De Profundis* was to be intoned was only one stop further on, so the general decided to continue on foot. He crossed to the central pavement and let his thoughts return to the colonel's remains as he walked along it.

He could no longer remember exactly what had happened. He could only recall that he had been in a black and somehow mindless mood. He had felt his soul being crushed under a great weight. But now, looking back, his action seemed to him to have been totally senseless.

But in any case there must surely be a way of setting the matter to rights. He would discuss it with the priest. There were quite a number of soldiers measuring six foot one – the colonel's height. As for the teeth, that could easily be arranged. And who would ever suspect that the colonel's remains weren't really his? The more he thought about it, the more he felt it should be possible to reach an agreement with the priest.

Then he tried to recall some of the soldiers who were the same height as Colonel Z., but without success. Every time during the course of their excavations that the expert had called out "Six foot one" he had been unable to prevent himself thinking: Like Colonel Z. But at this moment he just couldn't recall a single one of them.

He could only remember the British flyer they had found by chance under the ruts of a village road – and then reburied in the exact spot where they had found him.

Then he remembered the diary soldier. He certainly measured six foot one. The general began to imagine what it would be like if they were to substitute that soldier's remains for those of the colonel. He pictured to himself the reception that the colonel's assembled family would accord to the remains of that simple soldier, the grandiose funeral service, the solemn obsequies, Betty in deepest mourning, weeping while the dead man's old mother on her arm went on talking and talking relentlessly about her son to anyone who would listen. Then the poor fellow's bones would be transported to his murderer's magnificent tomb, the bells would ring out, a general would deliver a funeral oration, and the whole thing would be an outrage against nature, the whole thing would be a perversion, a cheat, a profanation. And if ghosts and spirits really did exist, then the soldier would rise from his tomb that very night.

No! the general thought. We had better find another. There must surely be one. He began to step out. He only had two more minutes before the Mass was due to begin. He was already in sight of the church, a handsome modern edifice with its main door leading almost directly onto the street. And parked along the pavement on either side of the entrance were a number of luxurious cars of various makes.

Members of the diplomatic corps, the general thought to himself, and walked swiftly up the marble steps. The Mass had barely begun as he entered the church. He dipped a finger in the stoup on his right, crossed himself and found a seat on the side. He fixed his eyes on the priest and listened to him speaking, but without actually managing to grasp the meaning of anything he said. He was only really aware of the customary black hangings covering the side walls of the church and the empty coffin in front of the choir, also draped with black cloth. The hangings and the congregation's black clothes seemed to deaden the guttering light of the candles; moreover the windows were set very high, and the light they gave had in any case been filtered through their multicoloured stained glass, so that the church seemed even darker and colder than it really was.

The priest was praying for the souls of the dead soldiers. Lack of sleep had made his face even paler than usual, and his eyes looked tired and tormented. The diplomats all sat listening attentively, their faces set in grave expressions, and mingling with the smell of the burning candles there was a faint whiff of scent hovering in the nave.

A woman in front of the general began to weep silently.

The priest's voice carried to the four corners of the church, solemn and sonorous:

Requiem aeternam dona eis!

The woman's sobs redoubled and she pulled a handkerchief out of her bag.

Et lux perpetua luceat eis! the priest went on, raising his eyes to the great crucifix.

Then his voice thundered out even more solemnly and sank to an even deeper note:

Requiescant in pace! he concluded, and his words echoed back from every corner of the church.

Amen! the deacon said.

For a few seconds the general thought he could hear the tiny sound of the candle flames burning.

May they rest in peace! he repeated to himself, and a sudden wave of emotion engulfed him.

So that as the priest raised the wafer and the chalice over the kneeling congregation, then went on to eat of the bread and drink of the wine for the salvation of the soldiers' souls, it suddenly seemed to the general that he was seeing them, thousand upon thousand of them, their aluminium mess-tins in their hands, queuing up for their evening stew from the big dixies, just at that moment of the day when the sun's last rays were lighting up their mess-tins and the steel of their helmets with glints of scarlet and eternal light.

And may light eternal shine on them! he breathed between his lips, after he had kneeled down, staring with wild and sombre gaze at the marble flagstones on the floor.

The little bell rang and everyone rose.

Ite, missa est! the priest's voice rang out.

Deo gratias! the deacon added.

People began to move towards the doors. Even from inside the church one could hear the car engines starting up, and as the general emerged through the main door he saw that the diplomats' cars were already moving off one by one. He walked over to wait for a bus at the stop just outside the church. Once in the bus he remained standing at the back of the vehicle, near the big rear window.

"Tickets, comrades," the conductress cried.

He understood the word for ticket and realized that of course he would have to buy one. He pulled a hundred-lek note out of his pocket and held it out to her.

"Haven't you anything smaller?"

Sensing what she said rather than actually understanding it he shook his head.

"It's three leks," the conductress said, and held up three fingers in front of his face. "Haven't you got three leks in coins?"

The general once more shook his head apologetically.

"He is a foreigner, comrade," a tall youth with an oddly sedate way of speaking said to the conductress.

"So it seems," she answered, and began counting out change.

"He must be an Albanian just back from America," an old man sitting behind the conductress broke in. "There are some that forget our language completely over there."

"No, grandad, he's a foreigner, I'm sure of that," the sedate-voiced youth repeated.

"Oh no," the old man insisted, "you mark my words, he's an Albanian just come home again. I can recognize them at a glance, I tell you."

The general sensed that they must be discussing him and

supposed that he had been taken for an American.

The pair continued to argue in front of his face, and went so far as to point at the general without the smallest inhibition. My goodness, he thought, even if I were a shade they ought to show me a little more respect!

Suddenly the idea that they and he belonged to utterly different worlds, with no point of contact be it physical or mental, and that they lived in complete mutual ignorance, froze him to the marrow.

When the bus stopped at the State Bank and the passengers alighted, he caught the old man's eye. "O.K." the old man said to him with a smile of self-satisfaction on his face before he disappeared.

The general made his way through the crowd of country people who were waiting for their bus and then turned into the main boulevard.

The pavements along Dibër Street were packed with people, particularly outside the buffet-bars and the People's Department Store. As he walked past the latter he suddenly had the idea of buying a souvenir.

He stopped and looked in the windows for a moment, then walked in. There were a number of little figures of all kinds on display along the counters and he examined them slowly one by one. He had always had a weakness for such objects – most of them figurines in various national costumes.

What would our soldiers leaving Albania have chosen? he wondered. All soldiers abroad seem to buy exactly the same knick-knack to bring back. Their telegrams are identical too. And even their letters as near as damn it.

Suddenly the gnome began playing its drum again inside his skull; slowly at first, then faster, faster, ever faster. Only now he wasn't sitting inside his head cross-legged, he was standing up, black and white and shining, in his red tunic with its black edging, his tall cap on his head. And there he was at the same time inside the glass display counter, standing beating his drum, neatly fashioned out of gleaming porcelain, and the general couldn't tear his eyes away.

He pointed to it.

"The mountain peasant with the drum?" the assistant asked.

The general nodded.

The girl removed the figure from the counter, wrapped it up and handed it to him.

"That will be eighteen leks twenty, please."

He paid, walked out of the shop and turned up towards the street of the Barricades.

XXIII

B OOM, BOOM, TARARABOOM . . .
        "Hello there!"

The general wheeled around in surprise.

"Oh, hello," he replied.

It was the lieutenant-general, standing outside the hotel on the pavement. He still had the left sleeve of his greatcoat tucked into his pocket, and the remaining hand still held a pipe.

"How are you?"

The lieutenant-general drew on his pipe, then removed it from between his lips and watched the smoke curling up out of his mouth.

"Before anything else, though it's a long time ago now of course, I do want to apologize to you over that nasty business last year. We did receive your complaint. I hope you will believe that I was in no way responsible, and that I was genuinely distressed at the incident."

The general let his gaze rest on the other somewhat absently.

"Who was to blame then?" he asked.

"My second-in-command. He was behind the whole hideous mess. But why don't we go and sit down somewhere, then I can explain the whole thing properly."

"I'm sorry, but I really haven't the time just now. Can't we just talk for a while here?"

"In that case it would be better if we postponed it till this evening. But tell me first, how are you getting on with your work here?"

"Badly, as I told you," the general answered. "The going is pretty tough."

"Indeed it is."

"And then on top of everything one of our workmen died."

"Died? What of? Did you have an accident?"

"No, it was an infection."

"How did he get it?"

"No one is quite certain. A bone perhaps, or a sliver of metal."

The lieutenant-general looked duly shocked.

"You will have to compensate the family of course?"

The general nodded. Then after a brief silence he added:

"I've never seen so many mountains!"

"And there are still a lot to come!"

"No, we've finished. We've just come back from our final tour."

"You've finished! You're damned lucky then! I've got a lot more mountains ahead of me."

"Mountains everywhere. And those young people everywhere terracing them into fields, have you seen them too?"

"Of course. They're always up there digging away."

"They're clearing new land to grow cereal crops on."

"In one place I noticed they'd sown wheat beside a railway track right up to the very edge of the ballast."

"They'll sow any scrap of land they can find. Presumably their present fields just aren't sufficient for their needs."

"They're in a state of blockade, remember. The U.S.S.R. has refused to let them have any more wheat."

"They're certainly delighted to see the back of our soldiers, that's for sure."

"Indeed they are. The cemeteries are sown almost before we've emptied them. Instant deconsecration it's called."

The general laughed.

"But your work, how is that going?"

"Very badly indeed," the other replied. "We've been rushing up hill and down dale all over Albania for eighteen months now, but the fact is that we've got very little to show for it."

"You've had a great many setbacks, I take it."

"A great many," the lieutenant-general agreed with a sigh. "And as if that weren't enough it now looks as though we're going to have a very ugly scandal on our hands."

"What do you mean?"

"Oh, it's a nasty business. Haven't you noticed that I'm on my own? By the way, I was about to ask you: where is your colleague, the reverend father?"

"Up in his room, I imagine."

The other chuckled.

"I'm afraid a nasty suspicion crossed my mind," he said. "Because you see my mayor is probably in very hot water just at this moment."

"Oh? What has happened to him then?"

"He received an urgent recall," the lieutenant-general said. "It's several weeks now since we suspended our operations on his account."

He waited for the other to show some curiosity, but as the general seemed to have his mind on other things, he repeated: "A very ugly scandal."

"You don't mean he's misappropriated funds intended to finance your search?" the general eventually asked.

"Worse. What's befallen is a great deal worse."

Then the general listened as the other described all that he had been suspecting for a good while: the promise given by the families to reward those who unearthed the remains of their nearest and dearest; the greed of the workers involved, who wanted above all to feather their own nests; the fraud practised on the first skeleton which had been falsely identified, then the second, then a whole string of others. Until one fine day . . .

Little by little the general continued to winkle the whole story out of him.

"Yes? What happened then?"

His colleague made a gesture as much as to say: what was bound to happen.

"The inevitable happened," he went on. "Apparently it was one of the families that discovered the original substitution, and you know how such things snowball. In no time at all the slightest hint of such a thing becomes an absolute avalanche of suspicions, enquiries, reporters agog for scandal, the opposition which . . ."

"I've got it," said the general without showing a hint of sympathy. "If I've understood you correctly, you've rebaptized the bones of unknown soldiers with the names of those men they had been particularly requested to look out for."

"Not me, the others!" the lieutenant-general broke in.

"Of course."

"The mistake arose because instead of doing as you did in collecting up your soldiers – I mean their skeletons – so as to send them off all together, we sent them a few at a time. If we'd done as you have, none of this horrible mix-up would have occurred."

"One hell of a mix-up," the general agreed.

He let his imagination run away with all that might constitute any general's nightmare: the dispersal of his troops. The first signs of disbanding, the privates going absent, the officers tearing off their shoulder insignia to avoid recognition, and eventually, a general rout. He had thought that such a thing could only befall an army of the living, never one in a deep freeze. Well, this is precisely what had happened to his colleague.

He remembered his last press conference, when he was still back home, during which the flashbulbs simply accentuated the provocative nature of the reporters' questions: "We're told, general, that you've been furnished with the most precise data enabling you to achieve your mission at every step. Do you personally trust the accuracy of those lists and data on each soldier's height?" They kept repeating the words "lists" and "data" to make quite clear their own scepticism as to the insensitive, bureaucratic temper of the top brass in charge of the exercise.

Time-servers, bar flies! he fumed as he called them to mind. It was thanks to those lists and data that I suffered not a single casualty to my army! There they were, all present and correct, officers, men, runners, scouts, chaplains, and of course the signals boys who were shouting "Hello! Hello!" even as they fell, as though answering Death's own call.

"A really nasty business," commented the general after a long silence.

The other kept watching him in a daze.

"I begin to be very weary of the whole business. And I'm entirely on my own. How I envy you leaving tomorrow!"

The general lit a cigarette.

"It's in the evening especially that the hours seem interminable. It's even more depressing than all that rushing around and sleeping under canvas."

"But what can you do about it!"

"To think that for a year and a half we've done nothing but hop from one mountain or valley to another as though we were geologists or something. And now, just when the end is in sight, we have this mess to face."

"Like geologists, yes, that's well said."

"And think what strange deposits we've been searching for," the lieutenant-general said. "What should we call them, geologically? Mortuary intrusions?"

The general smiled, then looked at his watch.

"You must excuse me," he said, "I have a very full day ahead."

"Well, general, I mustn't keep you. I look forward to seeing you again this evening."

"I shall be somewhere around. I shall come back here to the hotel when it's all over."

The general threw away his cigarette and set off towards the lifts. But at the last moment he turned about and walked back towards his colleague.

"Is there nothing that can be done about those eleven you took of ours?" he asked.

The lieutenant-general shrugged.

"Difficult, very difficult," he said.

"But why? You must have the addresses of the families you sent them to."

The other smiled bitterly.

"That's easily said, but just think of the consequences. Think what a shock it would be for those families suddenly to be asked to send back the remains!"

"Is that sufficient reason?"

"Possibly not, but there is even more to it than that," the lieutenant-general said, "The mind boggles at the legal complications it would lead to. But in any case, let's talk it over more fully this evening."

"Agreed," the general said, and walked off again towards the lifts.

XXIV

I T WAS A QUARTER past five when the banquet came to an end. The general waited until all the guests had left and only he and the priest remained. Then he drank two glasses of brandy straight off one after the other and walked out himself, without a word to the priest.

One more formality over and done with, he thought to himself with relief once he was outside on the boulevard again. You could hardly say the atmosphere was anything but lukewarm, but at least it's all over!

He had thanked the Albanian authorities, on behalf of his people and the thousands of mothers concerned, for all the facilities that had been made available to them in their search. To which an Albanian politician, the same one who had originally met them at the airport, had replied by saying that they had done no more than fulfil a humanitarian duty towards another people with whom it was Albania's wish to live in peace. At which they had all touched glasses and drunk a toast – and beneath the crystalline tinkling of the glasses it was as though a distant rumble of guns could be heard. No one can get rid of it, that muffled thunder, the general had thought to himself, and all of them here are aware of it, even though they refuse to admit it.

Now he walked slowly on among the crowds packing the streets, his ears assailed from every side by the babble of their foreign tongue against the deep background hum of the city.

In Skanderburg Square an open-air concert was in progress. He advanced a little through the human sea then stood on his toes in order to get a better view. From the balcony of the Executive Committee building behind him two spotlights were beaming down their light onto the backs of the crowd, and from a little further off he could just catch a distinctive whirring sound. They must be making a film.

The general, his mind elsewhere, stood watching the dancers move and turn up on the stage.

The thunder was there, I know it was there, he said to himself again, that thunder beneath the transparent tinkling of the glasses. And not just the thunder of the big guns but the crackling of the machine-guns too, and the clicking of bayonets, and the clinking of mess-tins in the evening queue for hash. It was all there in the tinkling of those glasses, they were all aware of it, they could all sense it.

He felt a stab of pain in his eyes from the white glare of the spotlights. Thousands of human heads were patterning the square with their bizarrely projected shadows. The general felt a shiver go up his spine and began to fight his way back through the crowd. The spotlights were continually on the move, sometimes brandishing their blinding beams just above the crowd's heads, sometimes just below them, sometimes on them, so that all the heads turned round, becoming uneasy faces, and making their shadows shift on the ground.

The general freed himself from the crowd and turned into the avenue that ran alongside the park towards his hotel.

He was still seeing the representatives of two peoples, two states, sitting face to face and separated only by a few bottles and a few bowls of fruit.

Is that all that stands between us? the general had asked himself as they had touched their glasses the first time. Nothing but those brightly labelled bottles and those beautiful fruits freshly picked in the orchards and the vineyards along the coast? Then he had remembered those vineyards and those orchards plunged in the growing dusk, lining the roads that gleamed so pale and bright in the moonlight, and from which he could just make out the distant, lonely barking of a dog, and further off still the brightness of a shepherd's fire.

"There is a telegram for you," the hotel receptionist told him as he handed over the key of his room.

"Thank you."

On the yellow envelope he noticed the word *urgent* in tiny letters. He opened it and read: "Have heard your noble mission accomplished stop Please send news colonel stop Z. family."

He felt the blood rushing to his head. His temples were throbbing as though they were about to burst. He nevertheless made a great effort to keep control of himself, walked slowly over to a lift and almost fell into it.

Whatever possessed you to get mixed up in this business anyway? he asked himself in the mirror. He observed the pallor of the skin, the drawn features, the irreversible wrinkles on the forehead, those three deep furrows, the middle one slightly longer than the others, calling to mind the three lines that typists type at the bottom of a report.

"You're washed out," he told himself. "Emptied."

He walked into his room and switched on the light. The first thing his eye encountered was the little porcelain figure beating its drum on top of the heap of letters and telegrams piled up on the bedside table.

He lay down and tried to sleep.

Outside, fireworks sputtered and exploded. The multicoloured lights came through the blinds and lay in stripes across the ceiling and walls of the room. He was back once more in that long room in the barracks, twenty years before, sitting with the rest of the recruiting board along one side of the big table. He saw the hands repeatedly unrolling the X-rays, then holding them up to the light, displaying the pale ribs against the ceiling; then came the verdict, a weary and disillusioned "Good!" They almost always said "good" even when there was a slight patch between the ribs. It was only when the patches were too obvious to be ignored that they murmured: "Rejected". And it went on like that all day, every day. And the conscripts with their shaven heads were taken straight from there to the barracks, and from the barracks to the front, where the war had just begun.

The light from outside, filtered into stripes by the blinds, kept whirling round and round in his head. He shut his eyes to shut everything out. But no sooner were his eyelids closed than the long, stark barrack room reappeared even more clearly, with those bewildered recruits standing in front of the long table, completely naked, like pale, pale candles.

The general got up again. It was dinner time. He went out into the corridor with the intention of finding the priest. A passing chambermaid told him the priest had gone out. He went back to his room and phoned down to the desk to ask if the lieutenant-general was in the hotel.

Then he walked out into the corridor again and saw him approaching. They walked slowly and in silence down the marble stairs. The lobby below was still as full of bustle as it had been earlier and the two telephones were still ringing non-stop.

In the lounge they had difficulty finding a place to sit. Through the nearby window, looking out onto the boulevard, they could see the sight-seers walking past, and up in the sky the rockets' blazing sheaves of light, opening and falling back down, like thick multicoloured snow, towards the crowd and the dark trees of the park, only to die after a moment and plunge everything back into a darkness that seemed even deeper than ever.

The lieutenant-general ordered raki, the general brandy.

The sounds of the dance band in the basement came wafting up to them, and the wooden stairs leading down to the taverna were constantly creaking beneath the feet of the customers arriving and leaving.

They touched glasses and drank. Then they sat there for a long while without speaking. The general refilled their glasses. It seemed easier than starting up a conversation.

Outside, the rockets continued to explode, and from time to time their reflections starred the window.

"They are celebrating their victory!" the general said.

"Yes, as you say."

They watched the sky light up as though a gigantic flaming helmet was sinking earthwards from it, glittering with innumerable sparks, only to pale suddenly, lose its warmth, and vanish back into the womb of night.

"A pretty mission, ours!"

Once more he was wondering which was the worse, the war or this funereal pilgrimage that came after.

The general looked at the empty sleeve tucked into the tunic pocket.

Yes, we can all see you've been in battle all right, he thought.

"Yet in a way it is war, what we deal with," the lieutenant-general went on. "The remains we dig up constitute war's very essence, you might say. What remains when it is all over; the precipitate after a chemical reaction."

The general gave a bitter smile. "Poetry!" he muttered to himself. He filled the glasses again.

"I'm sure you've heard that pearlfishers' lungs sometimes burst when they dive too deep. Well, that's what happens to your heart with this job of ours."

"It's true. Yes, it's sad enough to break your heart."

"We've reached our limit," said the general.

"We've been defeated by the shadow of their arms," said the other. "What would have happened if we had really had to fight?"

"If we'd fought here? Perhaps it would have been better if we had!"

They spoke further of the war and its double, without ever concluding which of the two they opted for.

The music was still coming up from the basement night club, and the coffee machine occasionally emitted a hissing jet of steam like a miniature locomotive.

"Do you remember the football stadium I told you about that first evening we talked together?" the lieutenant-general said.

"The one where they wouldn't let you start digging till the football championship was over?"

"Yes, that's it."

"Yes, I remember it, vaguely. You'd begun excavating round the edges of the field, as I remember, and you told me about the rain, how it streamed down the grey concrete tiers of the stands."

"Yes, the graves ran all round the football and basketball fields like a sinister black dotted line, and the rain did cascade down the stands. But that wasn't what I was thinking of."

"What then?"

"Didn't I tell you – I think I did – about the girl who used to come and wait for her young man every afternoon, while he was training?"

"Yes, you did tell me something about her, but I'm afraid I don't remember exactly what."

"Well, she came there every afternoon. And when it rained she used to pull up the hood of her raincoat and just stand there, in one corner of the stadium, under the pillars by the players' entrance, just following her young man with her eyes as he rushed about on the pitch."

"Ah yes, now I remember," the general said. "The raincoat she wore was blue, wasn't it?"

"Yes, that's right," the lieutenant-general said. "She wore a pretty blue raincoat, and her eyes were an even lighter blue. They were a little cold, perhaps, but I've never seen any more beautiful. So there she came and stood, every day, and we for our part just kept on digging, until in the end the field was totally surrounded by open graves."

"And what happened then?" the general asked without much interest.

"Nothing, nothing in particular. As evening approached the young men stopped training, and then one of them would throw his arm round her shoulders and they'd go off together like that. And at that moment every day, believe me, I felt such an emptiness all around me, I felt my heart so heavy that the whole world seemed to me as abandoned and as meaningless as that dark, empty stadium. Would you believe it? At my age!"

It's true he doesn't look like a great lover, the general thought.

"But life is like that," the other continued. "Just when you least expect it a crazy, senseless dream begins to take root in your mind – like a flower growing on the edge of a precipice! I was a foreign general, and what's more a middle-aged cripple, I told myself; my only reason for being in this country was to collect the bones of my fellow countrymen, so what could there possibly be between me and that young, foreign girl?"

"Nothing. Nothing of course. But as far as thinking about her goes – well there was nothing against that. We all of us have wild dreams sometimes, especially where women are concerned. Why, one summer not so long ago, at the seaside . . ."

"There were times," the lieutenant-general went on, paying no attention, "there were times when I attributed my nervous exhaustion entirely to her, to the fact that my thoughts were so totally obsessed with her; but even then I knew it didn't really explain my depression. It wasn't so much the girl herself troubling my mind as something else, something vague, more abstract, something that was attacking me indirectly, through her. Do you understand?"

"I think so, yes. What disturbed you in her, it seems to me, was her youth, the fact that she seemed such an absolute manifestation of life. It's such a long time now that we've been running up hill and down dale sniffing for death like hyenas, trying to find ways of coaxing it or smoking it out of its lair, that we have almost forgotten that beauty still exists on this earth ... Listen, last summer on the beach, as I told you, I myself ..."

"At my age!" his colleague broke in again.

The general almost gnashed his teeth. He couldn't stand people who were so wrapped up in themselves. That's how he'd been listening, with clenched jaws, while the other went on and on about the football stadium and the stands and the girl in the blue raincoat.

Some suitor! he mused.

Once he realized that this adventure he had been through ... the summer before last, on the beach ... even if the other gave him the leisure ... he no longer felt the slightest urge to speak of it (for a moment he had really believed in that little adventure he'd supposedly experienced that summer on the beach, but it had been so gossamer-thin that it only took his interlocutor's obvious lack of interest for it to turn to vapour, like dew); once he had lost all hope of getting it off his chest he felt a sullen fury.

Now I'm going to let you have it! he muttered to himself. You'd like me to listen to your little vapourings but you don't give a toss for anyone else's feelings ... He hadn't wanted to listen to the little story of the beach? Right, then he'd find another way

246

to galvanize him. The old woman at the wedding, with her mud-spattered black bag and her remarks, he still had them in the forefront of his mind.

"One evening I went to one of their wedding feasts and stood up to dance with them," the general broke in.

But the other did not allow him to continue.

"And do you know what I did?" he went on himself. "Despite my grey hair and my missing arm, do you know what I did when we went back to that town a month later? I went alone to the stadium one afternoon, just at the time I knew the players would be training. But the ground was shut, they weren't doing any training that day after all. I asked to be allowed in all the same, and the groundsman opened the gate for me. The stadium was more dismal and deserted than ever. The graves had been filled in again but you could see where they'd been, like scarred-over wounds all over the surface of the ground. I walked round the edge of the ground till I came to the pillars near the players' entrance, the spot where the girl always used to stand. And at that moment I felt a despair well up inside me that was so deep, so overwhelming that I thought somehow the life was just going to be crushed out of me by those long, wet, curving tiers, those empty grey stands rising in endless circles up to the sky. Are you listening?"

"Yes, yes, I'm listening," the general said, while inside what he was saying was: "Bully for you!"

He waited, seething, for the right moment to take his revenge. Old Nice now seemed to him to belong to the ghosts' punishment battalion. Let us confront him together, he thought, just as we confronted the mud and the rain!

"I was speaking to you about the wedding where I got up to dance . . ."

This time what interrupted him was a knock at the door.

Which did not prevent him, as he got up to open it, from darting a reproachful look at his colleague.

Another telegram.

"They send one missive after another," he said emphatically. "They imagine they can sort things out with a telegram! Do you know what an old woman in one of the villages here said to me one night at a wedding feast?" the general asked. "That I'd come here to see how they married off their sons so that I could come back one day and kill them."

"A terrible thing to say."

"A terrible thing to say? Ah, you think that's a terrible thing to say, do you? Then I wonder what you'd think if you knew what happened then!"

"I don't know," he conceded.

"Better to leave it that way."

"Drink up, soldier," the lieutenant-general put in. "Your good health! Here's wishing you a safe journey home. How I envy you!"

"Thank you, soldier," the general replied.

He could feel the drink gaining the upper hand. His irritation had subsided, although not completely. He was about to revert to the topic of Nice when, oddly, it was the infected workman he spoke of instead.

"We had a workman who caught an infection," he said.

"Yes, so you told me."

"He died."

"Yes, I know," the lieutenant-general said, looking him straight in the eye, as much as to say that he took this sort of thing in his stride.

"So you told me, so you told me," the general brooded. But what about you, boring me with your talk of stadiums, and I let you carry on.

The lounge was slowly emptying and the stairs down to the

night club were creaking less often, though the music was still wafting up them.

"So where is your reverend father?" the lieutenant-general asked suddenly.

"I've no idea. He must be lurking somewhere around the hotel. Answering all these telegrams."

The other glanced over at him once again with surprise and seemed about to ask for further clarification. But then he changed his mind.

Then the general leaned over his shoulder, as though about to entreat him. After a moment's hesitation he made up his mind:

"Do me a favour. Stop going on about that stadium of yours . . . and about blue raincoats and so forth."

"I give you my word, I promise not to mention the stadium again."

"One day we heard a song which to begin with we took for a provocation," the general resumed. "But it was a very ancient song, a love song."

"Oh really?" the other said with indifference.

"The words went more or less like this: 'Oh pretty Hanko, beautiful as the dawn, do not walk among the graves, or you'll bring the dead back to life.'"

"Well, well," the lieutenant-general said. "Well, well."

They went on to talk about a great many things after that, but the war and graveyards kept finding their way back into the conversation. Every one of our thoughts has a metal label on it like the graves themselves, the general thought to himself during a pause. A little metal label on a wooden cross, its inscription rusted away, hardly legible any more. A label that grates and squeaks when it's windy, and it's almost always windy. Like in that valley where the labels and the crosses were all leaning towards the west. And when we asked why they were all tilted in the same

249

direction like that, the villagers explained it was because of the wind, because the wind always blows from the same direction.

The lounge was almost entirely empty when the next telegram arrived. The general took it from the porter's hand and ripped it open without even looking to see the place of origin.

He crumpled it into a ball, as he had the previous one, without even reading it through to the end. Then he tossed it into the ashtray.

"You are receiving very mysterious telegrams tonight."

The general did not reply. The other sighed:

"I'm afraid of telegrams at night."

The music could still be heard from below, but the people using the stairs were getting very few and far between.

"What time is it?" the general asked.

"Nearly midnight."

They drank to something else that the general did not exactly grasp.

Never mind what we drink to. All he's got to do is stop and think . . .

For an instant old Nice came back to mind.

You thought you'd got away with it, he mused. You thought you were off the hook. Not true: you're not to slip out of her hands any more than I could.

"I wanted to ask you," he said, leaning over close to his companion's ear. "Have you ever drunk with a priest?"

"A priest? No, not as far as I remember. Though I wouldn't risk my hand in the fire over it."

The general could not help looking down at the empty sleeve tucked into the deep tunic pocket.

Yes, he thought, with only one you'd be a fool to risk it.

"Not as far as I remember," the lieutenant-general said again.

The general sat shaking his head for a while.

"Well, that's life," he commented meditatively. "One day you're travelling along in the rain and next day you're having a drink with a priest. Isn't that the truth?"

"Oh indeed, indeed."

"You really agree with me?"

"How could you think otherwise?"

"Excuse me. I apologize for doubting you."

"Oh please, please!"

The general, his eyes fixed on the ashtray, raised his hands and shoulders in a great shrug of bewilderment.

XXV

THE GENERAL HAD IMAGINED that it was his colleague who was mumbling and was startled to hear himself ask: "What's that you're mumbling about?"

"I was remembering the words spoken by someone that wretched night: 'Rain and death, it's everywhere.'"

The other gasped in dismay.

"Later on my dear old priest – he has the rank of colonel and is an interpreter as well, but also a lover and heaven knows what else – he told me that the old adage did not end there."

The other grunted.

"'Rain and death, it's everywhere, go and look for something else, old fellow . . .' Oh do stop whistling like that . . . In other words it's a bit of a reproach, a warning . . . All right but I, just like you, can't do anything else. People go hunting for oil, for chromium, antique statues. We, in our affliction, can do nothing else but this, aren't I right? We employees of the Standard Death Company. Ha ha ha!"

The other listened open-mouthed.

"The whole thing's turned into a mess," he continued pensively. "What with the chromium and the oil company getting into the act . . ." After a pause he added: "It's past midnight, I think they want to shut the lounge up for the night."

"Yes, I have that feeling too."

"Why don't we go up to my room? We could talk a little more.

I feel very happy in your company."

"Me too."

They staggered up the hotel stairs, each clutching his bottle.

"We mustn't make a noise," the general said. "The Albanians go to bed very early."

"Give me the key then. It looks to me as though your hands are shaking."

"The important thing is not to make any noise."

"Well I need noise," the lieutenant-general said. "I need noise because silence terrifies me. This battle we're fighting, it's silent like a silent film. I'd rather hear the guns thundering. But I'm talking like one of your people from a play, aren't I?"

"Shh! Someone's coughing at us."

"Give me your key. Yes, a silent battle! A battle between dead men!"

"Do come in, please. Sit down. I'm very happy to see you here like this."

"Yes, I am too. Being here with you. Happy, I mean."

A vast spread of death, the general brooded.

They sat down on opposite sides of the table and gazed at one another affectionately. The general filled the glasses.

"We are just two migrating birds, sitting at this table drinking raki and cognac," the lieutenant-general said with deep emotion.

The general nodded. They sat there for a while without speaking.

"We had a row over the sack," the general said at last, forcing his eyebrows into a frown.

He began staring at his companion as though he were trying to remember something. Then, in a confidential murmur, he added: "I pushed him over the edge."

"But you just said the priest was in his room!"

"No, I mean the sack," the general said. "Not the priest."

"Ah, I understand. Of course."

"He didn't want me to throw the sack in the water," the general went on, "but I wanted to get rid of those bones. At all costs, you realize?"

"Quite right. After all what possible importance can a sack have?" the lieutenant-general said, and took a puff at his cigarette.

"Yes, but you just try telling him that. He won't listen."

"And that's why you pushed him over the edge?"

"No, not him, the sack."

"Ah! I beg your pardon."

There was once a car and a lorry driving along in the rain, the general thought. Then, aloud, he began:

"There was once a car and a lorry driving along in the rain . . ."

"What? What did you say?" the other asked. "Are you in military transport yourself?"

"No. It's the beginning of the second story I shall tell my little grand-daughter."

"Ah. You collect stories then?"

"Of course."

"Just as I thought. Now I have always been very interested in where fables come from."

"That's a very important problem."

"Insoluble!"

"Ungraspable, I'd say."

"It's very good of you to admit it."

"Enough talk!" the lieutenant-general said in a peremptory tone.

The general stared at him in stupefaction, but his mind soon wandered off elsewhere.

"Do you know the song 'When the wild geese fly away'?" he asked. "One night I had a strange dream. I dreamed I saw a cemetery in the shape of a V flying through the sky."

"What fun!"

The general stared at him again.

"I have four priests among my dead," he said then.

"Really? I haven't a single one," the other said with a grieved air.

"You haven't even got a whore."

"No, I haven't a whore either."

"Don't let it upset you. You might still find one."

"Yes, perhaps I might," the lieutenant-general murmured. "You find all sorts of things under the ground. Where is your bathroom?"

"Through that door."

The general sat alone at the table for a long while. At last the other returned.

"Once, in a valley, we found mule bones all mixed up with the remains of our soldiers," he said.

"One of our reprisal battalions."

The lieutenant-general was having difficulty enunciating his words, and drunkenness had drained the colour from his face.

"Incompetent officers! I am here to sweep up the débris of your defeats!" the general announced.

"We mustn't be too hard on them. They didn't have an easy job."

"Ours was harder."

"Possibly."

"Report on Exhumation Number 104, Type B," the general muttered.

They sat silent for a moment.

"Mule bones are very different from human bones. Anybody at all could tell the difference. At a glance."

"Of course they could. I believe the human skeleton is made up of five hundred and seven bones."

"That isn't true, my friend," the lieutenant-general said, his mood suddenly dark. "It isn't always true anyway. Take me, for example. I have less than that."

"It's not possible."

"But it's a fact," the other insisted hoarsely. "I have quite a number of bones less. I am an invalid, a cripple."

"Now now," the general said consolingly, "you mustn't upset yourself like that."

"I am a cripple," the other went on. "I can see you don't believe me, but I intend to prove it to you here and now."

He began trying to remove his tunic with his one hand; but the general seized him by the shoulders.

"There's no need, my friend, there's no need! I believe you, I really believe you. And I beg your forgiveness. I can't say how sorry I am. I am very, very much to blame. Yes, I have behaved quite inexcusably."

"I have to show it to you. To everyone who doesn't believe it. I must show it to you here and now."

"Ssh!" the general said. "I think someone is knocking."

They were silent. There was another knock at the door.

"Who can it be? At this hour?"

"I don't like it, hearing knocks on a door like that in the middle of the night," the lieutenant-general said. "That's what the knocks sounded like on my door that night, when the urgent call came for me to go to the front. Rat! tat! tat! Then when I came home I couldn't open the door. It was the first time I'd tried it with only one hand."

The general staggered over and pulled open the door.

It was the porter, with another telegram.

"You seem very mysterious tonight," the lieutenant-general said. "All these telegrams in the night can't be a good sign."

"It's them again," the general said. "They seem very upset."

The white telephones are ringing away over there at this very moment, he thought. Hello? Hello? Hello? They are all telephoning one another, rushing from house to house like mad creatures, visiting one another, chattering to one another . . . And vaguely he tried to picture them all, all gathered together at the colonel's house, busy ringing all their friends, the old woman appearing at the top of the stairs with her hands stretched out to make a cross, Betty half out of bed in a state of shock, all of them muttering: "That wretched man, he still hasn't found him. What a wretched fellow!"

I'm not a wretched fellow, Betty! he told her in his mind, and then out loud:

"They're not going to get much sleep tonight."

"What is it they want?" the lieutenant-general asked.

"The sack."

"I would advise you to give it to them and have done with it. Be very careful!"

Oh arseholes! the general thought to himself.

He crumpled the telegram up into a ball and threw it onto the floor.

"You know something?" he said. "I'm rather afraid that priest of mine is a spy."

"It's quite possible. I wouldn't risk my hand in the fire over it though."

They were silent for a long while. Beyond the blinds it was possible to discern a whitish, murky glimmer.

"Look, dawn's breaking," the general said.

They could hear the gentle sound of rain falling on the balcony outside.

"Telegrams make me afraid," the lieutenant-general said with a slightly wild look. "There's always something unpleasant in them, something secret. And then other things are left out. I remember once, at the front, one of the staff officers got a telegram from one of his friends who'd been dead for ages."

"Oh my friend, what a sad story. What a terrible story!"

"Ssh!" the lieutenant-general said. "Do you hear?"

"What? Hear what?"

"Listen! Can't you hear anything?"

The general tilted his head and listened.

"Rain!"

"No, not that."

In the distance, far in the distance, an indistinct, rhythmical noise could be heard. Then voices, peremptory, abrupt, followed once more by just the sound of the rain.

"What can it be?"

"We must go out onto the balcony," the general said, and stood up.

As soon as they opened the french window the cold, wet night air froze their faces, and the distant, rhythmical noise became much clearer.

They both went out onto the balcony. A fine, soft rain was falling. Even the boulevard looked pale and grey under the cold neon street lights, and the park, facing the hotel, was no more than a black and ominous mass.

"That way," the lieutenant-general murmured, his face paler than ever now. "Look!"

The general turned his head, then started. At the far end of the boulevard, near the University, big, dark squares were advancing towards them.

The heavy tramp of feet could now be more clearly distinguished, and the orders, sudden and brief, carried icily through the darkness of the night.

The two generals remained there, leaning on the balustrade of the balcony, eyes fixed on the advancing shapes. As the dark squares neared the bridge they could make out the cold reflections on the wet helmets and bayonets, the long columns of soldiers, the officers with drawn swords, and the gaps between companies and battalions. The earth shook under the heavy boots, and the curt cries of command rang out like bayonets clashing.

The formations kept coming; the whole boulevard was now teeming with soldiers, and the street lamps lining the roadway were reflected to infinity on the wet, shiny helmets, looking as cold and mysterious as a world going putrid.

"An army," the lieutenant-general said. "What's going on?"

"It's their army. They must be rehearsing for tomorrow's parade."

"For their Liberation Day?"

"Yes, of course."

Now there was a sound like muffled thunder in the distance.

"The tanks!" the general said.

And the tanks duly appeared beyond the bridge, massive and black, their gun barrels aimed into the night.

The boulevard was now all troops, metal, marching feet, thundering engines, abrupt commands, and all of it, as in a single body, streaming relentlessly on towards Skanderburg Square.

When the last formation had disappeared behind the government buildings and the boulevard was once more empty, lying silent and pale beneath the street lights again as though after a night without sleep, they went back into the room.

"It was a whole army, out there."

"Yes, an entire army."

"I'm cold."

"We're soaked through."

"Drink, general, otherwise you'll catch cold."

The cold had made them both a little more lucid.

The general raised his head.

"You saw them out there, marching by?"

"I did."

"They make me think of my own army. They make me wonder how my soldiers would look, marching past in their blue bags with their black edgings."

"It would be even more difficult for me," the one-armed general said. "Mine are really only a rabble. How would I even recognize them, I wonder?"

"When you come before this vast stretch of death," the general mused. He wondered what lay behind this mute terror.

"When you come before this vast stretch of death," he said out loud.

"What?"

The general took his head in both hands, in an attitude that was quite unlike him, a posture totally alien to him, more than alien, as though its origin lay in the world of ancient crones.

No, he muttered to himself.

He could not stomach this playing with words blended with a sort of funereal music.

When you reach the place where . . . look for my son . . . look for my boy. In a haze he saw Countess Z. and old Nice deep in conversation. Give me back my son, foreign woman . . . Well have him, then, Countess. Take him home.

He was alone between the two of them.

"Do you know why I had my row with the priest?" he croaked, as if clambering out of a well.

"No," the lieutenant-general said.

"Over a skeleton. We're missing a six-foot-one skeleton."

"What a thing to row over," the other snorted.

Then he lifted his head suddenly, a gleam in his eyes.

"Six foot one? Would you like me to sell you one that height?"

"No," the general said.

"Why not? I've got heaps. You're a friend, I can let you have one for a hundred dollars."

"No!"

"But I've got so many that height! I've even got some six foot four if you want. And six foot six too. And even some seven foot!

Our soldiers were taller than yours. Would you like some?"

"No," the general said. "I don't want any."

The other shrugged.

"Well, it's your affair. I was only trying to help."

The general got up and made his way with difficulty over to his case. He opened it and tipped the contents onto the floor. The lists, the cards, the sheets of paper covered with notes all lay jumbled up in a heap with his towels and shirts. He picked up a bundle of lists and staggered over to the door.

What's got into him? the lieutenant-general wondered.

After weaving along the deserted corridor a short distance the general stopped outside a door.

Ah, he said to himself, this is the priest's door.

"Father!" he called out in a low voice, bending to peer through the keyhole. "Father, can you hear me? It's me! I've come to make it up with you. We were stupid to have that row about the colonel. Why should we quarrel over a sack? We can settle the whole business quite easily, father. We can make another colonel for you. All right? It's in both our interests, you know. You wantto be able to say: 'Oh Betty, how light you are!', don't you? So it's up to you. You need a skeleton, don't you? Well I've got one! I've brought the lists with me, father, do you hear me? Here they are! We've got any number of six-foot-one soldiers. If you'll just get up now we'll choose one. There's one here in the second machine-gun company, and another here in a tank regiment, yes and here's another. You get up and we'll go over the lists in detail. Ah, that one has two incisors missing, I see. Never mind, we could get a dentist to put two in for us. And there are two or three more I've found as well. Are you listening? And they're all six foot one. It's true, father, I'm not lying to you. Six foot one, six foot one . . . As a matter of fact, I think I'm six foot one myself."

261

The general went on for a long while muttering outside the door, bending down and trying to peer through the keyhole. Suddenly the door flew open and a stout woman stood there glaring at him in fury. Scornfully she spat at him:

"Aren't you ashamed of yourself, at your age!"

The general tried to open his eyes very wide. The door was slammed in his face and he remained standing there in silence for quite a while. Then he slowly bent down, and with great difficulty tried to gather together the lists, which he had in the meantime allowed to slide from his grasp.

At daybreak, when the pageboy brought the last telegram, they were still drinking. The general opened the envelope, pulled out the message, but was unable to make out a single letter of it. He held it for some while in front of his face, stretching his eyes open and furrowing his brow, but without any success. The printed strips looked to him like ribbons of mist against a white sky. He screwed the telegram up, made his way uncertainly over to the window, pulled it open.

"Unidentified!" he cried, and threw the crumpled piece of paper out.

The telegram fluttered earthwards in the cold half-light of dawn.

Last Chapter But One

IN THE MORNING, very early, one of the maids from the fourth floor came down to the night-porter.

"I found these papers," she said, showing him several sheets with typing on them. "One of the guests must have left them behind."

"Where did you find them?"

"In the corridor. Some were in front of number 429 and the rest in front of 403."

The night-porter looked surprised. Then his forehead creased in doubt.

"That's all right. Leave them here. Whoever lost them will come and ask for them."

They were typewritten lists of names. Many of the names were marked with little crosses in red and blue pencil, and there were quantities of notes in a shaky handwriting.

Last Chapter

RAIN MIXED WITH snow was falling on the foreign soil.

The heavy, damp flakes melted and were gone as soon as they touched the concrete of the esplanade outside the airport buildings. On the bare earth the snow lasted a little longer; though even there it was unable to form a white layer, because the rain gained the advantage over her companion as soon as they both touched the ground.

The general, in full dress, stood watching the snow. Now and again he looked up at the sky. But the sky was indifferent to her children's fate once they were on the ground and continued to release an endless supply of fresh snowflakes to their perdition.

"It's cold," said the Albanian politician who had come to see them off.

"Yes, very cold," answered the general.

With a touch of impatience they watched the progress of the aircraft as it taxied closer, while a woman's voice from the loudspeakers urged belated passengers to hurry. Shortly after, the roar of the engines became so loud, they might have gone on using the same words to complain – "It's cold," "Yes, awfully cold," "Terribly cold" – without anyone noticing the repetition. Nothing else could be heard and so it was, with the steam of their breath enwrapping heaven knows what words, that they reached the boarding steps.

The wind continued to blow, without respite.

Tirana, 1962–1966